NEVER

After ten years in London, working for a City law firm, Clare Donoghue moved back to her home town in Somerset to undertake an MA in creative writing at Bath Spa University. In 2011 the initial chapters of *Never Look Back*, previously entitled *Chasing Shadows*, were longlisted for the CWA Debut Dagger award. *Never Look Back* is Clare's first published novel.

CLARE DONOGHUE

NEVER LOOK BACK

PAN BOOKS

First published 2014 by Pan Books
an imprint of Pan Macmillan, a division of Macmillan Publishers Limited
Pan Macmillan, 20 New Wharf Road, London N1 9RR
Basingstoke and Oxford
Associated companies throughout the world
www.panmacmillan.com

ISBN 978-1-4472-3928-4

1 3 5 7 9 8 6 4 2

A CIP catalogue record for this book is available from the British Library.

Typeset by Palimpsest Book Production Limited, Falkirk, Stirlingshire
Printed and bound by CPI Group (UK) Ltd, Croydon, CR0 4YY

Visit **www.panmacmillan.com** to read more about all our books
and to buy them. You will also find features, author interviews and
news of any author events, and you can sign up for e-newsletters
so that you're always first to hear about our new releases.

To my mum and dad
for always being there

Acknowledgements

I would like to thank my editor Trisha Jackson, Natasha Harding and all of the Macmillan team for making my dream a reality. Hellie Ogden at Janklow & Nesbit for her time, enthusiasm and getting me here and Celia Brayfield and Bath Spa University for getting me started.

Thank you to my family for their love and assurance. Thanks also to Mark, for all the hours you've spent teaching me about London policing and Sue for always cooking up a storm. Huge thanks to my writing buddy and friend, Eve Wheaton. Your support and encouragement have been invaluable and to the rest of my writing group, Kes and Hannah, thank you. Finally, a big thank you to all the staff at the Beacon Centre at Musgrove Park Hospital in Taunton for their support and for looking after my father at a very difficult time.

PROLOGUE

21 January – Tuesday

He licked his thumb and forefinger, closed his right eye and pushed the thread through the eye of the needle. He never used machines. They snagged the material, pulling and ripping at his treasures. If a section was damaged, nothing could be done. He had no access to more and besides, a secondary piece wouldn't be the same. He looked down at his hands. His knuckles were red and chapped and his fingers were trembling. He needed to rest.

He climbed the stairs, walked into the bathroom, over to the sink, pulled on the shaving light and looked at his reflection. His hair stood up at odd angles. It looked almost sculpted. A chuckle rumbled in his throat but as it rose into his mouth it turned into a cough, hacking, tugging at his lungs. He turned and walked out, dragging his feet, aware of the stench wafting up from his body, his clothes, his hands.

His eyes felt heavy, his joints seeming to solidify as he made unsteady progress towards his bedroom at the back of the house. The rain was loud, the cold it brought seeping through the windows, chilling his bones. He stopped at the door to the spare room, pushed it open with the heel of his hand and looked in. His eyes drifted back and forth over colour, patterns, all different, all alive. It wouldn't be long before he was ready.

1

Debbie stepped off the train at East Dulwich station, misjudged the drop and stumbled onto the platform. Icy breezes found their way beneath her jacket, pinching at her skin. She could feel eyes on her as other commuters watched her unsteady progress towards the exit, her cheeks burning as the January wind snapped at her face. She had considered splashing out on a taxi but it was more hassle than it was worth. None of the black cabs wanted to go south of the river. Whenever she said, 'Nunhead, please,' she would invariably get the same response. 'Just clockin' off, luv,' or 'I'm on my way home, only got time for a local drop-off.' South-east London was essentially a dead zone. No chance of a return fare. No chance of a taxi.

She reached the steps, the cold concrete penetrating the thin soles of her shoes, her toes tingling. She slipped, dropping her handbag but managing to right herself as she watched it tumble down to the bottom of the steps, its contents spilling out onto the dirty pavement: an empty wallet, an empty jewellery case and two packets of paracetamol. She stood,

3

rearranging her grey pinstripe skirt, her fingers finding the broken zip. He had been rough tonight.

The night air was making her feel light-headed. She pressed the button at the traffic lights and waited, resting her head back on her shoulders, her body swaying. A bus stopped in front of her, its exhaust catching in her throat. She tipped her head forward and looked at her reflection in the shadowed windows. Her hair was a mess, strands hanging around her face, limp and lifeless. Even in this light she could see the smudges of mascara under her eyes. Why would he want her? She pushed the button for the lights again, her hand lingering, eager for the support.

She looked up the road at Lordship Lane. It was the 'in' place to be, trendy wine bars and gastropubs lining the streets, charging a fortune for their imported spirits with unpronounceable names. Groups of fashionable twenty-somethings huddled under the heaters outside The Bishop, their faces glowing red as they took drags on their cigarettes. Debbie doubted any of them had ever ventured into Peckham itself, despite it being less than a mile away. She watched as a group of girls waved and called to friends on the other side of the street, their smiles visible, their happiness evident. She would never be like them.

When the lights changed, she limped across the road. Goose Green Park stretched into the darkness on her left. The children's play area was shadowed and still. She turned away, preferring to focus on the houses and flats on the other side of the road. The lights glowing from numerous windows comforted her. She reached into her handbag, her cold fingers searching until they closed around her phone. She dialled her brother's number, thankful when it went straight to voice-mail. 'Hey, Tom, it's me,' she said, trying to control the slur in her voice. 'I'm gonna come over tomorrow night with Mum. I've had a tough day. Give my love to Jules and kiss baby Jake. Bye.' She ended the call and dropped her phone back into her bag. It was quarter to nine. The baby would be in bed by now anyway.

As she approached the lights of the Tesco Metro she was looking for a gap in the traffic to cross when something stopped her. A shiver worked its way up from her aching feet to her throbbing head. Now she was away from Lordship Lane, the pavements were almost empty. She stared into the park, at the trees. Was there someone standing there in the darkness? She turned away and ran across the road, the sound of a car horn echoing behind her.

'Damn it,' she said, slipping on a patch of ice. She needed cash for tomorrow. Another birthday in the office and another fiver she would never see again. She walked over to the cash machine at the side of the Tesco, struggling with her purse until she finally got her card out. She punched in her PIN and waited. A breeze brushed the hairs on her neck; it felt warm.

'Don't turn around . . . please.' The voice was low; the whisper sent his breath right into her ear.

'What . . .?' Her voice sounded hoarse.

'Good evening, Deborah.' He stretched out her name, enunciating the syllables as if talking to a child, flattening his body against hers. She felt something sharp digging into her ribs. Her eyes darted to either side but she couldn't see anyone. She replayed his words in her head. How did he know her name? Her stomach dropped, her mouth suddenly dry. 'I'd like you to take a few steps into the alley there,' he said, his voice calm.

She wanted to vomit but she remained motionless, mute, as he whispered like a lover in her ear. 'Please . . .' she croaked, 'just take what you want.' Tears fell onto her cheeks and lips. She knew she should shout, run, anything, but she couldn't.

'I can see I am going to have to be more direct.' His voice dropped to a low rumble.

It was then that she knew who he was. He was the eyes she had felt watching her on the platform, the shiver that ran down her spine when she had crossed the road. As the knife punctured her skin she realized he had been with her for weeks: following her. Her bladder let go. The warm urine soaked into her underwear and tights.

He put his arm around her waist, her feet barely touching the ground as he walked her towards the alleyway at the corner of the building. She had never felt so small in her life. 'Please . . . please, don't do this.' Debbie didn't recognize her own voice; her words slurred, her breathing laboured. She fought to stay conscious as he lifted her into his arms. The lights of the car park were fading but she could see a figure standing in the darkness. She tried to cry out but could make no sound. All she could hear was his voice, whispering in her ear.

2

23 January – Thursday

DI Mike Lockyer opened his eyes, unable to ignore the insistent buzzing of his mobile. He picked it up and rolled onto his back. 'Hello,' he said, stifling a yawn. There wasn't a trace of daylight around his curtains so it was early, very early.

'Morning, sir.'

He sat up and looked over at his alarm clock. A call at 4.10 a.m. from Jane Bennett, his senior detective sergeant on Lewisham's murder squad, wasn't good. 'Morning, Jane. What's up?'

'We are, sir,' she said, no trace of sleep in her voice.

He tried to engage his brain as he grabbed a pair of boxers from a pile of clean washing and dragged on yesterday's suit trousers, already scanning his bedroom for some deodorant. 'Go on.'

'The on-call team are on site. East Dulwich Road, Tesco Metro, SE22 9BD. Female. Eighteen. DOA . . . it looks like there might be a connection to the Atherton and Pearson cases, sir.' She might not sound tired but he recognized tension when he heard it.

'I'll be there in ten minutes. Anything else?' he asked, already walking out of his bedroom, down the hallway, grabbing his jacket and coat as he passed.

'No. Ballinger is the DI on call, so he'll fill you in when you arrive. I've called the team in. Do you want me with you, or shall I get things prepped here, for when you get into the office?'

'You stay put. I'll brief everyone as soon as I arrive.' He was about to hang up when he heard her clear her throat. 'Is there something else, Jane?'

There was a slight pause on the other end of the phone. 'The chief asked me to tell you . . . to mention that he wants the scene processed ASAP. He doesn't want . . . in his words, "a media circus" invading Peckham again.'

'I'm sure he doesn't,' Lockyer said, slamming his front door, a gust of freezing wind hitting him full in the face. 'I'll see you in a sec.'

Lockyer zipped up his jacket as he approached the officer in charge of the outer perimeter. He couldn't help but be slightly amused as she struggled to hold the police tape aloft for him. The scent of her perfume filled his nostrils as he brushed past. It was strong, way too strong for 4.30 in the morning.

'Thank you, Officer,' he said, trying not to breathe in any more of the musky odour.

A thin layer of ice crunched beneath his feet as he crossed the road. The temporary traffic lights were on red, the ice reflecting the colour onto his shoes and legs. It looked like he was walking through a pool of blood.

East Dulwich Road was deserted, apart from four police

vehicles, the SOCOs' van and a redundant ambulance. The squad cars' flashing lights cast an eerie glow over the supermarket car park. A low muttering was coming from the alleyway that ran alongside the Tesco Metro, a squat red-brick building. It had only opened three months ago and already its reputation was tarnished by violent crime. A sixteen-year-old had been stabbed two weeks ago for his mobile phone and last week three young people lost their lives in the car park in a gangland dispute over territory. Nothing stayed unblemished for long; not in his experience, anyway.

The Tesco itself was fronted by a wall of glass. The shadowed panes seemed to watch him, distorting his tall frame into a ghastly image. His head looked tiny, his torso stunted and his legs stick-thin and fun-house long. He looked away and veered towards the alley.

Three dead girls.

Phoebe Atherton, twenty, body found on 14 December on the edge of Camberwell New Cemetery. Katy Pearson, twenty-two, body found on 4 January by a group of twelve-year-olds in New Cross. An image of Katy Pearson's body, discarded like a piece of rubbish on scrubland behind the Hobgoblin pub, flashed into his mind. His team weren't dealing with the case but he had seen the crime-scene photographs. The poor girl had been no more than twenty feet away from help during the entire attack.

Both of the girls had had their wrists cut, then they were raped and finally their throats were slashed. The wrist wounds hadn't been the killing stroke, but the more the girls struggled during the sexual assault, the faster their blood would have been pumped out of their bodies. The thought made his palms sweat. He stopped and took a lungful of the January air, grateful now for the bite of cold on the back of his throat.

There was no confirmation of a link between Katy and Phoebe, not officially, but the whispers around the squad were getting louder. This body wasn't going to do anything to quieten the rumours. All three murder sites were within two miles of each other. If the modus operandi was consistent with the others, he and the murder squad could potentially be dealing with south-east London's first serial killer. It felt like he had wandered onto a film set instead of an unremarkable suburban street in East Dulwich.

He approached the inner cordon at the mouth of the alleyway and dragged on some shoe covers held out to him by another young officer. It was only then that the smell hit him. The cold would have slowed down the first stages of decomposition but there was no mistaking the sweet, metallic odour of blood.

The scene of the crime officers had laid down numerous three-by-two platforms of toughened plastic to protect the site. He stepped up onto one of them, aware that he was inches away from vital evidence. The platforms criss-crossing the piles of debris made the scene look like some sick collage, the forensics team hovering around the body, obscuring Lockyer's view. All he could see were two bare feet.

'Mike, delighted you could make it. I was entering rigor myself waiting for you.' Dave Simpson stood and walked towards him, removing his gloves.

'David. What have we got?' Lockyer asked, resting a hand on his friend's shoulder. Dave was the senior pathologist for

Southwark. His district included the boroughs of Greenwich, Lambeth and Lewisham. It was a massive area to cover and meant a lot of overtime. He dealt with everything: gang-related shootings, a young girl stabbed to death for twenty pounds, a mercy killing in New Cross, a man beaten to death by his neighbour because of a kid's bike, and that was a quiet week. Every hour the poor sod had worked seemed etched on his face.

'Female, Deborah Stevens, eighteen years old . . . and we're looking at the same MO as the others. It's too early for me to officially confirm but . . . unofficially, you're looking for the same man. Wrists, rape, throat.' Dave shrugged.

He stepped over to another platform to get a better look at the shrouded body. 'How long are these guys gonna be?' Lockyer motioned towards the SOCOs.

'They're almost done. Five minutes. Once they're done I'll talk you through what I have so far and we can discuss the . . . differences.'

'Differences? You just said it was the same MO?'

'It is, bar a couple of things.' Dave put his finger to his lips. 'I'd prefer to talk to you about them when this lot have gone. Lot of ears here.'

'Can we get this scene cleared, now?' Lockyer's tone left no room for interpretation. The group of bent figures finally acknowledged his presence and began shuffling out of the alley, their papery outfits crackling as they went. 'So? Come on. I don't want to waste any time if you've got something I can move on.' He took a step towards the body but Dave stopped him. 'What's up with you?' he asked, looking at Dave and the firm hand holding his arm.

'Before we go and look at her, there are two things,' Dave said.

'And they are?'

'Firstly, there are two additions to the MO. It appears that the attacker used a knife to initially subdue the victim and then drugged her. I won't know for certain until I have her on the table, but she has a puncture wound just below her ribs and an entry site and bruising on her neck.'

'I'll need confirmation on that ASAP. If the suspect bought or stole prescription drugs, it could be a great lead.' Lockyer was already thinking who in the Serious and Organized Crime Division would be the best person to ask about purchasing or stealing prescription medication. 'And . . . the second thing?' Dave didn't answer. Lockyer looked down at the hand still holding his arm. 'What the hell is up with you?' he asked, trying again to shake free of his friend's grip.

'I just want you to be prepared before you see her. She . . . I mean . . . there's a resemblance to . . .' Dave drifted into silence and seemed to be looking everywhere but at Lockyer.

'Come on, Dave . . . what resemblance?' He wrenched out of Dave's grip and stepped towards the body. Her bare feet were smeared with mud and filth from the alleyway. Her scraped knees were splayed outward, her right leg lying at an awkward angle with what looked like badly torn tights stuck to her thigh. Her skin was translucent. A sheet covered her torso but Lockyer could still see the blood. It looked viscous, like oil. It had pooled around her wrists where they had been cut.

As he took another step forward the victim's face came into view. Her auburn hair was plastered against her right cheek. He squatted next to her and tilted his head to look into her lifeless eyes. 'Oh my God,' he whispered.

'That's what I was trying to tell you,' Dave said, pulling him to his feet. 'I'm sorry, mate. I almost had a heart attack myself, when I arrived. Took me a couple of seconds to realize it wasn't her.'

Lockyer tried to focus, to move or speak.

'Mike . . . are you all right?'

The iron clamp crushing his heart suddenly released its grip. He swayed as his senses rushed back to him. '. . . I'm fine. It isn't . . . it isn't her,' he said, touching the chain around his neck, rolling the ring back and forth beneath his shirt.

'No, it isn't. I'm sorry, I handled that badly. I wasn't sure what to say,' Dave said with a shake of his head.

'It's fine, just knocked me off for a second, I'm fine . . . what else have you got for me?'

He tried to listen to Dave's preliminary report but all he could think about was Megan. All he could see was her face.

3

Sarah crossed the road and walked onto Peckham Rye, Antonia close behind her dragging a less than willing terrier. There were three joggers on the opposite side of the park but other than that they were the only ones braving the cold weather. That was good.

Cars queued at the temporary traffic lights at the bottom of the park, their cold engines sending white clouds into the air. She found the normality of it almost comforting. People still went to work, still effed and blinded when they missed the lights. Everything carried on as before. Only she had changed. 'So, whose dog is it?' she asked.

'Sally's. Well, her friend's, actually. She's dog-sitting. He's sweet, really, just a little hyper,' Toni said, tugging on the dog's lead as it struggled to go back the way they had come. 'Monty . . . stop it,' Toni said. Monty sniffed the air, looked up at them both and then resumed his game of tug of war.

'And why are you walking him?' Sarah asked, brushing her hair out of her face. It was cold but the sun had pushed through the clouds and she could do with the colour.

'No reason, really . . . I just thought it would give us a good reason to get out of the house,' Toni said, with a smile.

Sarah should have known the dog walk was just a ploy to drag her out of her flat. Toni had tried everything in the past week, suggesting cinema trips, shopping, dinner out. Sarah had refused them all with the same excuse. She was tired and just needed some rest. It was true, in a way, but it wasn't the real reason she didn't want to go out. 'You mean, get *me* out of the house,' she said, returning Toni's innocent smile.

'It's only a walk, Sarah. We can go back if you'd like?'

'No, it's fine,' Sarah said, glancing behind her. 'I'm out now. The fresh air will do me good.' She gave Toni a shove on the arm. What were friends for, if not forcing you to do something you didn't want to do, for your own good?

They walked arm in arm as they entered the manicured section of the park. Winter had removed all the warmth and colour. The lush green hideaway that had been created last spring was now bare wooded arches, dead leaves turning to mulch in the flower beds. She couldn't wait for the weather to change. The dark nights, the cold. She hated it. It only made things seem more bleak.

'William Blake saw visions here,' Toni said, gesticulating around her at the dormant garden.

'Really?' Sarah replied, with no interest.

'Yes, he did, trees filled with angels . . . imagine that? Angels,' she said, squeezing Sarah's arm.

She didn't know how to respond. It didn't feel like a place filled with anything even close to ethereal, but it was sweet of Toni to try to fill the silence between them.

'They kept Italian POWs here during the Second World War, too,' said Toni, raising her eyebrows.

'Fascinating,' Sarah teased, relieved to feel a natural smile spreading across her face.

'Someone has to educate you, *bella*,' Toni said, giving Sarah a friendly shove. 'So, how's work?' she asked in a sing-song voice, pulling the dog back onto the brick path, its paws already caked in mud.

Sarah's smile vanished as she stopped walking and turned in a circle. 'Oh, you know, same old, same old. I've got a job up in the City on Saturday. It's an easy job. Head shots for a management team.'

'That's good, good that you're still . . .' Toni's words were drowned out as Monty started to bark.

Sarah looked into the crush of pine trees that had been pinned and forced into an archway ahead of them. She heard a rustling and stepped back. The dog yelped as her heel connected with one of its paws. 'There's a good reason I don't have pets,' she said, hoping she didn't look as on edge as she felt. She watched as Toni bent down and petted the little terrier, talking to him quietly in Italian. Sarah let the words soothe her but the peace didn't last. A squirrel darted out of the line of trees, disappearing into the undergrowth. The dog started to bark again, pulling at the lead to escape. 'Are we done yet?' she asked, looking back. She could just see the end of her road. She wanted to be home, to close the door and put another day behind her.

'It's not good, Sarah. You can't keep doing this,' Toni said. 'Why don't you come and stay with me, just until this thing blows over?'

She wanted to ask how Toni knew it would blow over. Things were getting worse, not better. And there was no one to help her. 'I can't, not right now,' she said, not trusting herself to look up. 'I've got a couple of possible jobs that I need to confirm. I only heard about them this morning. Besides, I'm fine, there's no need.' This time she took a deep breath, tipped her chin up and looked across at Toni who was shaking her head. 'I'm fine, really.' She forced a smile but it was obvious Toni didn't believe her. 'Thanks for getting me out of the house. It's helped, honestly,' she said, reaching down and giving Toni's hand a squeeze.

They walked back to her flat in silence, the dog's sniffing the only sound interrupting Sarah's thoughts. Would he call tonight? She closed her eyes and shook her head. Of course he would.

4

Lockyer pushed against his eyelids with the tips of his fingers, but the image of the victim's bare feet and Megan's face refused to shift.

'Sir?'

He opened one eye and saw Jane standing in the doorway to his office. 'Jane. Perfect timing. As always.' The overhead spotlights were too bright. His head was thumping. He abandoned his attempt to open both eyes and maintained a lopsided view of his DS.

'I just wanted to report in and check you were . . . all right?' Her eyebrows disappeared beneath a severe black fringe: a new style that reminded him of a Lego man toy. The comparison suited both her petite frame and her demeanour. He had worked with Jane for years, watched her progress through the ranks, chosen her for his senior DS, and from his experience she was always immaculate, well presented, punctual, efficient; in essence the perfect copper. He was yet to find any faults. That couldn't be normal, surely? As the thought entered his head he caught sight of his own reflection in his computer screen. His dark hair was unbrushed and his olive skin was hidden beneath a day or two's stubble. Handsomely dishevelled? Possibly. He looked down. His shirt was buttoned up wrong. No. Just dishevelled.

'I'm fine, Jane.' He stood and walked over to his much-prized window, adjusting his shirt. They had moved him into this office when he had taken over as lead DI for Lewisham's MIT, Murder Investigation Team, part of the HSCC, the Homicide and Serious Crime Command. Neither title was used much, by him or his team. He was running the 'murder squad', plain and simple. Other branches in Hendon, Barnes, Belgravia and Barking dealt with north, south and central London, but the east and south-east were his domain. As he pushed back the vertical blinds to look out at the grey morning, his nose was assaulted by the smell of exhaust fumes and fried food drifting through his open window. He took a step back, watching as the human traffic of Lewisham collided, funnelled into a narrow pedestrian walkway. It was the fourth time the council had dug up this particular eight-foot-square section of the High Street. 'That is to say . . . I'm fine, considering I am dealing with three murdered girls, I've been up since four and listening to that jack-hammer since eight.' His voice echoed in his ears, trying to compete with the small boulders that were smashing against each other inside his skull. What he really wanted to do was drive the four miles home, close the shutters on his floor-to-ceiling Georgian windows, stretch out on his new sofa and go to sleep. The sofa had been delivered over a week ago and he still hadn't managed to sit in it for more than five minutes.

'I spoke to Dave. He told me about this morning, sir,' Jane said, interrupting his thoughts.

He glanced over his shoulder. Her concerned face was beginning to make sense. 'Dave shouldn't be telling anyone anything,' he said.

'Sorry, sir, Dave just thought . . . he thought someone on the team should know.'

He looked away and studied Jane's reflection in the glass. She looked up at the ceiling, down at the floor and then at both sides of his office. He hadn't seen her look this uncomfortable since that May Day bank holiday, four years ago. An ill-advised evening for sure but it had been Jane's facial expression the next morning, a combination of embarrassment and concern in her eyes, that had made Lockyer run. 'I don't want anyone else to hear about this. Is that clear?'

'Absolutely, sir. Dave's getting ready for the post. He'll call when he's good to go. Should be an hour and—' The jackhammer resumed and drowned out the rest of Jane's sentence. 'Are you sure you don't want to talk about it?'

'Jane. Enough. You sound like Clara, for God's sake. Close the door on your way out.' He took a deep breath and turned back to his desk. It still felt odd mentioning Clara.

An hour later, surrounded by white Formica and steel, Lockyer stood in the mortuary suite, looking down at Deborah Stevens' body. She looked so small, fragile. The skin over her cheeks was taut and colourless. A griping pain rippled across his stomach. He cocked his head to one side and looked into her milky eyes, still open, frozen in terror. There was no sign of the smiling girl from the photograph that was now attached to Debbie's file, given to him by her family. He leaned closer and whispered her name, 'Debbie,' then straightened and backed away from the table as Patrick, Dave's senior assistant, began laying out all of the instruments needed for the procedure.

'Did you see the bite mark?'

Lockyer turned to find Dave standing right next to him. 'What bite mark?' he asked, looking away, reluctant to look his friend in the eye.

Dave walked around to the other side of the table, pointed to Debbie's right shoulder and lifted a section of matted hair away from her pale face. 'Here . . . it's at the top of the trapezius muscle. I didn't see it in the prelim exam because it was hidden by the hairline.' Lockyer took a step forward and looked at the livid, purplish marks scattered over Debbie's neck. It looked like she had been attacked by a wild dog, not a man. He turned away, the image of the marks already burned into his memory. 'There isn't enough of an impression for dental recognition but Patrick has taken some deep tissue swabs and we might have some saliva.' Lockyer didn't respond. He couldn't. All he could see was Debbie's attacker, crouching over her, sinking his teeth into her like a vampire in the moonlight. 'OK . . . hard to please this morning, I see,' Dave said, walking to the end of the mortuary table. 'Would it make you happier if I said I had a fingerprint?'

He tore his mind away from the images in his head and finally looked at Dave. 'Fingerprint. How? The body was cleaned, wasn't it?' His voice rough, like flint on stone.

'He did . . . watered-down bleach, like the others. I guess he missed a spot,' Dave said with a shrug. 'It's a partial print, in blood. Right index finger. It's on the outside of the left thigh.' Dave held up his right hand to demonstrate the angle against Debbie's outstretched legs.

'I need that print,' Lockyer said.

'Already done. Patrick lifted it just before you came down. Your team are scanning it now,' Dave said. 'Who knows, maybe you'll have a suspect by the time we're done here.'

He looked down at Debbie, pushed his anger away and said a silent prayer that Dave was right. He resisted an urge to reach out, to touch her cheek, and without warning Megan's face pushed its way into his thoughts. His hand went automatically to the chain around his neck, the band of gold cool against his chest. He shook his head. Now wasn't the time. 'What about the drug?' he asked.

'It'll take a few days to get the toxicology report back but I think he used some kind of mild barbiturate.' Dave moved forward and gently lifted one of Debbie's arms. 'The defensive wounds here . . . and here, indicate she came to at some point but I doubt she was ever fully conscious,' he said, indicating several deep scratches on her hand and forearm. 'And he definitely used a knife to further subdue her,' he said. 'This is the puncture wound.'

'Can you check the others for any drug traces?' Lockyer asked, looking away from the welts on Debbie's arms and the small hole just beneath her ribs.

'Of course,' Dave said. 'We already have the blood work back on the first two victims but I haven't had time to look at it, what with this and the gang killing last week. I'll rush them through and get back to you. Now . . . if that's all . . . I think we're ready to begin.' Dave's voice had taken on a much softer tone. Respectful. He reached for a scalpel and paused like a conductor before a concert.

Lockyer watched Dave make the Y incision, constantly speaking into a Dictaphone, detailing every move he made, every cut. 'The outer chest cavity is clear, no evidence of trauma, oedema present but consistent with hypostasis. Patrick, please open the chest cavity.' Lockyer looked away. He wasn't squeamish but there were some things he just didn't need to see, and the removal of the chest plate was one of them.

'I am making my incision and opening the pericardial sac . . . heart clean, very little plaque build-up, consistent with the victim's age.' Dave's scalpel moved in a blur. 'I am taking blood from the inferior vena cava . . . Patrick.' Patrick stepped forward, placing a syringe into Dave's gloved hand. As Dave dissected the lungs he muttered, 'Smoker, not heavy.'

Bile rushed into Lockyer's mouth. Megan smoked. He could still hear Dave's voice but it was as if he was talking under water, his words muted. '. . . kidneys, clean . . . liver, clean . . . pancreas . . . stomach, very little to see here. She hadn't eaten in six hours, at least . . .' He swallowed and forced himself to focus. '. . . we'll move on to the reproductive system now,' Dave said, his blurred shape taking a step back, sidestepping before approaching the table again. A freezing hand snaked its way up Lockyer's body, touching his thighs, his stomach and the base of his spine. He hung his head and let out a long breath.

'Mike?' He could hear Dave's voice but it sounded far away. 'Lockyer!' Dave's harsh shout brought him back. He stood straight, blinking rapidly. Dave and his team were all staring at him. 'Are you all right?'

He cleared his throat. '. . . I'm fine,' he said, covering his face with his hands as he coughed. 'I'm sorry about that . . .' He fumbled for something to say, anything to explain his bizarre behaviour. 'I'm fine. Must be something I ate.' He waited for what felt like hours as David and Patrick continued to stare at him.

'Right,' Dave said, breaking the silence. 'Let's continue, shall we?'

He tried to ignore the look of concern on his friend's face, dropping his eyes to the floor as Dave made the incision to open up Debbie's reproductive cavity. He felt furious with himself. When he told Jane earlier that he was fine, that he didn't need to talk about this morning, about Megan, he had meant it. So why was his body going into some kind of meltdown?

'We've got something here,' Dave said, the grey bags under his eyes illuminated by the mortuary light as he looked up. 'She's had a D&C . . . very recently . . . last few days, I'd say, either the result of an incomplete miscarriage or a first trimester abortion.' Dave's shrug told Lockyer which his friend thought more likely.

'Jesus,' Lockyer said, shaking his head. 'Are we done?' he asked, watching as Patrick began positioning Debbie's head for the brain exam. He could do without seeing them remove a section of her head. He wanted out of this room.

'You are,' Dave said. 'We'll finish up here and I'll get my full report to you as soon as I can.'

'Right. Thanks,' he said, already turning to leave.

'Hey, buddy, you might want to get something for that stomach of yours,' Dave said. 'You look like shit.'

'Thank you, David,' he replied, without bothering to turn around.

*

Lockyer sat down at his desk as the office door clicked shut. He had been making lists in his head on the way back from the mortuary suite. Things he had to do, things he wanted Jane and his DSs to get started on and things for the DCs to be getting on with, but all he kept seeing was Megan's face. He needed to make the call. He pressed speed-dial three on his mobile, inhaled, held the breath and waited. It was on the fifth ring that she answered.

'Hello, Megan speaking.'

'Hello, Megan speaking. This is your father speaking.'

5

23 January – Thursday

Sarah turned out the main light and closed her bedroom door, her right eye twitching as the click of the latch echoed around the room. Her body, this flat, her life: nothing felt solid. Everything had been replaced with shadows, paper-thin imitations that threatened to blow apart at any moment, disintegrating into a million pieces. The floorboards creaked as she padded over to the window. Her blind was already down, so, careful not to touch it, she peered around the edge and looked out at her little strip of garden: roaming weeds, strangled flowers and light clumps of dead grass where her lawn had failed to grow.

She stepped back. He couldn't see her. She knew that. Her flat was on the first floor and the only thing that overlooked the back of the house was the Bredinghurst School playground. The fence separating her from the school was twenty feet high, covered in ivy. She sighed and sat down on the edge of her bed, her legs suddenly too weak to hold her. How many hours had she wasted trying to convince herself that he wasn't outside, that he couldn't see her, that he didn't exist?

She pulled up the hood of her sweatshirt. A low thud made her freeze. She held her breath and waited, straining her ears to identify the origin of the sound. Her heart hammered in her chest. As her body began to shake she heard three more thuds and the sound of rushing water. It was her central heating, just water and pipes. She rocked back and forth, dizzy as the adrenalin that had surged through her body just seconds ago abandoned her.

She turned and looked over at her alarm clock. It was almost midnight. He hadn't called tonight, not yet. For what felt like the hundredth time Sarah thought about calling Toni, but what would that achieve? She already knew what Toni would say. 'Call the police. I'll come over. You shouldn't be by yourself.' No. She wouldn't do that. If he called, he called. There was nothing Toni could do about it and there was nothing the police would do about it. Sarah was on her own. Her socks crackled against the sheet as she climbed into bed. She covered her bedside lamp with a pashmina. It made the room just dark enough. She picked up her notebook from the nightstand and opened it, unable to focus on the scribbled dates and times that swam on the pages. Tonight's entry was barely legible. It looked more like a scream on a page than actual words. Her arm brushed against the video camera where it nestled next to her. She shouldn't watch it again. It would only make things worse.

The calls had started six months ago, although the ache in her bones made it feel much longer. At first she had answered her phone without fear: 'Hello . . . hellooooo.' Why wouldn't she? Two months had gone by, dozens of the phantom calls and still the penny hadn't dropped. Even as fear started to take hold, she had convinced herself that it was a wrong number, a cold call from Abu Dhabi about Internet providers, or a friend on holiday, drunk and oblivious to the time difference. But then it changed. It was a Tuesday night in October. She had flopped into bed after a heavy vino session with Toni. When her phone rang she had answered it. She was too tired, too drunk to talk, so she just listened. That was when he had said her name: 'Sarah.' A man's voice. Not loud, not questioning. Just her name carried on an outward breath and then nothing. Nothing but his breathing. That was the night she had realized it wasn't a wrong number and it never had been. The presence she had sensed, the weird incidents she'd shrugged off, for months, had been him. She had called Peckham Police Station the next day and had recounted her story to four different officers before being put through to a sergeant who was either very old, very jaded or both. She told him everything: the phone calls, the phantom knocks on her door, the stuff with her car and, most importantly, the presence she had felt but not believed until that one call had brought everything into focus. What had the sergeant done? Nothing. He had patronized her, saying, 'My advice at this stage, Miss Grainger, would be to alter your routine. Small changes often result in an end to this kind of nuisance.' He had used words like 'nuisance', 'harassment' and 'harmless' as if he were reading them from a cheat sheet. He never said 'stalker'. Sarah had, she kept on saying it, but he had swerved and returned to his safe words. 'Ninety per cent of these nuisance cases turn out to be nothing. An old boyfriend, perhaps, or someone who would like to be a boyfriend. You are doing the right thing, Miss

Grainger. As long as you show him no further encouragement, he will get bored.'

She sat up and threw her duvet off, unable to stand the
weight pressing down on her. How had she encouraged him,
exactly? By answering her phone? Was that seen as a come-on
these days? She shook her head and stared at the bedroom
door. The sergeant had even told her not to change her
number. How would they prove anything if there wasn't a
clear log of all the calls she had received? 'Keep a journal of
further events, if there are any, but do call us at any time if
you are concerned. I assure you, Miss Grainger, we take these
cases very seriously.'

'What a load of crap,' she said to the empty room. The
police didn't care. Whenever she called to speak to them, to
tell them things were getting worse, to tell them she couldn't
take any more, the answer was always the same. 'Officer
Rayner will call you right back, Miss Grainger,' but he never
did.

Her eyes were again drawn to the video camera lying next
to her. She picked it up as if it was coated in acid and opened
the screen, her hands already beginning to shake. As she
pressed play, she shrank back into her pillows. She watched
as her street flickered to life on the display in front of her.
Parked cars lined the pavements. Lights shone out from
her neighbours' houses. The picture zoomed in. A dark car.
A dark figure sitting, motionless. She wasn't even sure what
kind of car it was. Maybe a Honda, like her brother's?
She couldn't see the registration. The man inside didn't move;
his shape could almost be a mannequin. The screen went
black. That was it.

When the man in the car had actually moved Sarah had dropped the camera and run through to the kitchen, gasping for air. She had crawled on her hands and knees to retrieve it an hour later when she was calm enough. He had made her crawl in her own home and cower under her own windowsill.

She pulled her duvet up around her chin and turned onto her side, staring at her white wall. She reached out a cold hand and let it hover over the switch on the bedside lamp. If he was outside, watching, he would know that she was in her bedroom. Her hand retreated under the covers. She was so thirsty but knew she couldn't make it to the kitchen. Now she had closed herself in, her bedroom door was both a comfort and a terror.

Unable to sleep, Sarah tossed and turned, watching the red numbers projected by her alarm clock onto the ceiling, counting the hours. Her mind drifted, sleep sucking her under for just a moment until her stomach lurched, forcing her eyes open, dragging her back to consciousness.

A ringing sound floated along her senses. As her mind moved in slow motion towards understanding, the ringing became louder, deafening. She sat up, staring. On the bedside table her mobile vibrated, the blue light from her phone illuminating the room. She edged towards the noise, keeping the covers tight around her. For a fleeting second she imagined seeing Toni's name or even her mother's. The face of her phone came into view. 'Call' was all the screen told her. She could answer. She wouldn't, but she could. It was 1 a.m. The phone stopped and after ten seconds the display went black. She tunnelled back into the centre of her bed, the duvet covering her completely. Her breathing slowed. The diary. 'Damn it,' she said as she stuck her head and one arm out of the warmth and grabbed the notebook and pen. She had made more notes in this last week than she had in the past four months. She looked at the time and scribbled: '1 a.m. call. Not answered. No message.' She closed the book, pushed it back onto the table, and once again retreated under her duvet, groggy with restless sleep. She tucked herself into a ball and wrapped her arms around her legs. She could feel her body giving in, exhaustion dragging her under.

Then she was dreaming about a series of doors. She was trying to find her room in a vast hotel. She recognized the concierge but she couldn't ask him where room 1497 was. None of the doors would open. Each time she turned a brass handle it buzzed. They must be locked. Sarah desperately looked at the white corridor in front of her, hoping for a sign, an arrow she could follow. She tried another door. This time a buzzing and ringing sounded with each twist of the doorknob. She opened her eyes. A blue light danced over her ceiling. Without moving she reached over and picked up her phone, bringing it close to her face. 'Call' the screen said. She looked up at the time projected in red on her ceiling. It was 2 a.m. She pushed the phone beneath her pillow and waited for the ringing to stop. With automatic movements she picked up the notebook and pen and wrote down the entry. She lay back on the bed, her brain telling her she was dreaming. She was still in the hotel. Sarah closed her eyes and continued her search for room 1497.

At 3 a.m. she was awake, staring at the ceiling. She had

been considering turning her phone off for the past thirty-four minutes, but then how would she log the calls? And what would be the point anyway? He would still be calling but without the ringing she wouldn't know. He would be sneaking into her bedroom without her knowledge and she couldn't bear the thought of that. When the phone jumped into life next to her she didn't even flinch. Her fear had been replaced with a kind of numb acceptance. The red numbers on her ceiling and the blue lights danced together now.

At 4 a.m. she started laughing. Deep in her stomach she felt tremors that ran haphazardly through her body as though she was having a fit. 'Come on,' she said to the gloom. 'Come on, then.' Almost immediately he answered her. The ringing, the buzzing, the lights. It was a party in her room at 4 a.m.

An hour later she lay looking at a hairline crack that ran the length of her bedroom wall. She counted the calls off in her head again, just to check she hadn't imagined them. Four calls, on the hour, every hour since 1 a.m.. 5 a.m. flickered red on the ceiling. Had he finally given up? She tensed her aching muscles and said a silent prayer that he had, but before she could finish the thought her mobile started to ring, buzzing next to her. She couldn't bring herself even to touch the phone any more. She rested on one elbow and looked at the screen. Her hands itched as she wrestled for the fifth time with whether to answer. He wanted her to answer. More than anything he wanted her to give in to him. The ringing stopped.

She had coped with a fortnightly call but every night this week and then five times last night – it was too much. The mobile beeped to let her know the caller had left a voicemail. She picked up her phone and threw it at the wall. It bounced and landed at the foot of her bed. Unharmed, indestructible. She looked over at her bedroom door, at the pale light surrounding it. She couldn't wait any longer. She threw back the duvet and dragged herself out of bed.

In the bathroom she splashed cold water on her face and blinked at her reflection in the mirror. Her eyelids were swollen. She tipped the contents of her make-up bag into the sink. The mirror had a crack running across the bottom left-hand corner where she had screwed it on too tight. The 'one coat' azure paint she had chosen looked tatty, with bits of the previous pink showing through where her brush strokes had been too quick. A film of dust and condensation clung to the cistern of the toilet. The tiles beneath her feet were coming loose, leaving tiny sharp corners that snagged her feet. She put her hands on either side of the basin, closing her fingers around the porcelain. Her reflection blurred at the edges but her eyes were on fire. Hers were the eyes of a hunted animal. She had nothing left to hold on to but her fear.

6

Lockyer reversed his Audi into a space opposite Cliffview Residential Home. The double-fronted Victorian terrace was only two miles from the centre of Lewisham, so there were no cliffs for twenty miles at least, and no view unless the identical row of houses sitting opposite could be deemed picturesque.

The warm leather of the Audi's curved headrest soothed his nerves as he attempted to clear his mind. He had dealt with cold-blooded murderers more times than he wanted to think about, but this guy was different, more organized, methodical. He took a deep breath and leaned forward against the steering wheel. His mind was still racing, Debbie's face so vivid it was making his chest ache. He pinched the bridge of his nose with his thumb and forefinger as images of the crime scene crowded in on him. He took the keys out of the ignition and climbed out of the car. The smog, even this close to town, had vanished. The air was crisp but the clouds looked heavy with snow.

The red brick of the house was damp, a shimmer of steam rising from the masonry as the sun burnt off the previous

34

night's downpour. He had never and would never take his work into this place. The staff didn't even know he was a copper. The idea of the macabre side of his profession somehow infecting the vulnerable minds within was too much to bear. He walked up the small driveway to the covered front door, a small keypad off to the side. The code changed once every three months. He punched in the new number.

As he entered the hallway he noticed Amber, one of the carers. She was on the phone, absently picking at a frayed edge of flowered wallpaper. He had been coming here for almost five years now, so he knew better than to disturb her. Amber was patient and kind to the four men and two women who called Cliffview their home but she had a quick temper for anyone else, particularly him, it seemed. She turned and gave him a curt nod. He had the feeling that she thought he didn't spend enough time here, wasn't as involved with his brother as he should be. He waited for her to finish the call.

'Morning, Amber. You look very nice today. How's it going?' he asked, giving her his best smile. He was hoping a bit of flattery would save him from her wrath. He had brushed his dark curls until they no longer resembled a Brillo pad, he was clean shaven and all of his clothes were clean, though the iron had eluded him. There wasn't a grey hair on his head, as yet, and Clara had always said that when he smiled his fleshy pink lips and Bushbaby eyes were his most disarming features. However, judging by Amber's withering expression, his efforts had fallen short of the mark.

'Mike. Bobby isn't expecting you. I assume you didn't call,' she said, turning and heading away from him towards the kitchen.

He raised his eyes and walked into the large communal lounge to his left. The four permanent staff kept the place immaculate but no amount of cleaning products could get rid of the smell that permeated the carpets, chairs and curtains. It was stale urine, antibacterial soap and something that he could almost taste; dry, sticking to the back of his throat. There was a disturbing similarity to the acrid, lingering smell of the mortuary suite. As he walked towards the double doors at the end of the lounge he looked out at the garden. It was too damp to sit outside. They would have to play cards in Bobby's room.

Lockyer had moved his brother here five years ago when he discovered he had a brother, and when he saw the shithole Bobby had been living in on the outskirts of Manchester. He thought back to the day he had found out about him; he'd been sifting through his father's effects and discovered numerous letters and bank statements, all relating to Robert Lockyer. He walked back through to the hall and up the stairs. The door leading to the rooms of Bobby and the other male resident, Ian, was wedged open with an ancient-looking fire extinguisher. He glanced into Ian's room as he passed.

'Hey, Ian,' he said, slowing his pace just enough for Ian to get his hand up and wave back at him. There was no such thing as a quick chat with Ian, so he knew better than to stop. Lockyer had attempted a couple of the house outings in the past but he hadn't coped very well. The excitement of a trip meant the staff spent most of their time keeping everyone calm: that had included him.

He stopped outside his brother's room and waited, staring at the pine door. It had been the right decision to move Bobby down here but every time he visited a pang of guilt tugged at his conscience. Bobby wasn't physically disabled – far from it – but he needed care, he needed the kind of help that Lockyer simply couldn't provide. Their own parents had washed their hands of Bobby and packed him off to Aunt Nancy's when he was seven. Lockyer had been four, but despite hours looking through family albums he couldn't stir even the slightest memory of his older brother from when they were children. Bobby's autism was too severe for his parents to handle. That was what his father's letters had said and, of course, that's what Aunt Nancy had eventually said, too. Other people had made Bobby's decisions for him his entire life. Anger and resentment for the life he and Bobby had been denied never failed to surface when he thought about what their parents had done.

'Hey, there.'

He turned to see Alice, another carer and possibly the happiest woman he had ever met, walking towards him. 'You here to see the Bobster? He'll be chuffed. And I see you've even shaved for the occasion,' she said, giving him a friendly punch on the arm.

'Hey, Alice. How are you?' he asked, doffing an invisible hat.

'Perfect,' she said, smiling.

'Good to hear. Any changes in the last few days I should know about? I saw Amber downstairs but she wasn't in the mood to chat.'

'Nah, Bobby never changes and you should ignore Amber. We all do.' Alice gave him a wink and walked away.

Grateful for the mood lift, he turned and knocked three times before opening the door to his brother's room. Bobby stood by the window, staring out at the garden below. He was tall, like Lockyer, but thinner: a reed, swaying gently. His hair was greying at the temples but his skin was pale and smooth, not a line in sight. More than Lockyer could say for his own weather-worn face.

This was Bobby's world; a world in a vacuum. The cream walls were covered with pictures of animals, birds mainly. Bobby loved birds. The bed was pushed up against the wall. It had blue cushions arranged neatly on top of the blue-and-grey striped duvet cover, a Christmas gift from Alice. Lockyer had bought an extra set not long afterwards because Bobby had apparently freaked out when they tried to change his bedding. Bobby's autism meant his ability to deal with change or the fast pace of the outside world was limited. As far as he was concerned his life was, and had always been, Cliffview. He remembered little else and little else interested him. He was content with his books, games and, most importantly, his routine. Five years Lockyer had been coming here, and Bobby still treated him like a new addition in his life.

As he watched Bobby at the window, oblivious to his presence, he wondered how Jane dealt with it, the emotional separation. Her son, Peter, was autistic. Lockyer wasn't sure of the severity of his condition and, if he was honest, was reluctant to ask. If he did, it would lead, no doubt, to talking about Bobby and he didn't want to talk about Bobby to Jane, or anyone else. It was his private family business. He was sure Jane must feel the same about her son.

'Hey, Bobby, how goes it?' He walked over to the window and into his brother's field of vision. Bobby turned his whole body to face him but didn't meet his eyes. He never did.

'It's your favourite card shark.'

'Cards,' Bobby repeated. His voice was quiet and gentle. He rocked from one foot to the other.

'That's right, buddy, cards. You up for a game?' He slowly reached his hand out and touched his brother's sleeve. Sudden movements disturbed Bobby. Lockyer had witnessed a few of Bobby's 'episodes' – that's what Amber had called them – and he never wanted to see another one. Bobby, eyes rolling, arms lashing out at anyone and anything, and the noise, the noise was unbearable, grinding teeth and a wail that seemed stuck in his throat. He turned and walked away, Bobby following him, as if compelled by a force field. He sat his brother down in one of the two leather wing-back chairs, already positioned facing each other. A pine table had been set up between the two chairs, a blue deck of cards resting in the centre.

Once Bobby was settled, Lockyer stood in front of him and offered his right hand. His brother lifted it to his face, focusing on the scar that ran from Lockyer's thumb to his wrist. Five years ago when they had met, it had been the first thing Bobby noticed. The nurses at the home in Manchester told him that Bobby assigned different rituals and indicators to each of the regular nurses and doctors. Something small and seemingly insignificant; a smell or a wedding band or a certain footfall but for Lockyer, Bobby had decided on a scar. That was how he recognized him five years ago and, according to the research Lockyer had done into autism, it was how he always would. He watched Bobby trace the imperfection three times before dropping his hand and picking up the cards in front of him.

'Cards,' Bobby said.

Lockyer sat down opposite his brother. 'That's right, cards. And I'm telling you, I'm not letting you win this time.' He thought he saw just the flash of a smile and comprehension on his brother's face, even though he knew in his heart it wasn't possible. He picked up his own cards and rubbed his chest with the heel of his hand as the pain of reality subsided.

7

24th January – Friday

Why hadn't she answered? He needed to hear her voice. Exhaustion had become his constant companion but it seemed to prolong the thrill in a way he couldn't have imagined.

He used the steering wheel as leverage, arched his back and stretched his legs out into the footwell. His muscles felt tight, unyielding. He groaned, looked at the clock on the dashboard. It was 8 a.m. He pulled his coat around him and turned up the collar. It had dropped to minus three during the night but just being this close to her seemed to warm his blood. He was dying to tell her, for her to experience it through him. But she was ignoring him. He felt like her puppet: she pulled his strings and he danced to her manipulative tune. It had been months since she had deigned to speak to him. All he had to sustain him were overheard snippets of conversations she had with her neighbours. As he leaned forward to ease the ache in his spine he rubbed his hands together. The joints on his fingers were red and swollen, his knuckles covered in scratches.

Surrey Road was quiet. The rustle of the ice-covered litter in the gutters and the wind whistling through the branches of the trees kept him company. Most of the Victorian terraces were split into flats. Hers was on the first floor: 10A. From his vantage point, sitting in his car, he could just see into her lounge, when the blinds were open. Her television was mounted on the wall next to the window. If she sat in just the right place he could see a perfect reflected image of her, curled up on a red sofa with a glass of wine and a book. But that hadn't happened in a while. Now, when she came home, she put down her blinds immediately. He was left with mere glimpses: her shadow behind a veil of maroon silk.

He pushed away his frustration, closed his eyes and imagined walking her home after one of her photo shoots, cooking for her and then sitting on her raggedy old sofa, just the two of them. Her long blonde hair would be pulled over one shoulder and she would be wearing her leggings, slippers and hooded jumper. She would probably rest her legs in his lap as she read. His trousers tightened around his crotch as his interest grew. He could almost feel her hands on him. The sound of a bicycle bell brought him back to the car and out of his fantasy. The warmth of her touch vanished.

She had known the effect she had on him the moment they met, all those months ago. It had been obvious. He had seen it in her eyes as she licked her lips when she talked to him, blowing on her coffee, her perfect lips pursed, as if waiting for a kiss. She was different from the others. As the cyclist disappeared around the corner, lights began to come on in some of the flats. Their warm glow bathed the dark street in little pools of gold. Her lights had been on all night.

He knew she was home because he had watched her walk up the street yesterday evening, unlock her front door (she had two Chubb locks now) and go inside. So why was she ignoring his calls? 'Selfish . . . bitch,' he whispered, his breath fogging the window. He opened it a bit further so he had an uninterrupted view.

As his anger subsided, cooled by an icy breeze, he heard a shout. His heart raced. Had it come from her flat? It was impossible to tell. He waited, straining his ears for another sound. He looked around at the deserted street. Nothing about it had changed but something felt different. Something was wrong. Condensation dripped down the windscreen. All his tiredness was gone. His eyes were fixed on her front door. 'Please,' he said, touching his cold hands to his hot face. He looked at the clock. It was almost 8.30. If she had a photo shoot she would leave her flat at 9 a.m. It wasn't fair; leaving him to sit here unacknowledged was cruel.

He watched as No. 12 drew back their curtains and No. 8 pulled up his blinds. Almost every flat showed signs of life now, except hers. The bald guy from No. 9 left his house at 8.45 a.m. He was wrapped up in a coat and scarf but had shiny brogues on his feet. He wouldn't make it to the station without slipping, that was for sure. As No. 9 slammed his front door half a dozen other doors seemed to open in sync.

As he opened his car door, a thin film of ice in the jamb cracked and broke. He paced up and down the pavement, hugging himself until a slamming sound made him turn. There she was. His anxiety, his anger, his weariness, they all disappeared. She was wearing her blue jeans and a black jacket he didn't recognize. She didn't have a scarf on or even any gloves. The coat was too big for her slim frame. She had lost weight. He was so relieved by her sudden appearance that he didn't move. He stood on the pavement not more than three houses away from her, staring. Without making a sound he stepped behind a white van parked at the side of the road and watched her lock her flat and walk to her car. It wouldn't do to startle her. She held up a delicate hand and clicked her keys. He noticed that she was muttering under her breath and her hands seemed to be shaking. The indicators flashed on her silver Golf as she pulled open the door and climbed in.

The sound of her engine starting dragged him from his stupor. He crossed the road. It was so hard not to look at her as he ran to his car. Once he was in he fumbled to get the key into the ignition. The engine faltered for a second before rumbling into life. He had parked facing Peckham Rye, as she had, so all he had to do was wait for her to pull away before following, a safe distance behind. It was a test of skill to follow her by car. She drove fast and rarely obeyed the traffic laws. Before they had even reached the lights at the edge of Peckham Rye she was four cars in front. He craned his neck to keep the back of the Golf in sight but he was having trouble keeping up with her as she swerved from one lane to another. His car groaned and wheezed as he pushed it harder and harder to keep pace. In Forest Hill she ran a red light, but the roadworks outside Catford Station forced her to slow down and he was able to weave in and out of the traffic until he was two cars behind her. He ignored the shouts of protest from angry commuters.

As they entered Lewisham and hit yet more roadworks

he let himself relax, just enough to think about where she was going. She hadn't been lugging her camera equipment when she had left her flat earlier. Her friend Toni, the rotund Italian, lived in Honor Oak, so she wasn't late for a coffee date. Two cars pulled off on a side street leaving just one car between them. The temporary traffic lights outside Lewisham Police Station changed and she accelerated and then swung her car, without indicating, across the road. She was blocking the traffic, causing chaos. Once her car was wedged into a space, the traffic began to move again. He was so busy watching her that he almost rear-ended the car in front. He dragged his eyes back to the road and kept going. He looked over his shoulder as he drove past. Sweat prickled in the hairs on the back of his neck. He needed to find somewhere to park. If he hadn't been right outside the police station he would have just mounted the kerb and left his car to its own fate. The bright yellow and orange of the Shell garage sign caught his eye. He indicated and pulled into one of the parking bays. He jumped out of the car and ran but by the time he reached her car she had disappeared. He scanned the street but couldn't see her.

The police station car park was on his left, teeming with people. Uniformed officers punctuated a meandering group of men and women as they drifted in and out of the station's electric double doors. Then he saw her. She was sat on a long red-brick wall that ran down from the entrance. She had her hands tucked in between her knees, head down, her hair covering her face. She was rocking back and forth. He stared at her, willing her to look up, to face him. He wrapped his fingers around the bars of the fence, his knuckles white, but when she finally raised her head he loosened his grip on the cold metal. He saw her wipe away a tear from her cheek. He wanted to kill whoever was responsible for the agony he could see on her face.

8

24 January – Friday

Lockyer sat back in his chair and stared at Debbie's file, relaxing his eyes until the words blurred on the scattered pages. He had been stuck in his office, reading and re-reading the post-mortem report, since 7.30 this morning. He pushed the section containing the photographic record of the procedure further to the back of the file. There wasn't one part of his brain that needed to see those images again. The first-hand experience had been enough.

He let his head hang forward and closed his eyes. Despite speaking to Megan and seeing her for a takeaway last night, he still felt odd, shaky. The smallest, seemingly inconsequential details about Debbie's case kept catching him off guard, liquefying his stomach, sending him running to the men's room. It didn't make sense. Her resemblance to his daughter was understandably unsettling but it hardly warranted this intense physical reaction. The only time he could remember feeling this emotionally drained and tense was when Megan was born. He had spent the first month of her life in a state of perpetual panic. The slightest thing had him convinced he was going to lose her. Even the memory made the muscles in his neck knot. But now, this case, this murdered teenager. Why couldn't he focus? Why couldn't he control his own body, for God's sake? He wiped his mouth with the back of his hand as bile pooled beneath his tongue.

It was no good. The more he tried to push Megan out of his thoughts and concentrate on Debbie, the more his daughter's face appeared in his mind. To top it off, there were no hits for the partial fingerprint or the DNA. That could change but he would have to be patient. And his calls to the organized crime unit hadn't turned up anything on the drugs. No missing prescriptions or stolen drug batches to chase up. Doors were closing faster than they were opening.

He picked up the transcripts of Jane's interviews with Debbie's family, work colleagues and friends. There was practically nothing to go on. Deborah Stevens had been an ordinary girl with a normal job, living with her mother and stepfather in a nondescript council house on a suburban street in Nunhead. They were separated from the darker, poorer streets of Peckham by Nunhead Cemetery and Dulwich proper – the posh part, by the Rye: a piece of parkland better described as a modest patch of grass. The family had been checked and ruled out, everyone but Debbie's real father, who hadn't been located, as yet. Wherever he was, he wasn't voting and he wasn't paying tax. Lockyer would have to call in some favours at MPS to see if they couldn't track Mr Stevens down using the missing persons' database. Mind you, if the CSA hadn't found him for child support, Lockyer doubted the MPS would fare much better.

Debbie had worked for Foster Advertising for six months

but none of her colleagues knew her well. In fact few seemed to know what her actual job entailed. Her manager, William Hodgson, spoke highly of her. He said she had been a hard worker; always on time, thorough and cheerful. Lockyer sat forward and looked again at the section on Debbie's aborted pregnancy. There was no mention in any of the interviews about a man, a boyfriend. Her mother was adamant there was no boyfriend. 'Debbie wasn't interested in boys,' the transcript read. 'She wanted to make something of herself.' Jane had told him that the mother's voice had been brimming with animosity. Not towards Debbie, of course, but towards the killer, the police, anyone she could blame for the death of her daughter. He shook his head and pushed himself away from his desk. He knew there would be no respite for the family. Debbie hadn't died of natural causes or been killed in some tragic accident. She had been viciously taken from the world. It wasn't something her family would get over.

He dropped the interviews back onto the file and pushed it to the edge of his desk, shifting in his chair. His arse was asleep. This office wasn't designed for him. He was six foot three and could barely get his legs under the curved plywood desk.

He closed his eyes and pictured the crime scene, images forming behind his eyelids. East Dulwich Road deserted but for some temporary traffic lights, the red light reflected by the patches of ice on the road, the pool of blood, the abandoned Rye, the grass standing to attention in the frost. The alley, narrow and dark, littered with bottles, fag butts and syringes. Her blood, black against the cement. Debbie, lying among the debris.

'I need a break,' he said, rubbing his eyes. The artificial lights were a killer. Lewisham's new Metropolitan station, home to the area murder squad and numerous other departments, was ultra-modern, lots of blue-tinted glass, red brick, aluminium and no atmosphere whatsoever. He stood up, pushed his hair off his forehead and walked out of the room. 'Penny, I'm heading out for five minutes. When Jane arrives tell her I want her in the briefing room at eleven to run through today's action list on the Stevens case. I want the Atherton and Pearson files too, and I want Chris in there, with the interview transcripts prepped.'

He was desperate for some air; even the smoggy air of Lewisham High Street would do. Five minutes, some breathing space and a coffee from Bella's. He was halfway across the car park when he saw Jane walking towards him.

'We might have something, sir,' she said, her breath clouding in front of her face as it mingled with the freezing January air.

'Tell me?'

'The hospital and GP notes didn't give us much, but I just got off the phone with records and they've confirmed that she wasn't referred for the procedure by her GP. She went through a private clinic.'

'What kind of clinic?' he asked, turning away from the gates and heading towards his car.

'They provide pregnancy and STD testing, treatment and counselling for young and underage women,' Jane said, keeping pace beside him. 'I've spoken to the manager, he's expecting us.'

'Good,' he said, shoving his hands into his pockets. 'We'll

take your car; my keys are upstairs.' He changed direction and headed towards Jane's Volvo.

As soon as they were out of the station car park, weaving in and out of the Friday mid-morning traffic, Lockyer noticed the silence. He turned and looked at Jane's profile as she honked the horn and swerved to avoid two buses whose drivers had decided to stop for a chat. Was she paler than normal? As if he would know. God, he hoped she wasn't about to go off sick.

'You OK?' he asked. She didn't reply; her eyes were still focused on the road ahead, but he could have sworn he saw her flinch when he spoke. 'Jane, did you hear me?' he said, hoping his impatience wasn't too obvious.

'Yes, sir,' she said, without turning to look at him. Her voice was hard but her cheeks were now flushed with colour. 'It's nothing, just the case and . . . home, you know.'

'Peter?' he said, his irritation vanishing.

'Yes, sir. I'm fine, really,' she said, turning to face him, displaying her most reassuring smile before returning her focus to the traffic surrounding them.

He should have known it was Peter. Jane's son was the only part of her personal life that ever encroached on her work, and even then the instances were few and far between. She rarely talked about her home life. Lockyer had been to her little flat in Blackheath once, maybe twice, but that was it. As far as he knew, Jane's mother took care of Peter when Jane was at work. He went to school during the day but had extra help because of his autism, although Lockyer didn't know what the 'extra help' really entailed. He had never asked.

Few people in the office knew what Jane's life was really like when she clocked off. What Lockyer did know about her past, he had gleaned from snippets of conversation over the years: her one-time boyfriend had buggered off when she was eight months pregnant. Jane had once told him that she felt like a stranger in her son's life because of his condition. Of course, that would have been the perfect opportunity for Lockyer to empathize, to let her talk about Peter, to tell her about Bobby, but he hadn't. He couldn't seem to find the words then, or now.

'We're almost there,' Jane said, swinging the car into a narrow lane running between two terraces.

'It's down here?' he asked, looking around at the high walls enclosing the back gardens of the houses.

At the end of the lane there was a newly tarmacked car park with a dozen spaces marked out by fresh white paint. The clinic sat at the back, a single-storey red-brick building with a gabled roof. Four gold letters hung over the door: LYWC. Underneath them was a smaller sign that read, 'Lewisham Young Women's Centre'.

'This is the place,' she said, pulling into one of the spaces.

'Not too busy for a Friday morning, is it?' he said, looking around him at the empty car park. He opened his door, got out and straightened his jacket.

'Maybe they're not open on Fridays,' Jane said, clicking the central locking on the squad car. 'It took me a couple of goes to get an answer when I called.'

He opened one of the double doors and gestured for Jane to go ahead of him. Lockyer realized he felt a lot better. Somehow the drive, the air and the change of scenery had lifted the emotional fug that had been suffocating him all morning. As he followed Jane over to the reception desk he could almost feel his head clearing. The desk was a traditional shiny pine, five feet high, and hiding behind it was a fifty-something receptionist who looked to be leafing through a women's gossip magazine. All Lockyer could see were bright colours and orange-looking girls staring up at him.

'Good morning,' Jane said, already holding out her warrant card. The receptionist jumped a clear foot in the air with an accompanying screech. He didn't know who was more surprised, her or him. He took a step back.

'Oh, my,' she said, her south-east London accent strong, her voice croaky. If there weren't twenty Benson & Hedges in this woman's purse he would hand in his badge right now. 'You frightened me to death, creeping up like that. The bell under the doormat's stopped working again. I've told them it needs fixing . . . I've asked a dozen times, at least . . .'

He looked over at Jane and saw that she was just as stunned by the woman's reaction as he was. He cleared his throat and gave her elbow a shove when he saw the corner of her mouth lift with amusement. The receptionist was still talking, not to either of them in particular, just chattering into the ether, her eyes alternating between looking up at the ceiling and then down at her feet.

'Mr Walsh said you'd be stopping by and to help you with whatever you needed . . . he's had to pop out, you see. Friday mornings is usually our quiet time, normally when we do the notes, that kinda thing, so, how can I help you? Mr Walsh didn't say, he just said something about notes . . . not that I can show you notes but I suppose I can look at them, and then . . . I don't know, I suppose it depends.' The woman finally stopped talking and looked from Jane to him and back again.

'And you are?' Jane asked, hiding her smile as she reached into her jacket for a notepad.

'Sheila Collins. I'm in charge when Mr Walsh isn't here . . . well, I answer the phones and look after reception if no one else is in,' the woman said, looking around her, blushing at her failed boast.

He turned away as Jane began to speak, tuning out her voice as she went through the basics with the verbose Ms Collins. The waiting room was bland. Despite the obvious newness of the building the interior looked tired. The white walls were faded to a dull cream and the brown carpet tiles were awash with shiny tracks from numerous pushchairs, no doubt. There were two dozen green plastic chairs and a pine table displaying a sad array of out-of-date women's magazines. For some reason he had been expecting something more swanky, all stainless steel and posh art.

An idea ran along the edge of his thoughts; his pulse quickened, but then it was gone. He shook his head and turned back to Jane. From her facial expression he could tell she'd had enough of talking to Ms Collins. He was about to save her when the door to the office opened.

'Can I help?'

Lockyer stepped sideways to see a guy standing in the doorway. He was wearing a shirt and tie and a black pair of ill-fitting skinny jeans. The receptionist's shoulders dropped as she let out an exaggerated sigh. 'No, Danny, I'm fine,' she said, turning and giving him a wide grin, revealing a large amount of lipstick on her two front teeth. 'Mr Walsh said the police would be coming by, to ask some questions . . . I'm dealing with it.'

'And you are?' Lockyer asked, aware of Ms Collins' dismay at being ignored.

The man stepped forward, holding out his hand. 'Danny. Danny Armstrong. I work with Sheila on Fridays – just wanted to see if I could help.'

'I can handle this,' Sheila said, her voice hardening. 'Mr Walsh said I was to deal with the police.' She puffed out her chest and folded her arms securely over her generous bust, her nose turned up to the ceiling. 'I am quite capable.'

'Ms Collins,' Lockyer said, 'if you can answer my colleague's questions . . . that would be most helpful, as you're the most senior member of staff here.' Sheila looked about ready to explode with pride.

'Oh, yes, yes, of course,' she said.

'I'll just ask Mr Armstrong a couple of questions while you two finish up,' Lockyer said, turning away, nodding to the guy to follow, gesturing for him to take a seat as far away from the reception desk as possible. 'So, Mr Armstrong . . .'

'Call me Danny,' he said, smiling.

'OK. How long have you worked here, Danny?' Lockyer asked, keeping his voice low. He didn't want Sheila eavesdropping or chipping in to the conversation.

'Six, seven months, something like that . . . Walsh hired me over the summer.'

'And before?'

'Nothing special, general admin-type jobs. I used to get work through an agency but Mr Walsh offered me a permanent position. It was good money and the hours were good, you know, so I took it,' he said with a shrug.

'I see,' Lockyer said. 'And do you have much contact with the patients?'

Danny shook his head. 'No, not really. I'm mainly in the back office. As Sheila said, she deals with the front desk.'

'I can see that,' Lockyer said, glancing over his shoulder. Ms Collins was in full flow. Jane was now leaning on the desk. He would have to buy her a bacon sandwich on the way back to say thank you. 'Did you ever see or speak to a Deborah Stevens? She was a patient here.'

'No, the name doesn't ring a bell. I usually remember patients' names, even if I never see their faces. I enter all their information onto the computer but her name isn't familiar. One of the others must have input her record.' Danny sniffed, sat back and adjusted his jeans.

'Right, thank you, Danny,' Lockyer said, deciding how long he and Jane should wait around for Walsh. 'Do you know when Mr Walsh will be back?'

'Not a clue. He had a couple of appointments this morning, I think,' Danny said, raising his eyebrows. 'Sorry,' he said, pointing at his head. 'I had a heavy night last night, not feeling my best.'

'How long has Mr Walsh been here?' Lockyer asked.

'Since the place opened . . .' Danny seemed to be about to say something else but stopped, covering his mouth with his hand.

'And does he have much interaction with the patients, in his capacity as manager?' he asked, reaching for the notepad in his jacket pocket.

'Some . . . it depends. If he's here, he sometimes talks to them in the waiting room,' Danny said, shifting in his seat. His relaxed demeanour seemed to be changing as he looked increasingly uncomfortable.

'Is that unusual?' Lockyer asked.

'I don't know,' Danny said, staring out of the window.

'Is Mr Walsh a good employer?' That question seemed to hit a nerve. Armstrong crossed his legs and started jiggling his foot.

'Yes,' Danny said, not looking at him. Instead he looked over at Sheila and then at the double doors before his eyes finally settled back on Lockyer. 'Look, I like working here.' He laughed and covered his mouth but there was no humour in the sound. Lockyer recognized the gesture and wondered whether Armstrong had had braces as a child but still hadn't grown out of the habit of trying to hide them. 'I guess he can be difficult, sometimes.'

'Difficult?' Lockyer asked, aware of Jane's voice in the background.

'He's . . . he's not that nice to Sheila or the other women . . . I know Sheila's a bit much, but Walsh can be . . . cruel. He . . .'

'Officers . . . I'm so sorry I'm late,' a voice boomed from behind them. Lockyer turned to see a man, mid-forties maybe, wearing round black-framed glasses and a blue-and-white wide-pinstripe suit that looked expensive. 'I had some business to attend to in town that couldn't wait . . . please,' Walsh said, gesturing to a door at the end of the reception desk. Lockyer thanked Armstrong and stood, waiting for Jane to join him. Sheila wasn't verbose any more. She stood behind the desk, mute, her eyes wide. 'I do hope Sheila and Danny have been helpful,' Walsh said. 'Please, do come through to my office and we'll see what we can do about helping you, shall we?' Walsh opened the door to a long hallway and waved Lockyer and Jane inside. 'Sheila . . . fag butts . . . now,' he hissed as the door closed behind them.

Lockyer covered his mouth to disguise a yawn as Walsh continued to regale them. He was on to the highlights of his career at the moment. He caught Jane's eye and nodded for her to take control, otherwise they were liable to be here all day. This guy was half smarm, half comedy vicar. Thirty minutes had gone by and they already had the majority of his life story. Walsh had given them alibis not only for Debbie and the other girls' murders but also, it seemed, all unexplained deaths dating back to Roman times. Despite the barrage of irrelevant information Lockyer had noticed one thing. When Jane said they would have to verify Walsh's alibi with his wife, the guy had been reluctant, to say the least.

'Mr Walsh,' Jane said, holding up her notepad to halt the diatribe. It worked. Walsh sat back and folded his hands in his lap. 'What can you tell us about Deborah Stevens?'

Walsh now clasped his hands together, as if in prayer. 'How awful for something like this to happen? It's so . . . senseless isn't it?' he said, shaking his head. 'I don't know how helpful I can be, I'm afraid. Of course I looked over her medical notes before you arrived but there wasn't much of interest, I don't think. You know she had an abortion, I assume?' Walsh said in a stage whisper.

'Yes, a D&C. Did you arrange that?' Jane asked.

'Not personally. One of my doctors, Dr Bird, referred her . . . once she was definite about her decision. I have asked him to make himself available to you, as I assumed you would want to talk to him.' Walsh cleared his throat. 'There's nothing in her notes in relation to the father of the baby, or anything really, only that she was dead set on having a termination.'

'How many weeks was she?' Jane asked.

'She was at the end of her first trimester . . . twelve weeks, according to her notes. A D&C isn't the simplest or nicest of procedures, I'm afraid.' Walsh stretched out his mouth, the corners turning down like a toad. He seemed an odd fit for this kind of job. He clearly found the whole thing upsetting and a bit distasteful. Lockyer couldn't decide what to make of him; Walsh seemed genuinely distressed to be talking about abortion, let alone murder. There was a tremor at the corner of his mouth but perhaps it was just his nervous disposition. Lockyer felt on edge just sitting across from the guy. 'I only saw her, Deborah, a handful of times, sitting out in the waiting room mainly. I did speak to her once, only for a moment. She and I were sheltering under the porch during a downpour and we got to talking.' Lockyer watched as Jane scribbled notes in her pad, nodding for Walsh to continue. 'Well, she was ever so young – not our youngest, naturally, but she seemed young for her age, if you know what I mean?'

'What did you talk about?' Jane asked.

Walsh seemed put off his stride when his question was ignored. His eyebrows were knitted together in an anxious bundle. 'Well,' he said, all but wringing his hands. 'She was saying that she didn't like the rain. It meant she had to take the bus and she wasn't keen on being around too many people . . . I certainly remember that because I thought at the time it was such an odd thing for a girl of her age to say. She seemed shy but not so much with me, I guess.' Walsh tipped his head to one side. 'I don't know why.' Lockyer didn't either.

'What else, Mr Walsh? It would really help if you could tell us as much as you can recall.' Jane sat forward in her chair, trying to get Walsh to look at her.

Lockyer looked around at the consulting room, intrigued by how un-medical it appeared. There were the obligatory boxes of surgical gloves and a yellow bin marked with a hazard sticker but that was about it. Both he and Jane were sitting on a grey couch, while Walsh sat on a comfy-looking armchair. The bulk of the furniture would have been better suited to someone's lounge or some fancy hotel lobby.

'. . . I offered her a lift but she said her mother didn't like her to take favours from people . . . you never know what they'll want in return,' Walsh said. 'Another funny thing to say, I thought, but I guess young girls have to be careful.' He covered his face with his hands. 'Oh, how dreadful.'

Lockyer looked out of the window as Walsh wiped away a tear. The emotion appeared genuine, but then Sheila and Armstrong's reactions had looked genuine too. It seemed Walsh had two personas. But which was the real one?

'Mr Walsh, we will need full access to your database and records for our investigation,' Lockyer said, holding up his hand before Walsh could protest. 'I am aware of the confidentiality issue, but it is necessary, I'm afraid. You will be provided with the relevant legal paperwork so there's no breach on your part.'

'Of course. I understand, Detective. I will assist wherever I can,' Walsh said.

'I will need a comprehensive list of all your employees for interviewing purposes,' he said.

Walsh nodded at him enthusiastically. 'Of course, of course.'

'Would you be happy to provide a fingerprint sample and some DNA?' Lockyer asked, picking up his jacket, getting ready to leave. The yes, yes, response he had expected wasn't forthcoming. He looked over at Walsh. The guy was motionless.

'Me . . .' Walsh stuttered. 'Why would you . . .?'

Jane leaned forward; she was so good at this. Cop bedside-manner wasn't his strong suit. 'It's merely procedure, Mr Walsh. It's important to eliminate those connected with the victim as early as possible.'

Walsh looked as if he was going to be sick. 'Well . . .' he said, his eyes resuming their crazed journey around the consulting room. 'I will need to speak to my lawyer . . . first.'

'If you feel that is necessary, Mr Walsh, feel free to do so.' He sat back on the couch, his jacket draped over his knees, listening to Jane as she finished off the details. He was looking at Walsh. Was the guy really as distraught as he looked?

9

24 January – Friday

Sarah sat on the long wall that ran from the pavement up to the doors of Lewisham Police Station. She had talked to herself in the car on the drive over, practising what she would say, but now, sitting here, she was frightened. She lifted her head, her hair hiding most of her face, and watched people walking in and out of the station as the damp from the freezing concrete seeped into her bones. She studied their faces through a veil of hair.

She stood up, wrapped her arms around herself and walked up to the double doors. She could see an officer behind the reception desk, his eyes fixed on the computer screen in front of him. Should she tell them about her conversations with Officer Rayner at Peckham Police Station? She didn't want to. The main reason she had come to Lewisham was so she wouldn't have to deal with Rayner ever again. If they thought he was her point of contact would they send her away, refuse to help? She shook her head. 'Just walk in, all you have to do is walk in,' she said under her breath, each step sending icy air through her jeans. She wanted to go home but when the doors hissed apart she felt compelled to keep moving.

The foyer was vast but still held the smell of industrial cleaner and something else: vomit. She imagined the kind of people who staggered or were dragged in here. Everything was blue glass and chrome. She approached the desk, her throat drying and her mind emptying with each step forward. The officer looked up and smiled at her.

'Good morning. How can I help you?' His voice was soft.

'Yes, I need to speak to someone, I've spoken to an officer before but he was . . . he said to . . . I mean, it's probably nothing but I wanted to come and talk to someone else.' She stared at her hands. She wanted to disappear.

'I will just need some details from you, madam.'

She stuttered and stumbled over her words, holding up her diary as some kind of talisman: proof that she wasn't crazy. The officer nodded after each faltering sentence and tapped away on his computer. God knows what he had put: 'Female, 35, deranged.' That would be about right. He gave her a clipboard and a form to fill in and ushered her away.

A blue plastic bench ran the length of the foyer opposite the reception desk. She sat down and filled in her name and address. Her handwriting looked childlike. Other people were scattered along the bench with their own clipboards. All of them were either staring at the floor or into the middle distance. At least she didn't seem to be the only one struggling. She couldn't get past her own name. Her pen hovered over the box marked 'Detail of Complaint'. She was afraid that if she started writing, nothing would be there. The more she wrote, the emptier the page would become.

'Miss Grainger?' Sarah looked up as a short female officer with a badly cut, Dawn-French-style fringe walked towards her.

'Yes,' she said, unsure whether she should stand or stay where she was.

'My name is Jane Bennett, Detective Sergeant.' She shook the officer's hand, surprised by how tiny and fragile the woman's fingers felt. 'If you would like to come with me, we can talk about what's been happening with you?'

What an odd thing to say. Happening with you. Not happening to you, but with you.

Sarah pulled the zipper on her jacket up and then pushed it back down again. The repetitive action was soothing. The buzz of the zip created a kind of white noise. Sergeant Bennett had excused herself to go and speak to her boss, ten minutes ago. She had taken Sarah's phone with her after they had listened to the voicemail he had left. The message had been whispered, only a few words audible above a hiss of static. 'Sarah . . . I . . . wanted to tell you . . . I helped . . . was cold . . . I did it . . . I did it.' It didn't make any sense but at least it meant she had something.

She was sitting at the edge of a large open-plan office. Partitions separated desks into groups of two or four. She guessed Bennett was a senior officer because she had a desk to herself, against a window. The sergeant had been polite, knowledgeable, sincere and conscientious. What had Rayner been? None of those things, and he certainly hadn't been a detective. Who knew, maybe he wasn't a policeman at all. Bennett had made notes. Not into a computer but actual handwritten notes. The old-fashioned familiarity of it had made Sarah smile for the first time in days. Computer records could be lost but paper felt more permanent. She swivelled the office chair to the right and then back to the left, syncing the action with her zipper routine. She stared at her hands and was relieved to see that they had stopped shaking, for now.

10

24 January – Friday

His feet were turning into blocks of ice waiting for her. He wiggled his toes to encourage at least a little life back into them, closing his mind to the people who jostled him as they rushed by.

Everyone around him was oblivious to what he saw, what he knew. She was so close he could almost smell her and yet no one else seemed to feel her presence. He smiled and looked again at the double doors, willing her to appear. Saliva wet his tongue as anticipation hummed through his body.

There she was, walking carefully to avoid patches of ice. He tipped his head to one side and watched, transfixed by her face, her shape, even the way she moved. Her skin was pale, her hair dragged back into a ponytail at the nape of her neck. He couldn't wait to touch her there, a place so soft, so delicate. He stamped his feet, rolled his head around his aching shoulders and followed her as she walked towards her car. As he passed, only inches behind her, her scent filling his senses, he reached out, his fingers touching her hair for one exquisite second. She didn't see him. It wasn't their time.

11

24 January – Friday

Lockyer was sitting alone in the briefing room, staring at the floor-to-ceiling glass that separated him from the main office. The bottom third was frosted so all he could see was the shadowed bodies of his team wandering back and forth, only their heads in focus. No one looked in at him but he still felt observed. Everyone was waiting for his lead.

He had been ignoring a strong impulse to call Clara, though what he hoped Megan's mother would say eluded him. Without thinking he started turning the ring that hung around his neck. It had become a kind of talisman or touch-stone since their separation, over five years ago. It maintained a connection. She didn't know he had it and would no doubt be livid if she did. The memories conjured when he touched the small circle of gold were happy. He knew Clara didn't feel the same way and that was the reality he had to live with. 'Work and women. That's all you care about, Mike.' The memory of her words still stung. It took almost nothing to stir his guilt. He let out a frustrated breath, feeling his anger build but knowing it had nowhere to go but inward. He took his hand away and started to shuffle the papers in front of him, refocusing his mind.

The notes Jane had given him from their interview with Walsh were extensive, but there was no information or clue as to the identity of the father of Debbie's baby. From the notes Walsh had shown them, Debbie hadn't said much, other than she needed a termination because having the baby 'wasn't an option'. There was still something about Walsh that didn't seem quite right, though. He had been too emotional, almost over the top. Jane was running a full background check now. She agreed that Walsh seemed to have a strong influence over his staff that wasn't quite 'normal'.

'You ready for me?'

He looked up to see Phil Bathgate, their consultant forensic psychologist, leaning against the glass door. For someone whose job entailed putting himself into the mind of some seriously disturbed individuals, he had an oddly relaxed demeanour.

'Sure. Take a seat . . . and shut the door,' he said.

Phil sat down and began adjusting his seat; higher, lower, tipped back. 'Thirty million and they can't afford decent chairs,' he said, all but fighting with the chair.

As Lockyer watched the performance he thought it was pretty obvious why the vast majority of the office thought Phil was a grade-A arse-wipe. 'So, what do you have for me, Phil?' he asked.

With an exaggerated sigh and a roll of his eyes Phil gave up on the chair and took a blue ring binder out of his briefcase. He pulled out several sheets of paper and with-out speaking slid them across the table. 'Well . . . the psychological and geographical profiles are really coming together. The third body has given me an excellent sense of the suspect's motivations.'

'I assume, when you say the "third body", you're referring to Deborah Stevens,' he said, biting his tongue, already wishing this particular meeting was over. The sheer delight evident on Phil's face wasn't right. 'Can you just run me through what you've got, Phil?'

'Absolutely, that's what I'm here for . . . no problemo.' Phil smiled, oblivious to Lockyer's mood. 'I've approached the profile with four aspects in mind. Firstly, the antecedent, meaning the fantasy or plan the suspect had before the act, and what triggered his activities on those days and not others. Secondly, the method and manner of the murder. I think that's self-explanatory. Thirdly, body disposal. Obviously, we know he didn't transport his victims after their deaths but that in itself is interesting. And finally, post-offence behaviour. Is he following you? I mean to say, following the case, enjoying being part of such an exciting investigation.' Phil took a deep breath and sat back. He looked delighted by his own brilliance.

'This isn't my first profile briefing,' Lockyer said, rubbing his right eyebrow where a twitch was taking hold.

'Naturally . . . I'll talk you through the crime scenes and highlight where your man is speaking to you.'

Lockyer decided to ignore the emphasis Phil placed on 'your man' and 'speaking to you'. Instead he looked down at the first sheet of paper and scanned the details printed in tight black ink. Phoebe Atherton, the first victim, had been reduced to ten bullet points.

Phil began reading them out. 'The first victim was found

at 14.00 hours at the edge of Camberwell New Cemetery; very significant.'

'What? The time or the location?' Lockyer asked.

'Both. Dr Simpson put the time of death in the early hours of the morning. So, it's fair to say he likes to work at night . . . the killer, that is . . . not Dave,' Phil said, chuckling at his own poor attempt at humour. 'The cemetery itself may represent the suspect's mindset at the time of the attack. If this was his first victim . . . doubtful . . . but if it was, the cemetery would be a logical choice.'

Lockyer turned his chair so he could stare at the white-board at the end of the room. Pictures and documents had been attached to it and interlinking arrows drawn on with a green marker pen. Somehow, the chaos of the board helped him concentrate and absorb Phil's assertions without having to absorb Phil's manner as well. 'Go on,' he said.

'Of course . . . he may not have killed like this before but he will have practised. I would imagine that he started small, scaring young women, that kind of thing. Nothing major, jumping out of bushes or following them home, so they knew he was there,' Phil said.

'How long would you say he's been building up to this?' Lockyer asked.

'Years – five, maybe more. As I say, he would have started small.'

Lockyer thought of all the unreported assaults or unsolved sexual attacks he had seen in his years of service. Any one of them could have been a starting point, a building block. 'What are we talking about here, Phil, sociopath . . . psycho-path, what?'

'Certainly not a sociopath. The suspect will be above-average intelligence, organized, ritualistic and functioning on all cylinders. Top of his game, you might say?' Phil smiled, exposing two rows of straight, bleached teeth.

'Jesus, Phil. Try and rein in your weird-shit phrases, will you?' Lockyer said, shaking his head. 'Top of his game . . . unbelievable.' Phil nodded, but said nothing. That was the trouble. The guy was so good at his job it was impossible to tell what he was thinking. At least the creep didn't know about Debbie's resemblance to Megan. If he did there would be questions, endless questions. 'What did you feel when you saw what you thought was your daughter's face?' 'Of course, you would have begun to grieve on a subconscious level. Are you aware that your ability to perform your duties may be impaired?'

'What I want to emphasize here, Lockyer, is the suspect's desire for power. The attacks, the locations, even the murders themselves . . . they're all secondary.'

'Secondary?' he asked, again stunned by Phil's glib attitude.

'Yes. The locations, though significant, are hardly discreet. The Stevens girl was even moved, mid-attack, no doubt because of the alley's proximity to the general public. That's what I mean by power, Lockyer. Rape, though violent, is rarely about sex. Carrying out these attacks in built-up areas is the suspect's way of demonstrating his superiority and dominance over not only his victims, but everyone else. You included.'

He felt the muscles in the back of his neck tighten. 'Just what I needed to hear . . . so what about the wrist wounds? What's that about?'

'I couldn't say, although I would suggest that they are inextricably linked with his "performance" during the rape. In my opinion, he is able to perform sexually but only in a perfunctory way. Meaning, the excitement of the blood and rape would be enough to maintain his erection but he will be unable to climax. This could explain the throat wound. He would go as far as he could and then the frustration of not being able to ejaculate would be so intense that he would have to do something to bring the attack to an end. He certainly wouldn't want the victim to witness his shortcomings, shall we say?'

'And the bite on the victim's neck?' he asked, aware that the image of Debbie's killer struggling to climax on top of her was going to stay with him for some time.

Phil looked down at the pages on the table. 'Yes, no such marks were found on either of the first two victims. I think it is safe to assume that it represents a further stimulant for him and a further assault on the victim's body. However, it does worry me. There is something very basic about biting. To be honest, I'm surprised he indulged himself . . . potentially leaving dental impressions, DNA . . . It doesn't seem to be this killer's style,' Phil said with a careless shrug of his shoulders, as though disappointed that Debbie's murderer had so little self-control.

It didn't take a genius to figure out what was coming next but Lockyer knew he had to ask. 'There will be others?'

'Yes, without doubt. Altering his technique, as he has done with the Stevens girl, demonstrates that, and . . .' Before Phil could continue, Jane knocked on the glass door.

Lockyer waved her in, relieved to have the distraction.

'Phil . . . sir,' she said.

'Yes, Jane?' he said.

'I've had the report back on Walsh . . . he's got two priors,' she said, glancing down at a piece of paper she was holding. 'One for drunk and disorderly. He was eighteen at the time.'

'And the other?' Lockyer asked, struggling with the thought of Walsh at eighteen, let alone drunk.

'ABH, sir,' Jane said, one eyebrow disappearing beneath her fringe. 'He was charged but the CPS didn't pursue it. Seems he had a "disagreement" with a colleague some time ago,' she continued, looking again at the paper in front of her. 'He would have been thirty-five. I'm pulling the file for more details.'

'Interesting,' he said, remembering the sheer panic on Walsh's face at the mention of fingerprints being taken. No wonder, if he had priors. It also explained why Sheila and Armstrong were so nervous around him. A guy charged with ABH must have a pretty impressive temper. 'Double check his alibis for the murders and come back to me,' Lockyer said, aware that Phil was starting to huff and puff on the other side of the table. 'Anything about the other girls from the clinic's records?'

'No, sir. Nothing. Neither Atherton or Pearson are listed as patients and none of the employees recognize them from the photographs I took down there,' she said, looking despondent.

He knew how she felt. Katy, Phoebe and now Debbie. They didn't work near each other or socialize in the same places. Other than living in roughly the same postcode, there was nothing to link any one of them. Nothing to show Lockyer how or why they were being targeted by a killer. 'Go on,' he said.

'I've arranged second interviews with Stacey Clemments, the best friend, and William Hodgson, the boss. They're both coming back in Sunday at 09.00.'

'Good.'

'Who do you want to run the interviews, sir?' she asked.

He sat back in his chair and looked at the ceiling. The transcript of the interview Penny had done with Debbie's boss had bothered him most. 'Tell you what. You do the best friend and I'll do Hodgson myself.'

'No problem, sir.'

She didn't leave.

'Is there something else, Jane?' he asked. Now he was looking at her face, he noticed the little crease between her eyebrows.

'Yes, are you nearly done? I have a case I think could be of interest. I'd like to talk it through with you?'

'Give me five minutes, Jane,' he said, seizing the opportunity to escape with both hands. 'I'll meet you in my office.'

As the door closed he turned to Phil. 'Apologies. Can we wrap this up and I'll go over your full report and come back to you?'

'Right, well, if you have to go.' Phil sounded like a peeved child.

'Yes, I do. Quick rundown if you can?'

'Fine. As far as I see it . . .'

'Main points, Phil. Just the main points.'

'Yes . . . ' Phil looked down at his notes; his confidence seemed momentarily absent. 'Main points. Excellent geographical knowledge. Lives and works locally. Broken home, possible abuse, possible alcoholic parent. Sexual inadequacies. Twenty-five to forty-five. White male, hunting within his own ethnic group. Above-average height. Above-average intelligence. Strong . . .'

Lockyer struggled to concentrate on the rest of Phil's summary as an image of a possible killer appeared in his mind, followed closely by Debbie Stevens' body, lying in the alleyway. He could see her face, her mouth. It looked like it was moving, like she was trying to tell him something.

12

24 January – Friday

Sarah was sitting alone at Bennett's desk, staring at her diary. The cheerful daisy pattern on the cover looked out of place. She pulled it towards her and flicked over the pages, each entry tugging at her nerves as she remembered so many sleepless nights. The impression of her black biro had left deep grooves, making the backs of each page look like Braille.

'Sarah?'

As she turned she saw Bennett and standing next to her a tall guy wearing a crumpled charcoal suit.

'Sarah, this is Detective Inspector Mike Lockyer, my boss.'

She shook the proffered hand, his grip suggesting he was more accustomed to shaking hands with men, demonstrating his power with this simple gesture. Despite his rather dishevelled appearance he was an imposing figure, handsome even.

'Good morning, Miss Grainger,' he said, smiling. When he released her hand it flopped like a dead fish back onto her lap.

'Please, call me Sarah,' she said, trying to ignore the tightening in her throat.

'Apologies . . . Sarah it is,' he said, looking from her to Bennett. His expression was hard to read. There was sympathy or pity but it was tinged with something else she couldn't quite place. Frustration, maybe, at having his time wasted. 'Yet another pathetic female with an overactive imagination.' She could almost hear him saying it.

'Sarah, my colleague DS Bennett will remain your point of contact. However, she has just briefed me on your case, and if you don't mind, I would like to ask you a few questions?'

She was finding it difficult not to stare. He looked like a Hollywood movie star who had been roughed up for an art-house film role. But more questions? She wasn't sure she could stand any more, the disbelieving looks. Her exhaustion was suffocating her. 'Go ahead,' she said, flinching as he pulled a chair up next to her. He must have noticed her reaction because he pushed his chair back half a foot before sitting down. He was still close but not too close.

His questions made her dizzy. They made no sense. She could hear herself answering but her brain was aching with the weight of each bizarre inquiry.

'Tell me, did contact increase or decrease at any particular time of the month? Is there a pattern in your diary that is easily identifiable?'

'What time and where did you receive these calls?'

'How long have you lived in the area?'

'Do you work with an agency or privately?'

'How do your clients get in contact with you?'

'We will need to keep your mobile phone for a day or two for interrogation.'

'Have you told anyone else about these incidents?'

'Where were you on the nights of the 14th of December, 4th of January and 22nd of January?'

'I will need details of the contact on those days.'

'I will want to make a copy of your diary.'

She found herself staring into his round brown eyes, unable to look away.

'Thank you. We will be in touch. You've been very helpful,' he said, shaking her hand, more gently this time.

She didn't understand. They were meant to be helping her, not the other way around, but before she could say as much, he stood, turned on his heel and walked away. Sergeant Bennett sat down in the seat vacated by her boss. Sarah had almost forgotten Bennett was still there.

'Thank you, Sarah. I know it's been a very long day for you. We won't be too much longer.'

'What was all that about? It felt like those questions were meant for someone else,' Sarah said, swallowing hard. Bennett leaned forward, and for just a moment Sarah thought she was going to hug her, but instead she reached over and picked up the diary.

'We need to get details from your phone of all the calls you've received. You'll be able to collect it tomorrow afternoon.' Bennett rose from her chair. 'I'll make a quick copy of your diary. Just wait here for one more minute.' Like her boss before her, Bennett was gone in a second, leaving Sarah alone. Alone. That's what he had done to her. He had made her feel alone, even in an office full of people.

Her mobile buzzed on Bennett's desk. Was she allowed to answer it? She leaned forward and looked at the screen.

It was a London number, a City number. She picked it up and pushed 'answer'. 'Sarah Grainger speaking,' she said. Her voice sounded hollow.

'Good morning, this is Scott Abrahams, from Stephenson Harwood. I just wanted to confirm times for tomorrow's appointment?'

A weight dropped into Sarah's stomach. She had totally forgotten. 'Err, Scott . . . yes. I . . . what time did we say? Sorry, I don't have my appointment book with me.'

'Two p.m. was arranged . . . until five p.m. We have called people in specially, as it's a Saturday. I assume that is still convenient with you?' Scott asked, but Sarah could tell from his tone of voice that not only would she get an earful if she even tried to cancel but she would never be working for that firm again.

'Two, yes . . . absolutely, I'll be there.' Sarah tried to put some enthusiasm into her voice, to at least feign an upbeat attitude.

'Good. Thank you. Come to reception, ask for me and we'll get you set up. How long will you need?'

'Twenty minutes, half an hour tops. I'll get to you for 1.30 to give me enough time, if that's OK?'

'Fine. See you tomorrow, Miss Grainger.' The line went dead.

Sarah put the phone back on the desk. She had never forgotten a meeting. It was because of him. He was infecting every part of her life, dismantling it from the inside out.

13

Lockyer looked again at the post-mortem pictures spread out on his desk, the late afternoon sun casting shadows on the girls' faces. The cuts made on Debbie's wrists were the same as those on Katy's and Phoebe's; similar length and depth. The rape was violent: just like the others. Dave's report said Debbie's attack had been more prolonged than the other victims'. The drugs would explain that; but that wasn't what was bothering him. Something was different. Yes, there were the bite mark and the fingerprint, but that wasn't it. There was something about the murder scene that was bugging him.

He glanced over at his notepad, lying on the edge of his desk. The letters D&C stood out. Dilation and curettage. Even the words made him wince. He turned and looked out through the blinds, but instead of seeing the winter sunshine he saw Clara, lying on a bed, in a green hospital gown. It had happened after the marriage but before the separation. He had been in the process of moving his stuff out of the family home when she had walked in the front door and announced that she was pregnant. For a second he had felt happy but then her face had brought him crashing back down to reality. 'I'm not keeping it, Mike. Not now. Not like this.' It felt like someone had reached into his chest and ripped out his lungs. He couldn't breathe. He could barely believe the words coming out of her mouth. But he hadn't fought her. Instead he had taken her to the hospital, sat quietly and held her hand while the surgeon explained what was about to happen: 'The procedure will involve the opening or dilation of the cervix before surgically removing the lining of the uterus, or in your case, Mrs Lockyer, the contents of the womb.'

He turned back to his desk. Now was not the time for some sick trip down memory lane; he resisted the urge to reach for his chain and Clara's ring.

'So, what did you think?'

He looked up to see Jane standing in the doorway to his office, her eyebrows bunched.

'Of what?' Lockyer asked. Although, at this point, he wasn't sure he cared. He felt exhausted. Rays of sunshine shone through his office blinds like arrows.

'Grainger – what did you think?'

He turned his chair, stood up and began pacing in the four-foot-square space between his desk and a row of filing cabinets. 'We need to look into it, yes. Find out if Debbie or either of the first two victims reported being followed or harassed,' he said, picturing Grainger's face from their meeting earlier, her skin pale, her eyes dark and sunken. She looked utterly hollowed out by her ordeal. Weirdly, he could relate. 'A predator hunting on the street adjacent to Debbie's certainly warrants a closer look.'

'Do you want me to speak to the surveillance team about Grainger?' Jane asked, turning to leave.

'Not yet. I'll need to speak to Phil again about the geographical profile, see what he thinks.' A conversation he could do without. 'We can't afford to go off half-arsed, Jane, not on a hunch.' He knew it was a cheap shot. A lame way of sharing his frustrations, trying to make someone, anyone, feel what he felt. Jane blinked but seemed impassive to his tone. She would take whatever crap he dished out, even though sometimes he wished she wouldn't.

'Right, I'll wait for your word, then, sir. Is there anything else, before I head out?' she asked.

'Any holes in Walsh's alibis?' he asked.

'Not yet, sir,' she said, 'but with a bit of luck I should have confirmation by close of business.'

As Lockyer stared out through the blinds at Lewisham High Street he thought that luck wasn't a factor in this case, not yet. 'Right, thanks Jane,' he said, blocking out the almost constant blare of car horns from the road below.

'Sir, would you . . . can I get you anything from across the road, a bacon sandwich or something?'

He looked over his shoulder to see yet another concerned expression on Jane's pinched face. Was his fatigue that obvious? What could she see when she looked at him?

'No, Jane, but thanks,' he said, turning his back on her. 'I'll see you at the 18.00 briefing.'

He waited for Jane to leave before closing his eyes and picturing the crime scene again. It came as flashing bright images. Debbie's feet, her bare legs splayed out in an unnatural position. He refocused on the alley itself, blurring her body to just an outline. There was rubbish: cans, bottles and discarded crisp packets mingling with the mud and water from the nearby drain. Her blood pooled as though she was in a depression in the concrete. Drag marks. Yes, there had been drag marks, showing her attacker had begun the assault before deciding to pull Debbie further into the alleyway. But why move her? She was maybe ten or twelve feet from her original position. Perhaps noises from the Tesco car park had intruded, forcing him to retreat further into the darkness. A thought ran along the edge of his consciousness but he couldn't quite grasp it: a ghost.

Two hours later Lockyer crossed the office to the conference room where Jane and a few members of the team were waiting. She had set up a whiteboard and scribbled out various timelines. Her laptop was linked to the wall-mounted TV screen so they could see all the evidence in forty-inch splendour. Full-size post-mortem pictures. He walked in and sat down opposite the screen. 'Right, Jane, take us from the beginning. What do we know?'

Jane cleared her throat. 'Deborah Stevens, 135 pounds, five foot six, redhead, eighteen years old, advertising assistant, single, lived with her parents in Nunhead. She has one brother, here in London, Petts Wood, with a wife and three kids. Stevens left her office at just gone 18.00 hours. CCTV has her passing St Paul's, Moorgate and then heading towards the Barbican, but after that we lose her. We pick her up again at 20.05 boarding a train at Blackfriars station, the 20.09. According to her brother she was heading down to Petts Wood for a visit, new baby in the family. For some reason she decided against it. She changed trains at London Bridge and went on to East Dulwich station instead. She telephoned the brother around 20.40 to say . . . ' Jane consulted notes in front of her and on the computer before continuing, 'to say . . . she wasn't coming, she would see them the following evening. She mentioned that she'd had a bad day but didn't elaborate. We're checking her phone for any other relevant contacts, calls or messages. We have CCTV footage of her outside the Tesco Metro at 20.46 but she doesn't go into the shop. She walks away, to her left; there the CCTV ends. It covers the doorway and the parking area out front but the camera that covers the left-hand side of the building where the cash machine and side alley are situated was broken. Had been for a week or so. Security guard does a walk around at 04.00 and finds the body behind the building and calls 999.' Jane took a breath, looking over at him.

'Right,' he said, taking charge. 'Let's take it up to there and make sure we've covered everything. We need to establish where she was for those two hours before boarding the train at Blackfriars. I want a clear picture of her movements from the time she left her office until the final image at the Tesco's. We'll need it for the reconstruction.'

'Penny and Chris are looking at the CCTV. I'll get an update from them and come back to you.'

'OK. Next . . .' He sucked in his cheeks and looked out of the window, letting his eyes drift out of focus and then refocus.

'We've already questioned and accessed information from the Tesco staff, security guard included, but we need to take a closer look at all of the customers and get access to credit-card records.'

'What did her bank say about recent transactions? Did she withdraw cash from the machine outside the shop?' he asked.

'They haven't come back to us, as yet. If she was approached that close to the shop someone would have seen something, surely?' Jane said.

'I agree, it's unlikely, but remember the puncture wound on her torso and Benzo element. If he was able to subdue her with a knife, it would allow him time to drug her, near or even at the cash point. She would have been semi-conscious to begin with and he could have simply walked her around the corner with little resistance.' He sat back in the chair, trying to ignore the images of Debbie and a faceless killer.

'Has Dave come back about the toxicology reports on the others?' he asked.

'Yes. Neither Atherton or Pearson was drugged and, so far, there's nothing linking the three women, other than the MO similarities, obviously,' Jane said, with a shake of her head.

'Right. Let's move on to the scene and the post-mortem and see if there's anything there. You get the stuff ready. I'll be back in two.'

Lockyer got up and headed to his office to grab his own copy of the post-mortem. As he pushed open the door the face of Jane's client, Sarah Grainger, appeared in front of him but was gone again, in an instant. What had Phil said? That the killer would have started off small, 'jumping out of bushes or following them home, so they knew he was there'.

14

25 January – Saturday

Sarah pushed her front door open with her foot, juggling her camera bag and lighting disc in one hand and her briefcase and umbrella in the other. The rain was turning into sleet, soaking the bottom of her trousers and dripping down the back of her neck as she tried to shake off her umbrella and shut the door. She wanted to get inside. She could hear a car pulling into a space nearby.

She slipped on a pile of letters and flyers that were littering her downstairs hallway but managed to steady herself as she flicked on the light with her elbow. There was a fizzing sound, followed by a loud pop as the bulb blew, returning her and the hall to darkness. 'Great,' she said, dumping everything on the floor. She closed the door, turned the deadbolt, put the chain on and double-locked the two new locks Toni had helped her install a couple of weeks ago. She bent down and used both hands to scoop the mail into one pile, and shoved the mess of paper under her arm before picking up her camera and briefcase. The lighting disc could stay down here for now. She struggled up the stairs, her feet thudding against the wooden floorboards.

As she reached for the mail, wedged under her arm, it fell, scattering all over the kitchen floor. She pushed it aside with her foot and headed for the bottle of Jack Daniel's on the work surface. She took a glass from the cupboard and poured herself a measure. She wanted to be numb. Sarah took a swig, shuddering as she swallowed, staring beyond her reflection in the kitchen window to her garden below. The trees separating her from the school playground swayed back and forth in the wind. Every crack of a branch tightened her spine.

She kicked off her shoes, padded down the hallway to her lounge and collapsed into her sofa. Her book rested next to her. She stroked the cover. Maybe she could escape into someone else's world for a couple of hours. She opened it to the marked page and let her eyes drift over the words but she couldn't concentrate. With a sigh she closed it and tossed it onto the sofa next to her. She rested her head in her hands, closed her eyes and tried to focus on her breathing: in through the nose, out through the mouth. Her hair was damp from the rain she had failed to avoid and the smell of her coconut shampoo, normally a comfort, irritated her. A loud bang made her jump. She sat forward, ready to run. As she looked around, tears blurring her vision, she saw the book lying askew on the floor. 'I can't stand this,' she whispered. She was exhausted, her emotions raw.

Today had been her first proper photo shoot in weeks. The boardroom where she had set up for simple corporate head-shots felt too small, with no escape. Every time a male solicitor walked through the door, disgruntled that they had been called in on a Saturday, her heart had pounded in her chest as the question whirled in her mind like a maelstrom. Are you him? She pushed herself up from the sofa, swaying on her feet. She hadn't eaten all day, but it wasn't food she wanted.

Sarah walked through to the kitchen and poured herself another generous measure of Jack Daniel's. She took a swig. She was determined to sleep tonight. The sound of the doorbell made her choke. She put the glass on the worktop and walked to the top of the stairs. She crouched down but couldn't see anyone through the obscured glass of her front door. She crept down the stairs, carefully avoiding the floorboards that creaked, relieved now that the bulb had blown, for the darkness that covered her. She approached the door, her rushing blood deafening in her ears. 'Who is it?' she asked, her voice trembling. She stood and waited but no one answered.

As she turned, something on the floor caught on her tights. It looked like a business card but bigger. It was about four inches square and blank. She bent down, picked it up and turned it over in her hand. The note fluttered to the floor as she staggered backwards, tripping on the bottom step, landing hard on her back. She pushed herself into a sitting position and stared at the piece of paper. It had landed face up, a scrawl of words, written in black ink, underlined four times.

HOW COULD YOU?

She turned and scrambled up the stairs to the kitchen, snatching the phone from the hallway as she passed, and punched in Toni's number. As she waited for her to answer she slid down until she was sitting on the floor, huddled against her Ikea cabinets, the yellow plastic cold and hard against her back.

'Bennett will call me back,' she said, slumping down into Toni's sofa, reaching for her wine glass and waving it in Toni's general direction.

'But surely they must do more? What did she say about the note?' Toni asked, filling Sarah's glass and settling herself on a large blue armchair.

Sarah crossed her legs and rested back on the sofa. It was almost as old and knackered as hers, the springs creaking every time she moved. 'Bennett said I shouldn't worry, that "contact in cases like these sometimes spikes after a report". She said she would call me later and I can go into the station next week . . . if I want to.'

'If you want to?' Toni threw up her hands, spilling droplets of white wine on herself and the mauve carpet. 'It is ridiculous, outrageous. They should be helping you. They should be stopping this man. It's not right.' Toni pushed her mass of black hair off her face with what must have been a wine-soaked hand.

Sarah managed a half-hearted smile. To see Toni beside herself with rage on her behalf was comforting. It proved that someone cared. She had made the mistake of phoning her mother for support, perhaps even an invitation to come and stay. However, instead of understanding or sympathy she had received a tirade of doubt and disdain. 'Don't be so hysterical, Sarah. It's probably just a note from a neighbour or a passing tradesman, a window cleaner drumming up business. Your father and I are inundated with cards and flyers from competing firms. It's disgraceful, aggressive marketing. It shouldn't be allowed. I don't have the time to sort through mountains of junk mail . . .' Sarah had tuned out the rest of her mother's complaints.

'My mum thinks it's from a neighbour or some over-zealous window cleaner,' she said, taking a large gulp of wine. Toni had tried to entice her with crisps and dips from her well-stocked cupboards but Sarah couldn't face anything solid.

'I am sorry to say this, *bella*, but your mother is an idiot.' Toni looked at her, lips pursed, seemingly waiting for a challenge to the accusation. 'The policewoman must do something. This man should be in jail.'

Sarah couldn't disagree. Over the last month her grip on her home and work life had slipped beyond her control. Her earnings had disappeared to practically nothing. She had enough in her savings account to cover the mortgage but for how much longer? How long would she be a hostage in her own home? Feeling his presence, knowing he had touched her letterbox to post his poisoned note made her want to vomit. 'What am I meant to do now?'

'You stay here. That is what you will do. You are not going back to that flat until this policewoman has seen the note. She will read it, she will see you.' Toni came and sat next to her and pulled her into a suffocating hug.

She thought about what Bennett had said, that contact sometimes spiked after a report. But that would mean he knew she had reported him and the only way he could know that was if the police had already spoken to him and not told her. No, they couldn't have; she only made the report yesterday. Sarah closed her eyes tight trying to squeeze away the realization that was chilling her stomach. The only way he could know about the police was if he had been there, watching her.

15

26 January – Sunday

Lockyer closed the door to the interview room and pulled out one of the two orange plastic chairs facing William Hodgson. As he sat down he began flicking through the file Jane had given him that morning, running his eyes over Hodgson's initial statement. Penny had been over to Foster Advertising to take it last week. 'Fancy' was the word she had used to describe Hodgson's office.

Walsh had failed to provide fingerprints or DNA as yet, but two of his three alibis seemed solid. The only alibi that was even remotely shaky was for the night of Debbie's murder. Walsh had initially said hc was at home with his wife, but when Jane had made it clear they would need to speak to Mrs Walsh to verify his statement, he changed his story. He had been with his chiropractor, all night. The woman had confirmed it, but it would need to be double checked. Lovers lied.

Debbie's boss was hardly an intimidating figure. He was five foot nine at most, wearing a navy-blue tailored suit. From the cut of the jacket, Lockyer would hazard a guess that it was handmade. Not surprising, really. A guy like Hodgson, taking home a six-figure salary, wouldn't be a likely customer at M&S. Without thinking, he straightened his own jacket. 'Good morning, Mr Hodgson. My name is Detective Inspector Mike Lockyer.'

'Pleased to meet you, Detective,' Hodgson said, without so much as a flicker of anxiety.

'My colleague will be along in a moment and then we can get started. We appreciate you coming in on such short notice.'

'Not at all. I am happy to help in any way I can. It's an awful situation. The office is still reeling from the shock.' Hodgson spoke with an air of disdain, as if Debbie had been the victim of some minor infraction and he was, in his capacity as managing director of Foster Advertising, trying to deal with it sensitively. It clearly didn't come naturally. Hodgson shifted in his seat as he straightened his tie. There was no warmth or compassion in his eyes.

'Murder is a devastating crime, Mr Hodgson. It affects people in different ways,' he said, waiting for Hodgson's response to the word 'murder'. Nothing.

However, Hodgson's body language was beginning to contradict his calm expression. He was fingering his wedding band and seemed to have found something on the back wall to focus on. Most people were unnerved by the interview rooms at Lewisham nick, even if they had nothing whatsoever to be worried about. Each room had white walls, uncomfortable plastic chairs, a nailed-down table and a large glass mirror along one wall. Even the uninitiated recognized a two-way screen when they saw one. Hodgson looked pale under the harsh strip lighting.

'Of course, it's very sad. I'm sure Debbie will be sorely missed,' Hodgson said with not one ounce of sincerity in his voice.

Despite himself, Lockyer could feel his anger surfacing. The muscles across his shoulders were solid, forcing a pain up his neck and over his scalp. He wondered how Hodgson had treated Debbie when she worked for him. The poor girl didn't seem to have more than a handful of people who really cared about her. Lockyer cleared his throat and sat back in his chair, willing Penny to arrive so they could get started. Jane was already conducting her second interview with Stacey Clemments, Debbie's best friend, in an interview room three doors down. A knock at the door interrupted his thoughts and he turned as Penny walked in and came to sit next to him.

'Mr Hodgson, you know my colleague, Detective Constable Penelope Groves. She will be sitting in on the interview.'

'Pleased to see you again, Miss Groves,' Hodgson said, giving her what Lockyer assumed was his best smile, showing off his impossibly white, straight teeth. He felt sorry for any woman who had to work with this prick.

Penny pressed the button on the recorder and gave Hodgson a rundown of how the interview would work – that he was here to provide further information on Deborah Stevens, as her employer. A red light on the digital recorder flashed to indicate they were now on the record. Hodgson didn't look perturbed at the idea of being taped. In fact he seemed to have regained his initial composure.

'You are not under arrest and are free to leave at any time,' Lockyer said, searching for any reaction.

Hodgson just stared straight ahead. 'Thank you, Detective. How can I help you today?'

'Mr Hodgson, how long was Deborah Stevens in your employ?' he asked.

'Six months.' Hodgson sat back in his seat.

'Did you interview Miss Stevens yourself?' he asked.

'No.'

'In your first statement . . .' Lockyer glanced down at the folder open in his lap, 'you said that Miss Stevens was your personal assistant. Is that correct?'

'Yes, that's right,' Hodgson said.

'But you didn't interview her?'

'No.'

'When did you first meet Miss Stevens?' Let him try to answer yes or no to that question.

'On her second interview,' Hodgson said, looking from Lockyer to Penny. He seemed to be relaxing further into his role of helpful employer.

'So, you did interview her, then?' Lockyer asked.

'No,' Hodgson said.

'Do you think you could elaborate on that, Mr Hodgson? I am finding it difficult to understand how meeting someone on a second interview isn't classed as "interviewing".' This was going to take longer than he wanted or needed, and he was already keen to know how Jane was getting on with Clemments.

Hodgson looked at Penny when he answered Lockyer's question. 'Originally she was interviewed as an admin assistant for my team but I decided, given the lack of experience on her CV, that she would be better placed starting off as a secretary, directly under me, where her progress could be closely monitored.' Hodgson turned his attention back to Lockyer. 'So, when she was called in for the second interview, I went to meet her. To check she was suitable for the position.'

'And was she?' Lockyer asked.

'Was she what?'

'Suitable for the position.'

'Yes. She was friendly, enthusiastic and keen to learn.'

'What was her exact role in your agency?'

Hodgson seemed to consider the question for a moment, looking up at the ceiling. Maybe it was hard, trying to recall what people less important than him did with their days. 'Her role was to assist me and the outdoor team. My team. We specialize in outdoor-space advertising: buses, trains, Tube, that kind of thing. She was a PA, of sorts. I wanted her to learn the ropes before having face-to-face contact with my clients.'

So, if he was talking about work he was able to muster up three whole sentences. 'And would you say, Mr Hodgson, that she was good at her job?'

'Yes. She struggled at first. She was young, new to the industry, but I managed to bring her on,' Hodgson said with real pride in his voice. It was the first time Lockyer had heard or seen genuine emotion, although he suspected it was from what Hodgson perceived as his own achievements rather than Debbie's.

'When you say "bring her on", what do you mean by that, Mr Hodgson?' Lockyer asked.

'I explained how the advertising business works and what was expected of her. She was, as I say, keen to learn. I have been building my agency for twenty years. We are one of the leading advertising agencies in London. I have a lot to offer my employees, and I expect them to learn and excel in everything they do.'

'Would you say Deborah Stevens, once she had settled in, excelled?' He knew this wasn't how she had been described by other colleagues. Several had said they were unsure what she did, other than run around after Hodgson.

'Excelled . . . I wouldn't say that, no, but she was certainly improving. Some people take longer than others to pick up the pace of things.'

Lockyer frowned, aware that during their entire conversation Hodgson had talked quite happily about Debbie in the past tense. 'Can you tell me your whereabouts on the night of the 14th of December, the 4th of January and the 22nd of January, Mr Hodgson?' he asked.

Hodgson reached into his inside jacket pocket and pulled out an iPhone, navigating to his diary using just his thumb. 'The 14th of December, you said?' Hodgson asked, not bothering to look up.

'That's right, between the hours of 21.00 and 02.00.'

'I have given this information . . . but, as I said, I am happy to help. I was at a dinner function in the City with four business associates. It went on until at least eleven and then I drove home. I was home with my family from 11.30, 11.45 at the latest.'

'Did you drink at this "dinner function"?'

'No, Detective. I like to keep a clear head when I'm talking business, even in a social situation. I am sure you appreciate that, in your profession?'

'And the other dates?' Lockyer asked, ignoring Hodgson's attempts to goad him.

Hodgson continued to flick through his phone, a smile creeping onto his face. 'That's right. On the 4th of January I was attending a Lord Mayor's function. I couldn't confirm the number of guests, but in excess of fifty, if I had to guess. They are always well-attended gatherings.' Hodgson looked up at Lockyer and then gave Penny a nod and a smile. And the 22nd . . . let me see. Ah, yes. I was attending the Metropolitan Police's Annual Advertising dinner. I have worked with the MPS for many years now.' Hodgson's smile widened.

Lockyer hadn't spotted that when he had read through the transcript of Hodgson's first interview. Hodgson certainly had friends in high places. 'Could you excuse me for a moment, Mr Hodgson? Constable, can you pause the session, please?' He stood but kept his eyes on Penny.

'Yes, sir. Interview suspended at 09.25,' she said, stopping the digital recording.

As he pulled the door of the interview room closed he rubbed his forehead. So far there was absolutely no connection to any of the other victims, but that didn't mean one wouldn't be found. In the same way that Walsh had been too nervous, too emotional, Hodgson seemed too comfortable, too confident. He needed to find something to unsettle the guy.

Lockyer knocked on the door of the interview room and waited.

'Yes.' He heard Jane call out.

He turned the handle, pushed open the door and poked his head through the gap. 'You got a second?' he asked, glancing at the girl sitting on the other side of the table. Stacey Clemments didn't look a day over twelve.

'Of course, sir,' Jane said, pushing her chair back and joining him in the hallway.

He waited for the door to close before speaking. 'So, how's it going?'

'Good,' Jane said in a hushed voice. 'She's pretty nervous but I think she's being truthful, so far. Do you want to sit in?'

Lockyer wanted to know more about Debbie from someone who actually cared about her, something that he could use to push Hodgson off balance. 'Yes, I will. Just for a few minutes,' he said, his hand already on the door handle.

After the introductions he sat back in his chair, to give Jane space to work and Stacey space to breathe. The young girl looked about ready to collapse. Her cheeks were flushed, her eyes huge, like a startled animal. He listened as Jane talked to her, her voice soothing, her words supportive, encouraging. There was a knack in interviews like this. If you could build on a level of trust there was no end to what people would tell you. Jane was a master. She was far better at this aspect of the job than he was and he was more than happy to admit it as he watched Stacey wipe a tear from her chin, nod and start to talk.

'I'd seen her two days before,' Stacey said, swallowing. 'We'd been to The Ivy House, listened to a load of performance poets and a band . . . well, sort of a band,' she said, closing her eyes as if to remember. When she opened them she looked totally different, almost defiant. 'You may as well know we were smoking, smoking gear, I mean. I guess you test her hair for that kinda thing. It wasn't a regular thing, not every day or anything, but her mother didn't know, doesn't know. You don't have to tell her, do you?'

As he listened to Jane reassuring the teenager he was struck by just how young Stacey sounded. He imagined Debbie had been much the same; a small squeak to her voice, a strong south-east London accent. He thought about Megan. She was the same age as Debbie and Stacey. When she left uni and went out to work, if that was her decision, would she find it as hard? He looked over at Stacey as she talked and realized just how vulnerable Debbie had been. She would never have seen him coming.

'We mainly went out locally, The Ivy House, EDT, The Bishop, Liquorice . . . places like that,' Stacey said, counting off the different pubs on her fingers.

'Is there a group of you?' Jane asked.

Stacey shook her head. 'No, just me and Debbie. She wasn't always allowed out . . . her mum was quite strict, wanted her to do well in the new job. It was in the City. None of their family have ever been to the City, let alone worked there,' Stacey said, a small sneer crossing her face. He guessed Stacey hadn't been approved of by Debbie's mother and the dislike seemed to be mutual.

'Go on, Stacey,' Jane said, her voice so soothing that he even found himself relaxing under its influence.

'Well, it was always just me and Debbie, really, since school. Debs was quiet, a bit dyslexic, the teacher said. The other kids picked on her, took the piss,' Stacey said, her eyes brimming with tears. 'She was so quiet and gentle, you know? She wouldn't hurt anyone. All she wanted was to get a job . . . have a career, meet a guy, get married.' Tears were now flowing freely down Stacey's cheeks. 'She should have had better. She deserved better . . . better than him.'

He sat forward almost in sync with Jane.

'Him?' they said in unison.

'Sorry about that, Mr Hodgson,' Lockyer said as he walked back into the interview room half an hour later. He sat down and nodded for Penny to resume the interview.

'Interview resumed at 09.55,' she said. The red light on the digital recorder flashed.

Hodgson looked, if it was possible, even calmer than before. He thought he was going to be walking out of here any second, swanning out of the station in his three-grand suit. Lockyer smiled: he was wrong.

'Did you ever see Miss Stevens socially?' he asked.

Hodgson looked at the digital tape recorder. Lockyer could tell he was making a decision about how much he was prepared to say. 'I saw her on work social occasions. Drinks out, that kind of thing. I allow a generous budget for entertaining. I like to keep my staff happy.'

'And your wife?' Lockyer asked.

Hodgson sat forward. 'My wife?' His face was beginning to show some semblance of disquiet.

'Your wife, Mr Hodgson.'

'I'm not sure what that has to do with anything, Detective.'

'Does your wife ever attend these "social occasions", Mr Hodgson?'

'No, she doesn't. She travels a lot, with her work, but again, Detective, I am unsure how this is relevant to your investigation. My wife never even met Debbie.'

Lockyer felt the adrenalin fizz through his veins. Now he had him. 'Have you ever been to Deborah Stevens' home, Mr Hodgson?'

'No. There would be no reason for me to do so.' Hodgson ran his fingers through his hair. His immaculate and calm demeanour was slipping.

'Did you ever see Miss Stevens . . . privately?'

'No, I did not, and I do not appreciate the implication, Detective,' Hodgson said, stifling a coughing fit.

'Were you aware that Miss Stevens was pregnant?'

Hodgson's face froze. He opened his mouth to speak but shut it again. Lockyer waited. 'I . . . she was going to . . . yes,' he said, looking down at his hands.

Lockyer looked at Penny. Her hand was already hovering over the pause button on the digital recorder. 'In light of what you have just said, Mr Hodgson, I must advise you that this interview will be terminated and resumed under caution.' Hodgson's tan was all but non-existent now as his face dropped several shades until he was almost grey. Lockyer looked at Penny and nodded.

'Interview terminated at 10.10,' she said as she pressed the stop button. The red light on the recorder disappeared.

Lockyer nodded again and Penny resumed the tape, the light flickering back to life. He leaned forward and said, 'Mr Hodgson, I am obliged to advise you that this is now a formal interview under caution. You do not have to say anything but it may harm your defence if you do not mention when questioned something which you later rely on in court. Anything you do say may be given in evidence. Do you understand your rights as they have been explained to you?' he asked.

'Yes, I do,' Hodgson said, with a nod of his head.

'Would you like to have legal representation, Mr Hodgson?' Lockyer asked.

'No.' Hodgson couldn't seem to take his eyes off the table top.

'I would strongly urge you to reconsider, Mr Hodgson. You are entitled and are advised to have legal representation.'

'No. I don't want it,' Hodgson said, puffing out his chest, looking Lockyer straight in the eye. 'I understand my rights as you have explained them to me, Detective, and I waive my right to a solicitor. I do not need one.'

It was Hodgson's turn to squirm.

'You seem upset, Mr Hodgson. Are you all right?' Penny asked.

'Thank you, Constable, I'm fine.'

'Are you prepared to continue, Mr Hodgson?' she asked.

'Yes.'

'Good. Mr Hodgson, did you know that Deborah Stevens was pregnant?' Lockyer asked again.

'Yes,' Hodgson said, his voice suddenly quiet.

'Mr Hodgson. Did you have an affair with Deborah Stevens while she was in your employ and did that affair result in a pregnancy?' Lockyer asked.

Hodgson paused but only for a second. 'Yes, I did, but it

was brief, a couple of months at the most. She looked up to me. As for the pregnancy . . . she assured me that she was going to get rid of it. I gave her money for a clinic that dealt with . . . abortions.'

'How did you feel when Miss Stevens told you she was pregnant?' Lockyer asked.

Hodgson looked down at his hands, turning his wedding band round and round on his finger. 'I didn't believe her at first. She had become . . . clingy.' He said the word 'clingy' like it was some kind of disease.

'When did the relationship end?' Lockyer had a pretty good idea. He remembered Debbie's phone message to her brother the night she died. Lockyer suspected the 'bad day' and the two hours when Debbie dropped off the grid were both down to Hodgson.

'I told her we could no longer see each other on the day . . . on the day she died.' Hodgson's veneer had all but vanished. There was a tremor in his voice that even a man as slick as him couldn't hide.

Lockyer needed to push harder. 'As far as you were aware, did Miss Stevens go through with the abortion?' He watched as his question pushed a doubt into Hodgson's mind and then to an inevitable question of his own.

'Didn't she?' Hodgson asked. His eyes were beginning to gloss over.

Lockyer looked over at Penny. She turned to look at him and raised her eyebrows. He nodded. Penny sat forward. 'We understand this may be distressing, Mr Hodgson, but we need you to talk us through the affair. How it began, who initiated it, the duration, where you met, how you felt about her and the fact that she was pregnant, she said.

Lockyer sat back and watched as Hodgson relived the last three months. The late nights in the office. The glass of wine after a hard day. The inevitable pass, made by her, apparently. The clandestine meetings in hotel bars. They met in Holiday Inns around the City. They signed in under the name Mr and Mrs Hodvens, their shared joke.

'We agreed that an abortion was the only option. She was young. I was married. We both agreed. I can't believe she wouldn't have gone through with it. If I had known I could have . . . I wouldn't have.' Hodgson drifted into silence.

'Did you see Deborah Stevens after office hours on the 22nd, Mr Hodgson?'

Hodgson took a deep breath. 'Yes,' he said, avoiding Lockyer's gaze. 'I didn't mention it before because . . . well, because it was a private matter.' He finally looked up, defiance in his eyes. 'A friend has an apartment in the City that I sometimes use. Debbie and I . . . I took Miss Stevens there to end the relationship.'

'How long were you there?' Lockyer asked.

'A couple of hours at the most,' Hodgson said. 'At most.'

'That seems like rather a long time for a "break-up" conversation, wouldn't you say?' Lockyer didn't know why he was asking the question. It was clear from Hodgson's expression what those two hours had entailed and it made him sick.

'What's your question, Detective?' Hodgson asked, tipping up his chin.

He looked down at the file and composed himself. He

couldn't let Hodgson throw him off track. 'Were you angry about the pregnancy?' he asked.

If Debbie's lover was surprised by the change in direction he didn't show it. 'Yes. It was a shock. I was in shock, Detective.' Hodgson looked at Lockyer with raw anger in his eyes. Lockyer could hardly believe the change of atmosphere in the interview room. Maybe Dave was wrong for once. The three murders weren't linked, or at least Debbie's wasn't. Her murderer was potentially sitting two feet away from Lockyer on the verge of confessing everything before his lawyers could swoop in to save the day. He couldn't deny that it would be a relief. He was far happier solving crimes committed not by some phantom, but by ordinary people, like Hodgson, for the good old-fashioned motive of 'covering his own arse'.

'Do you think that Miss Stevens would have exposed your affair?' he asked. He could feel the hairs on his arms vibrating as another shot of adrenalin surged through his system.

'No. She would never have done that. It wasn't like that, Detective.'

'How would you have felt if Miss Stevens had told you she was going to keep the baby? I can appreciate that for a man in your position, married, a pillar of the business community, this would be most inconvenient.' He rested his hands on the table. He was trying to get eye contact with Hodgson but the man's eyes were darting all over the place, and then he was up and out of his chair, pacing round the room, muttering to himself.

'No,' Hodgson said, 'I ended it. She told me she'd already

had the abortion. I said we shouldn't see each other any more. She was upset. I think she thought that we would be able to continue, but if my wife found out, if my colleagues knew, my reputation would have been tarnished.'

'How would you classify your feelings at that time, Mr Hodgson?' Lockyer asked.

'I was confused, I was . . .'

'Angry?' Lockyer suggested.

Hodgson turned and his eyes focused. 'What?'

'Mr Hodgson, would you be willing to provide a DNA sample and fingerprints to assist our investigation?' he asked.

As soon as the words were out of his mouth he saw the change in Hodgson. It was as if a cold wind had blown into the interview room and turned the guy to stone.

'I would like to speak to my lawyer,' Hodgson said, his eyes hard.

Lockyer pushed back his chair, stood and leaned over the table towards Hodgson. 'Mr Hodgson has requested legal counsel. Interview suspended at . . . 10.57.' He nodded to Penny who stopped the tape. 'We'll speak again, Mr Hodgson. Thank you for your time.'

As Lockyer walked out of the room and closed the door behind him he felt his shoulders tighten once more. He was meant to come out of this interview with answers but all he had was more questions. He pushed his brain to pull the threads together. If Hodgson killed Debbie to stop her ratting him out to his wife, what about the other two girls? The MOs were the same – not similar, the same – Dave had said so. He shook his head, willing the pieces to fit into place, but they wouldn't. There was something about Hodgson, a cold-hearted narcissism, a frightening detachment. Lockyer needed to find the link, something that connected all three girls. Once he had that he would be one step closer to a killer.

16

26 January – Sunday

It was late and he was tired. He rubbed his eyes and resumed his task, the scissors slicing through the newspaper without effort. He applied some glue to a new page in his scrapbook and placed the picture of the detective in the centre. In the article DI Mike Lockyer was painted as some kind of super-cop. Since his promotion to leading DI for Lewisham's Murder Investigation Team, part of the Homicide and Serious Crime Command, Lockyer had apparently lectured at the Crime Academy, set up a task force to deal with south-east London's violent crime and had great success reviewing cold cases dating back to 2001. Almost twenty years of service, a cop to be reckoned with, adept at catching criminals. He shook his head. As far as he was concerned DI Lockyer wasn't living up to the hype.

He looked out at his garden, at the waterlogged grass, the soaked hedgerow and the crush of houses beyond. By morning all would be crisp, ice forming in the smallest of cracks. But the weather didn't bother him. He pushed himself away from the kitchen table, closed his scrapbook and tucked it into a drawer, safe from prying eyes.

There was nothing in the article about the detective's private life, marital status, sexual preference. The thought made him laugh. 'Never underestimate your opponent.' A phrase his father used often. He would do some more research, a bit of digging to find out what else there was to know about Detective Inspector Mike Lockyer.

As he climbed the stairs a rumble of thunder echoed high above him. He walked into the bedroom and lay down, too exhausted to change. Images of her, as she had been, crowded his mind. Her smell, her delicate hands, her skin so pure. She allowed the girls, helped him to choose them, but she wouldn't be ignored, sullied by a comparison to those not worthy of her. 'Never,' he whispered. He closed his eyes, his hands resting on his chest as her voice soothed him to sleep.

17

27 January – Monday

'Here you are, sir,' Jane said, handing Lockyer three folders, each at least two inches thick. She gave him a small smile and walked out of his office. He looked down at the first file. Phoebe Atherton. The second was Katy Pearson's. The last file, compiled by Jane, was Debbie's case history, so far.

The interview with Hodgson yesterday had ended too soon. To get the guy to confess to the affair was a breakthrough, without doubt. But he had pushed too hard, too fast. If Hodgson was as cold-blooded a killer as the MOs suggested, he wasn't likely to be lured into incriminating himself that easily. Lockyer had barely made it back to his office before Roger, his senior investigating officer, had called to tell him that Hodgson's lawyer was lodging a complaint. Lockyer should have insisted that Debbie's boss had legal representation before the interview under caution had taken place. Of course, the fact that Hodgson had refused several times made not a scrap of difference. It was all about the procedure. He had gone above and beyond his pay grade, but if Hodgson was their man, Lockyer didn't have time to tiptoe around the guy.

'Sir.'

He looked up to see Jane leaning into his office.

'Yes, Jane.'

'I meant to say, I checked with Hodgson's colleague regarding the two hours Hodgson and Stevens allegedly spent in the apartment over near Moorgate,' she said. 'The colleague confirmed Hodgson borrowed the keys to the flat late afternoon on the day of the murder and returned them at the MPS dinner function that evening, about nine-ish.'

'Right,' he said, waiting for Jane to leave.

As the door clicked shut he looked down at the piles of paper covering his desk. He picked up Phoebe's file and scanned the contents page. There were three sections devoted to the crime scene, the post-mortem and all the physical evidence collected, but he had already read the summaries, so he doubted he would find any new information there. There was only one exhibits section so he flicked to the relevant pages and began to read. Phoebe's clothes were listed, their condition photographed. A sentence, highlighted in yellow, caught his attention. A section of lining material, four-inch square in diameter, was missing from the trousers she was wearing. Not ripped out but carefully cut and removed. He opened Katy's file, turning to the exhibits notes. He put his finger on the page over another highlighted note. A piece of Katy's coat was missing too but it hadn't been cut out like Phoebe's. An entire section had been ripped away and taken.

He tipped his head back, his neck cracking. He didn't need to look at Debbie's file. He knew it by heart. Her clothing was listed and described: jacket, removed prior to attack, intact. Jumper, on victim, intact. Skirt and tights torn. He ran his fingers through his hair. Her skirt and tights were so badly damaged it was almost impossible to decipher what the original garment had looked like. There was no way of knowing if her killer had taken something from her too. And even if there was, what did it mean? He remembered the bite mark on Debbie's shoulder, as if she had been attacked by a wild dog, not a man. He let out a frustrated breath and flicked to the contents page of Phoebe's file. The interviews with her family and friends were as good a place to start as any. He opened his laptop and logged in to the audio files section. There were fourteen statements. It was going to be a long day.

An hour had passed and he was only on the third interview. The temperature in the room had dropped enough for him to put on his jacket. He looked out at the practically empty office and drained his fifth cup of coffee. The last two had been decaf but his heart still felt like it was hammering in his chest. With a shake of his head he went back to the audio transcript of the interview with Stefan Riste, Phoebe's partner. Riste had already been cleared of any involvement as he had been visiting friends in Manchester at the time of his girlfriend's murder. A Post-it note attached to the bottom of the page also confirmed he had alibis for the dates of Katy's and Debbie's murders too. As Lockyer listened, he was struck by the pain. Every answer seemed to tap into a new part of the poor man's grief. He sat back, the January sun casting intermittent shadows around his office. His breath fogged up his screen as he let out a weary sigh. As he pressed play again he decided to finish Riste's statement and then take a break. He would head to Bella's cafe across the road and get some lunch, or anything to stop the endless cups of coffee tearing a hole in his stomach lining.

He closed his eyes and listened to Riste talk. The guy was beyond distraught, his words laced with misery. And then Lockyer heard something. He clicked back ten seconds and listened again. Then again. Another officer had come into the interview room. Lockyer could hear the two officers talking. But underneath their voices he heard Riste's voice, barely audible. It was a few whispered words among thousands but it could mean everything. Riste's voice echoed in his mind. '. . . We hoped to try again.'

He dialled Jane's extension and waited. She answered on the second ring.

'Sir,' she said.

'I've got news,' he said, unable to stop a smile spreading across his face. He didn't feel sick. He didn't feel angry. His emotions had quietened. Finally, he felt focused.

'I'm on my way. I have news for you, too, on the Grainger case,' she said.

'Good. We have work to do.'

Lockyer had spent the past hour on the phone, speaking to Phil, Dave, the SIO and Stefan Riste. Jane was sitting opposite him on her mobile talking to Katy Pearson's husband.

'Thank you, Mr Pearson . . . yes, we will keep you informed . . . of course . . . thank you again.' Jane ended the call and slumped back in her chair. 'Pearson sounds terrible,' she said, her face pale.

'What did he say?' he asked.

Jane sat forward and took a deep breath. He knew she

was trying to shake off the trauma of the conversation she'd just had. 'Katy Pearson had a termination in October of last year . . . two months before she was killed.'

'But it's not on her medical records,' he said, slapping his hand down on the files on the desk.

'It is, sir. I double checked with her GP,' Jane said. 'Pearson's medical file was a mess. She was diagnosed with breast cancer in November, so the documentation relating to that was extensive. The termination paperwork wasn't attached when they sent over her file,' she said, her shoulders dropping.

He rubbed his temple, trying to push away the thought that they had lost valuable time. He couldn't stop thinking about his conversation with Riste. They had spoken for over half an hour, the poor guy sobbing throughout. An amnio-centesis test had shown chromosome abnormalities in the foetus: Down's syndrome. They had made the decision to abort the pregnancy but, according to Riste, Phoebe refused to go through their GP, who was not only their family doctor but a friend as well. She had used a private clinic that provided total anonymity. The hospital that carried out the procedure would have her details but wouldn't have been allowed to forward any information to her GP, as per Phoebe's instructions. Lockyer kept hearing Riste's words over and over in his mind. '. . . We hoped to try again.' But now they never could.

'He must be using their hospital records,' Jane said, dragging him out of his stupor. 'It's the only way he could know that all three victims underwent abortions, and have access to their real names and addresses.'

Lockyer blinked several times and took a deep breath in through his nose, blowing it out again, hoping Riste's words would go with it. He wasn't thinking about Debbie, Katy or Phoebe. He was thinking about Clara and the decision she'd made all those years ago.

'Sir, the hospital records?' Jane said, tapping her fingers on the table.

As he lifted his head to look at her everything seemed to rush back into focus. He saw Debbie's face. 'Right,' he said, clapping his hands together. 'We need to find out which hospitals looked after Phoebe and Katy, whether each hospital feeds their data into a centralized database, and if so, who would have access to that information . . .' Jane was out of her chair and out of his office before he had finished speaking.

He leaned back in his chair, his hands clasped at the base of his neck. All three victims had abortions within two months of their deaths. There was no way that was a co-incidence. It was the link. There was no doubt in his mind. His only frustration was that it had taken him this long to unearth it. He stood up and walked over to his window, pulling back his blinds to watch the people of Lewisham rushing back and forth, trying to escape the cold. The ice had melted and the snow was holding off, for now. He was thinking about Hodgson and the advertising work he did for the Met. It was feasible he worked with the NHS too. Could his high-powered connections have given him access to the girls' hospital records? Lockyer thought they just might.

18

28 January – Tuesday

Sarah sat alone in the interview room, her diary and the note on the table in front of her. She found herself moving them closer together, then further apart, straightening them against the edge of the table top.

She hadn't been home since Saturday. She couldn't face being alone. Of course, Toni had been great, fussing around her, making her soup, endless cups of tea and running interference with her phone. Sarah didn't know how many times he had called because Toni wouldn't let her look. Was he calling to get her answer, the answer to his note, a note she didn't understand? She pushed the piece of paper away and fixed her eyes on the door of the interview room. How long was she going to be here?

Bennett had called last night to ask her to come in, to bring the note, so they could 'talk things through'. But now that she was here all she wanted to do was go home, shut her front door and forget the whole thing. She had barely slept, disturbed by every noise, the unfamiliar creaks and bangs of a strange place. It shouldn't feel strange, she knew that. Toni's home usually felt warm and comforting but now, nothing and nowhere did. In the early hours of the morning she had stood in the kitchen, sipping tea, watching as night gave way to the grey of dawn, aware of the ache in her bones from a fatigue that threatened to consume her. Toni's house was at the top of a steep hill with an enviable view of London: Canary Wharf, the Shard, St Paul's Cathedral, the London Eye. But Sarah had turned away. It only served to remind her of a life she no longer had. Out there, beyond her world, millions of people would be waking up, taking a shower, eating toast while watching breakfast television and dressing for the day ahead. They were free.

As she sat back the knotted muscles at the base of her neck throbbed. She couldn't avoid looking sideways at herself in the large mirror on the opposite wall. Her hair looked awful; split ends stood straight up from her head as if she had been electrocuted. She touched her cheek. It was hot but her reflection showed no warmth, no life at all. The black jacket she had chosen hung off her bones. She knew she had lost weight but until now she hadn't realized quite how much. Her skinny jeans were baggy, excess material folding around her thighs.

She turned away, rested her elbows on the table and covered her face with her hands, tunnelling her vision. All she could see was the edge of the note and her diary. She began comparing her handwriting to his. Their W was the same, with a slight curve on the final upward stroke of the letter. The depression left by his pen and hers matched. Both were deep, cutting scratches on the page.

'Miss Grainger . . . apologies . . . Sarah.'

She looked up and saw Bennett's boss, the tall detective inspector.

'My name is Detective Inspector Mike Lockyer. We met last week.' He walked into the room, closed the door and took a chair opposite her. The sound of the metal chair legs scraping on the tiled floor sent a shiver right through her. She sat back and looked at him and then at the door. Where was Bennett? She reached out her hand as if in slow motion, and he took it, applying only the slightest pressure. It looked as if he was wearing the same charcoal suit she had seen him in last week. She could see that his shirt hadn't been ironed, the creases not quite hidden beneath his jacket. He looked tired.

'I'm sorry to have kept you waiting. Sergeant Bennett will be along shortly,' he said.

'OK.' She couldn't think of anything else to say.

'I would like to ask you a few more questions,' he said, taking a notepad and an expensive-looking pen from his jacket pocket. It was the kind of gift you received from a not-so-close friend on a significant birthday. His fortieth maybe.

'Sarah?'

She realized she was just staring at his pen, not speaking. 'Yes. That's fine.'

'How you are feeling?'

She looked at his face, his eyes, his mouth. There was no hint of a smile, or humour. He was really asking her how she was. Other than Toni, she couldn't remember the last time someone had asked her that. 'I'm . . .' She wasn't sure how to answer. 'I'm OK . . . I'm tired. I'm scared.'

'I understand. It must be very difficult for you. I want you to take your time. If you need a break, please do ask. We'll do this as quickly as we can. I appreciate how distressing it must be to talk about what is happening.' He nodded his head and rested one hand on the desk, palm down, fingers splayed, as if reaching out to her. His voice was soft, his words gentle. Despite herself she felt the tears coming. She swallowed them back and looked up into his face.

'Thank you,' she said.

She watched as he reached into his jacket again and pulled out a handkerchief. He passed it to her and smiled. Such a simple gesture; but at that moment it felt like the first time in her life someone had shown her any kindness. The Grainger family were tough. You didn't cry, you didn't shout. Nothing warranted a scene, an unnecessary show of emotion. 'Buck up,' her father would say, 'worse things happen at sea.' He had been repeating the same phrase since her childhood. It had never made sense when she was a little girl, running to her father when she had fallen and scraped her knee, and it didn't make sense to her now. She took the handkerchief and held it under her eyes. It smelled of washing powder. She hadn't seen anyone use an old-fashioned-style handkerchief in years. Her grandfather used to have one. With a loud snort he would pretend to blow his nose, the crisp white material flapping around his face. It used to be their in-joke.

'Can I get you anything? A glass of water . . . tea?' he asked.

Sarah composed herself. 'No, I'm fine. Thank you.' She

pushed her shoulders back and placed her hands in her lap, pulling the handkerchief between her fingers. It felt soft.

'I've read Sergeant Bennett's report from your meeting last week. Is this the note you received?' he asked, pointing at the piece of paper on the table.

'Yes.'

He turned it around to face him, barely touching the edges. He studied it and made some notes before pushing it away with the end of his pen. 'When did you receive it?' he asked.

'Saturday evening, the day after I saw Sergeant Bennett and talked to you,' she said.

'At what time, approximately?'

'About six o'clock. I called Sergeant Bennett. She phoned me back yesterday to say she wanted to see me this morning.'

'That's right. OK. What I would like to establish today is what has occurred, in what order and, if possible, why.'

'I don't know why . . .' She felt her chest tighten. She didn't know if she could go through it all again. She took a deep breath, her shoulders rising and falling.

'It's all right, Sarah. In your previous statement you said contact began approximately six months ago. Is that correct?'

'Yes. Like I told Sergeant Bennett, I didn't notice at first. It was just little things. Phone calls. Someone ringing my doorbell. My car was tampered with.' She watched as he made scribbled notes. His handwriting was worse than hers. His other hand was at the nape of his neck, pulling at something beneath his shirt.

'When you say "tampered with"?' he asked, lifting his pen as an accompanying gesture to his question.

'It was nothing really,' she said, feeling weak. 'Scratches, messing with my wing mirrors, stealing my hubcaps. That kind of thing. One of my neighbours said it was probably just kids.'

'Which neighbour?'

'Ash, he lives five doors down. I don't actually know his surname. But groups of kids hang around the corner shop in the evenings. He said it was probably them mucking about.'

'Did you report any of this?' he asked.

'No. I didn't. These things happen, don't they? There was never any significant damage. Kids get bored, nothing else to do, so they . . .' She trailed off. Her explanations sounded ludicrous but he was writing furiously in his little notepad. Maybe he was writing, 'This woman is an idiot,' over and over again in shorthand.

'Sarah . . .' he said.

She looked up. Again he stretched out his hand on the table top. 'It's all right. In cases like yours it is quite common for the individual not to realize what is happening. As you say, you shrug off one incident, you shrug off another. You were not to know, and indeed we don't know that these incidents are related,' he said. She noticed his hand go up to his chest again, to touch whatever lay beneath his shirt.

'But, if I had reported it. If I had told someone then, maybe none of this would be happening. I let this happen.' She covered her face with the handkerchief, shaking her head.

'No, Sarah. This individual who has, for whatever reason, taken it upon himself to harass you is at fault. He is the one who is in the wrong and he has broken the law.'

Sarah looked into his eyes. They did believe her. They were going to help her. Relief flooded through her body.

'When did you change your car?' he asked.

'Four months ago, in October.'

'Right,' he said, as he scribbled down another illegible note. 'In your meeting with Sergeant Bennett, you said that you received a phone call where the caller said your name. This was also in October? This was the point at which you realized there was a problem?'

'Yes, yes. He just said my name, nothing else.' The sound of his voice was still as fresh in her mind as if it had happened yesterday.

'And you didn't recognize the voice?'

'No.'

'And you have no idea who this man might be?'

'No, none.'

'So, other than the phone calls, ringing your door, the incidents with your car and the note, you have never had any other contact with him? You have never seen him?'

'No,' she said, thinking about the seven minutes of tape she had of the man sitting in his car outside her house. 'No, I have never seen him.' This was hard enough. If she brought up the video he would probably have her committed.

'It was after the telephone call that you spoke to Peckham police, to . . .' He flicked to the back of his notebook. 'Officer Rayner?'

'Yes. He told me to keep a journal, to record all the phone calls, the knocks at the door. Officer Rayner wasn't . . . he didn't seem . . .' She searched for the right words. She didn't want to be sent away. 'He didn't believe me.'

'It's OK, Sarah,' he said, his eyes soft, understanding. 'At which point would you say that matters escalated?'

'Only in the last couple of weeks. I used to get calls once a fortnight, maybe once a week. But then he started to call every night and then last week . . .' She could barely stand to think of that night. 'He called five times in one night, all through the night.'

'And this was Thursday the 23rd of January. Is that correct?'

'Yes, he left a voice message. I played it to Sergeant Bennett . . . he said . . . it was difficult to hear but he said something about someone being cold and helping, I can't remember exactly.' She stopped speaking, unable to continue.

'I've heard the message, Sarah. It's all right.'

Sarah tried to speak but her mouth had gone dry.

'You're a freelance photographer, is that correct?'

'Yes, for the last five years, give or take,' she said, her eyes stinging.

'What kind of clients do you normally work with?'

His voice was calm and restrained. She wanted to shout, to scream that she didn't want to answer any more questions. She wanted to lie down and sleep and when she woke up she wanted all of this to be over.

'Sarah?' he prompted.

'I work in the City . . . solicitors, accountancy firms, advertising agencies, large corporate companies, mainly,' she said, swallowing a rush of bile that was swamping her mouth.

'I see. And are you registered with a local doctor?' he asked.

She finally cleared her throat and answered, 'Yes, Dr Yermolov, Nunhead Surgery.' What did all this have to do with anything?

'Are you currently taking any prescription medication?'

'No . . . I mean, I was prescribed some Vistaril to help me sleep, but I haven't been taking it.' Was he checking that this whole thing wasn't some elaborate drug-induced hallucination?

'Have you had any medical procedures in the last twelve months?' he asked.

'I . . . no . . . I'm sorry, I don't understand the question.' She didn't understand any of this.

'I mean any surgical procedures,' he said, his pen poised over his notebook. He looked uncomfortable.

'No. I haven't.' She slumped forward and rested her arms on the desk. Without the table she was sure she would just slither to the floor, a boneless, empty shell. She was so confused. So tired. They had barely talked about the note or what it meant but she was already exhausted to the point of passing out, right here, in front of him. Would he leave her to sleep or pick her up and carry her to another room, where she could lie down? She imagined his strong arms around her, protecting her.

'Sarah?'

'Sorry, yes?' If he had been talking, she hadn't noticed. Her mind was wandering. She couldn't stay focused.

'Sarah?'

She dragged her eyes up to meet his.

'I think it's time we took a break. I will send an officer in with some tea. Would you like something to eat?' He was already standing. She couldn't look up, her head felt too heavy.

'I'll get some sandwiches sent down for you. There's always some left over from the morning briefing. I'll be back with Sergeant Bennett shortly. You relax for a minute.'

Before she could say anything he was gone. She let her head fall onto her arms. Her eyelids were so heavy, her mind drifting as she fell asleep.

Lockyer walked away from the interview room. Sarah Grainger was a totally different woman to the one he had met last week. Had she been that thin? There was an almost waxy sheen to her skin.

The calls had escalated after Katy's murder, that much was clear. The tech guys had tried to put a trace on the number without success. Triangulation only worked when the phone was in use and so far it hadn't been. All they could tell Lockyer was that it was a standard pay-as-you-go mobile phone. There was no way to track the purchase back to its owner.

The five calls in one night had happened the night after Debbie's murder. Hodgson's face flashed into his mind and he heard Phil's words in his head: 'He may not have killed like this before but he will have practised. I would imagine that he started with scaring young women. Nothing major, jumping out of bushes or following them home, so they knew he was there.'

But Grainger's stalker had been following her for six months, she hadn't had an abortion to his knowledge and she was, more to the point, still alive. Something about her case didn't quite fit but that didn't stop Lockyer quickening his pace. He wanted to speak to Phil and he needed to get permission to arrange some surveillance. He needed to get it sorted now, before Sarah left the building. The threads of this case were multiplying, flying as the momentum increased but, as yet, nothing felt strong enough to hold on to.

19

Something was wrong. Why was she here again? His hands closed around the bars surrounding the police car park. The metal felt cold but the action was familiar. He had stood right here not four days ago, watching her walk in and waiting for her to walk out again. The blare of a dozen car horns sent fresh pain into his head. He felt unsure.

What could she possibly gain from coming here? He had thought it might be some kind of game, something private between them, but he didn't feel confident about that any more. She seemed to have forgotten that he was the only one who could help her, the only one devoted only to her. He felt his cheeks heating at the lie. Of course, there had been others, but none of them had compared to her. He crossed the busy road, ignoring the shouts when his elbow struck a car's wing mirror.

The smell of grease was overwhelming as he passed a string of takeaways. Each was serving foods from different parts of the world and yet they all smelled the same. He swallowed and covered his mouth with his hand. The crush of Lewisham's pedestrians was too much. He stopped and stood, his back pressed flat against the window of a betting shop. The grey of the pavement was barely visible beneath dozens of feet. He looked up at the sky, the clouds heavy and white. The snow the weatherman had promised was on its way. But that wouldn't slow London's pace. Nothing did. He closed his eyes, assaulted by the sheer volume and variety of noises. People talking, shouting, screaming. Cars revving, their horns blaring, their exhausts rumbling. As he listened he began to be able to pick out individual sounds, the minutiae of London life. Someone ordering fish and chips, a small child pleading for a bag of sweeties. And then a voice he knew, a sound so beautiful it made his heart ache.

'. . . A bottle of Jack Daniel's, please.'

It was her; but where was she? He opened his eyes, his head snapping forward. He looked around him but there were bodies and machinery everywhere, blocking his view. His blood was pounding in his ears as his excitement began to build.

As he turned towards the police station he saw her. She was standing between some parked cars, her head bobbing from side to side as she looked for a gap in the traffic to cross. He stumbled out of his hiding place, reaching out to her as he got closer, but at the last moment she stepped out, jogged across the road and was gone behind a line of buses.

He was left only with the sounds of Lewisham, hard and angry.

20

Lockyer bent down, took his house key out of his left sock and let himself into the flat. The run had made him feel better. Just being out in the fresh air, even if it was freezing, had helped to clear his head. Snow had fallen overnight but it hadn't really settled. The streets on his circuit still looked grey.

He walked through to the kitchen, poured some coffee beans into the grinder and set it for twenty seconds. As he picked up his dented silver coffee pot he thought again about replacing it but he couldn't. It made two perfect cups and kept the coffee warm. He ran the pot under the hot tap while he waited for the kettle to boil. His favourite mug wouldn't fit on the pine stand by the sink, so it had pride of place on top of the microwave. He filled his mug and left it to cool. Bobby loved to drink coffee but he wasn't allowed to have it hot, just in case he spilt it on himself. Lockyer realized he would be lucky to fit in a visit this week. He picked up his mobile from the kitchen counter and pressed speed dial four.

'Hello, Cliffview.'

Just hearing Alice's voice made him smile. How could one person be that cheerful? It wasn't natural. 'Hi, Alice, it's Mike,' he said, resting his hand against his mug, glad of the heat. He was sweating but his hands were freezing.

'Michael, good to hear from you. You coming over later?' she asked, her voice bright.

As always, he felt a pang of jealousy that his voice had never and probably would never sound like that. 'I can't today, I'm afraid,' he said, taking a sip of his coffee. 'I just wanted to see how things were your end.'

'Things are good. I'm knee-deep organizing the Greenwich trip for next week. I've been showing Bobby pictures of the *Cutty Sark*. To say he is excited would be an understatement,' she said, laughing.

'I can imagine,' he said, walking through to his office, carrying his coffee in the palm of his hand. 'Will you tell him I'll be in tomorrow or over the weekend?'

'Of course, he'll be thrilled,' she said.

Bobby wouldn't be anything like thrilled. Today, two days from now, he wouldn't really know the difference, but Lockyer was grateful to Alice for maintaining at least the charade of normality, for his sake, no doubt. 'Thanks, I appreciate it.'

'Cool. I'm out tomorrow, though . . . my new man is taking me away for the day, so if you come then you'll have to face Amber.' She cackled.

'Thanks for the heads-up,' he said, turning on his computer. 'I'll certainly bear that in mind. Speak to you later.'

As he hung up he thought about Bobby's life before Alice, before Cliffview. A familiar combination of guilt and anger settled on his shoulders. Had Bobby's childhood been happy?

Lockyer didn't really know and there was no one to ask. Their parents were dead and gone, Aunt Nancy was in a home losing her mind to dementia and Bobby, the one person who should be able to tell him, was locked away, shut off in his own world. All Lockyer had were a few letters and pictures. Nothing, really. It was as if Bobby's life had been airbrushed so only the present existed, all the lines of his past erased. He stared at his mug and forced the thoughts away. He needed to believe that Bobby had been happy with their parents, and that his life had been full at Aunt Nancy's. It was the only reality he could handle right now.

Throughout his run, as he passed row upon row of Victorian terraces peppered with snow, he had been turning the case over in his mind, thinking about Debbie, about Hodgson. But as one avenue of enquiry opened, another closed behind him, trapping him inside. The more he tried to make Hodgson fit the profile, the less the guy did. According to Phil, the abortions might mean the girls' killer was fuelled by revenge, a life for a life, but even Phil had admitted he was reaching. This wasn't some anti-abortion campaigner on the rampage. Hodgson wasn't against abortion. He had wanted Debbie to have an abortion, even paid for it.

The surveillance team he'd put on Grainger were monitoring a potential suspect for her stalker, but the description didn't fit Hodgson. The more Lockyer looked at it, the more holes he saw. Grainger had said she did work for corporate companies in the City, advertising agencies included. Hodgson could easily have employed her services and decided she was worth closer attention. Lockyer could link Hodgson to

Debbie, definitely, to Grainger, potentially, but Phoebe and Katy were still a no go.

He stared at the peeling wallpaper. This had been Megan's bedroom when he and Clara had first separated. He'd spent hours choosing just the right pattern, so it was girly but not wall-to-wall pink and princesses. For the first couple of years he had Megan to stay every other weekend. Of course, it hadn't worked out quite like it should have done. He leaned forward and pushed out a bubble that formed and re-formed where two sheets of the badly hung wallpaper met. He needed to redecorate. He couldn't remember the last time his daughter had stayed over.

He looked at the files on his desk. Jane had organized them, as she always did. Red for the post-mortem, green for the crime-scene documents, blue for the interviews and yellow for the profile. He opened the green folder and scanned the exhibits form. Debbie had been wearing a sterling-silver snake bracelet. Lockyer couldn't picture it so he flicked to the back of the report to the photographs of each item listed on the form. It was a tightly woven rope of silver with a hook clasp. It didn't look cheap either, not something Debbie would buy for herself, but exactly the kind of present Hodgson would buy. Lockyer remembered the empty jewellery case found in Debbie's handbag. The bracelet was probably a softener before the sex and before Hodgson unceremoniously dumped her. He shook his head.

He looked back at the file. A single silver stud earring with a turquoise stone was found next to Debbie's body. It hadn't been ripped out of her ear, so it had either fallen out in the struggle or the attacker had removed it. He turned to the back of the folder again and looked at the on-scene photo. The butterfly back rested right next to the earring. This looked more like the type of jewellery Debbie would own. The exhibits sheet showed only one earring had been recovered, so either the killer had removed one from the scene as a souvenir or, more likely, it was still caught up in the array of debris recovered from the scene. The forensic team would be sifting through everything for days to come. He had asked Phil what the removal of the earring or earrings might mean, considering the piece of material cut out of Phoebe Atherton's trousers and the torn section of Katy Pearson's coat. Phil had been his usual cryptic self. 'It could be significant . . . but I wouldn't want to speculate at this stage.' Significant. That appeared to be Phil's word of the month. Every question he asked Phil, the answer began with 'It could be significant . . .'

Outside the window, rain was coming down in torrents, hitting the overflowing gutter with a repetitive thudding sound. He had timed his run just right. As he took a sip of his now cold coffee, he realized the smell he was trying to ignore was his own body, as his sweat dried into his running clothes. He stood up and arched his back. He would just work for another hour and then he could shower. He picked up the folder and shuffled out handfuls of crime-scene pictures and threw them onto the mahogany coffee table behind him.

He knelt on the pale pink carpet and began sorting through the images. Each had a sticker on the top left-hand corner. In black ink an exhibits clerk had written a number and a letter. These represented the sequence in which the pictures were taken and the proximity to the body; A being the closest, J being the furthest away from the final resting place of the victim. He arranged the As on the table in order. Even with the flash, the images were still dark. All he could really see was mud, chewing gum, the black of Debbie's blood and an assortment of bottles, cans and cigarette butts. He swept the pictures off the table onto the carpet and picked up the pile of B photographs. As before, he laid them out in order and studied them for any anomalies. Anything that he might have missed.

His doorbell rang just as he was arranging the F pictures on the table. He stood up, his knees popping as he hobbled down the hallway. He looked into the lounge, at his new sofa that he still hadn't managed to spend any quality time on. Maybe at the weekend he would get a spare couple of hours. He could chuck on a bit of Santana or the Eagles, lie back, close his eyes and relax. The idea was painful in its unlikelihood. He pulled open the front door as he pushed aside a pile of junk mail.

'Hey, I was in the area . . .' Megan stood on tiptoe, kissed his cheek and bounced straight past him and down the hallway, leaving a trail of water as she went. She was talking all the while. 'Have you spoken to Mum? Have you had lunch?' The red in Megan's hair shone as she passed underneath the hall light, shaking off the rain. He was almost overwhelmed by an urge to hold her.

She was already filling the kettle when he walked into the kitchen. He watched, smiling. She was so like her mother, who could also talk for England and rarely noticed if he was listening. Megan would be nineteen in April but watching her fuss with mugs, tea bags and milk, he saw a little girl trying to make breakfast in bed for her parents, struggling up the stairs with a heavy tray, uncooked eggs and cremated toast.

'How are you, Megs?' he said, sitting down at the kitchen table. He might be the boss at work but when it came to his daughter he was merely a prop. He had perfected silent acquiescence.

'Good, good . . . fine. Tea?' she asked.

'No, thanks.'

'My marketing and ethics modules are interesting but accounting is beyond me. I'd drop it but it's too late in the semester to start a new module. It'll be fine. I just need to get my head down,' she said, passing him a mug of tea despite his refusal.

He had little or no influence when it came to his daughter's education. A degree in Business Studies would give her a chance to study a broad spectrum of subjects, she said. He would have been happier if she had chosen a more focused path, one that actually led to a career. However, he had apparently given up the right to have his say when he had cheated on her mother, or so she had told him on more than one occasion during her early adolescence. 'Sounds like you've got it under control,' he said.

She sat down opposite him and started taking slurps of tea. 'You look tired, Dad. You need to take better care of yourself.'

'I'm fine, Megs, just busy.'

'You're always busy.' She put down her mug and rested her elbows on the table. 'I read about the murders of those girls in the paper,' she said, shaking her head. 'I don't know how you do it, dealing with that every day. I get upset just reading about it.'

'My team deal with murders every day,' he said, hoping that would be the end of it.

She seemed to sense his reluctance because she just nodded, took a sip of her tea and then said, 'So . . . do you have time for some lunch?'

He could tell by her facial expression that she was preparing for him to say no. 'Sure, I'll cook us something. I've got plenty here.' A slight exaggeration as he hadn't been to the shops for a week. He certainly didn't have time to drive into Lewisham, find somewhere they both wanted to eat, wait to be served and all the while be thinking about the murders.

'I'll help,' she said, her face lifting.

'No, no. I can manage. Why don't you go and watch some TV and I'll shout you when it's ready?'

'OK, if you're sure?' She got up, planted another kiss on his forehead and walked out of the room. When she had taken on the role of concerned parent he wasn't sure, but it made him uncomfortable. She seemed to have grown up overnight, her teenage temper tantrums replaced with a self-awareness and compassion that felt too advanced for her years. He couldn't help thinking that his job and performance as a father had facilitated her rapid ascent into adulthood.

After a search he managed to find pasta, a decent pesto sauce and some bacon. It was curling at the edges but it smelled OK. Once he had the water boiling he dumped in a couple of handfuls of penne. If he made extra that would do for dinner or lunch tomorrow. The smell of the frying bacon reminded his stomach that he hadn't eaten a proper meal in days. He burnt his finger and his tongue as he tried to scoop up a piece of the crisping bacon. As he sucked the end of his finger he looked out at his back garden. The decking he had laid last summer would be slick with all this rain. It wasn't quite the haven of outside space he had envisioned.

It was already midday by his oven clock. He must have been looking at the crime-scene photos for a couple of hours, at least. He took two bowls from the cupboard and set two places at the table. The pasta would be done in a couple of minutes. It was hardly a feast but he was quite impressed that he had managed to produce anything.

'Five minutes, Megs,' he shouted through to the lounge. She didn't respond.

He still hadn't bought a drainer, so he used the pan lid to drain off the boiling water. He spooned in the pesto and tipped in the bacon, stirring it with a teaspoon. It looked pretty good. 'Right, Megs. Grub's up.' He filled both bowls to the brim and waited. 'Megs . . . did you hear me?' He threw the tea towel over his shoulder and set the bowls on the table before walking through to the lounge. The television was on but Megan wasn't there.

'Megan?' he called, walking out into the hallway. The door to the bathroom was open. He glanced in but she wasn't there. With that, he knew where she was. He pushed open the door to his office. She was on her knees, her hands hovering over the crime-scene photos. She didn't look upset, just puzzled.

'Megan, you know how I feel about you coming in here.

This is not for you to see.' As he approached he saw what she was looking at. It was a close-up of Deborah Stevens' face.

'Dad?' she said, looking up at him.

'You shouldn't be in here, Megan.' She didn't move.

'Is this why?' she asked, pointing at the face in the picture.

'Why what? Come on . . . out of here, now.' He was getting angry. It was bad enough that his life was suffocated by images of pain but for his daughter to witness the harsh reality of his job was too much. 'Megan, I mean it. Out. Now.'

She pushed herself up on the table and stood, facing him, challenging him. 'Is this why you called me?'

He took her arm and pulled her out of the room, shutting the door behind him. She walked into the kitchen and sat down but she didn't even look at the bowl in front of her. Her eyes were on him. 'I don't know what you mean. Now, can we have some lunch?' He sat down opposite her.

'Why didn't you just say? I thought you sounded upset on the phone last week.'

He looked up and saw pity and sympathy in his daughter's eyes. 'Megan. I don't know what you're talking about. I've told you more than once that you're not allowed in my office. Those pictures are from a crime scene, they're not for entertainment.' He shovelled a forkful of the pasta into his mouth. The bacon tasted sour.

'Dad, she looked just like me. You must have noticed. You did notice . . . are you OK?'

'The bacon is off.' He slammed down his fork and stood up. He snatched his bowl and Megan's and threw them both into the sink. There was a loud crack as one of the bowls broke, a jagged line running right down the centre.

'Hey, hey . . . it doesn't matter. Let's go out. I'll buy you lunch? I wanted to talk to you about . . . something,' she said.

He couldn't look at her. He took a deep breath and put both his hands on the edge of the sink. 'I can't. I have to go into the office.'

'Right,' she said. He heard the scrape of her chair as she stood to leave.

They walked to the door without speaking. She turned on the doorstep, went up on her toes and kissed his cheek, but she didn't look at him.

'I'll call you,' he said, knowing he wouldn't. She just nodded and walked away.

He pushed away from the door and went back down the hallway and into his office. He stared at the peeling pink-and-white wallpaper, and then looked down at the photo of Debbie's face. He thought about her parents. They had lost their daughter. They would never again sit down for a meal, or feel her warmth when they hugged her. They had lost all that and he still struggled even to come close to having a meaningful conversation with his daughter who was alive and well. Why did he find it so hard to talk? At work, when he was on a case his voice was constant, his thoughts and ideas flowing freely, but here, in his personal domain, he was inhibited, dismissive; angry, even.

He knelt down and looked at the photos spread out on the table. Megan had pulled one of the pictures forward. It showed the drag marks down the alleyway. Like father, like daughter. The thought that had been swimming around in his head, out of reach, rushed into focus. He stood up, grabbed his phone off the desk and dialled Jane's number.

'Hello,' she said.

'Jane, it's me. I want to run something by you.'

'OK. I'm heading into the office in an hour. Do you want to do it then?'

'Fine, we can go over it then, but let me ask you something . . . the fingerprint on the victim's thigh.'

'Yes,' Jane said.

'Why would the killer go to the trouble of wearing gloves, a condom, cleaning his victims after the attack and then leave one single fingerprint?'

'Nothing has come back on the database. Maybe he just wanted to touch her, skin to skin,' Jane said.

'That's what I thought too, but Phil said that behaviour doesn't fit the profile.'

'So, what do you think now, sir?' she asked.

'We know she was moved mid-attack, but why?' He couldn't get the words out fast enough. 'I think someone else was there. I think our guy got spooked and moved Debbie further into the alley but didn't know he was still being watched.' He pictured the new scenario in his mind. 'I think someone watched the attack and only approached the body once the killer had left the scene.' Every nerve ending in his body told him he was right.

'But, sir, if someone was there why wouldn't they call the police? If they found the body after she was killed, why wouldn't they report it? Anonymously, if necessary?'

'I don't know. But I'm going to find out. We've got to look at the CCTV again. If someone else was there, Jane, then they saw Hodgson. They can identify him.' He let the words hang in the air.

'Sir . . . Hodgson's in the clear,' Jane said.

All he could hear was the blood rushing in his ears. 'Say that again.'

'Hodgson provided DNA yesterday, through his solicitor . . . he's clear, sir.'

Lockyer couldn't take Jane's words in. 'That can't be right. Grainger's stalker, the profile, his involvement with Debbie, it all fits.' Even as the words came out of his mouth the holes in his Hodgson theory, the holes he'd been trying to ignore for days, crowded in on him. 'It doesn't matter,' he heard himself say, his voice portraying a confidence he didn't feel. 'Hodgson was a long shot.' He hadn't thought that for a minute. Hodgson was his prime suspect. He looked at the pictures scattered all around his office as he felt another door slamming shut in his face. 'We've still got Grainger's stalker. Surveillance are in place. We're making progress on the termin- ations link and we have a potential witness, with whoever left the partial fingerprint. It might not be Hodgson but we're getting close, Jane. I can feel it.' He finished his rush of words, almost hollowed out by his own hypocrisy. He had been hell bent on it being Hodgson. The entire indoor team had been searching for a link for the past three days. Wasted time.

'Yes, sir,' she said, without enthusiasm. She was as disap- pointed as he was.

'I'll be in the office in thirty minutes,' he said, feeling his composure returning. 'I want the team in the briefing room. We need the list of who had access to the girls' hospital records. Call Phil, I want him there. If someone watched, then they know who our killer is, or at least can describe him.' He hung up the phone without waiting for a response.

As he gathered all the photographs together his mind shifted back to the fingerprint, to the person who had touched Debbie's thigh. What kind of person would have the stomach to witness a murder and not act? Whatever their character or motivation, that person was potentially as dangerous as the killer himself.

21

1 February – Saturday

'Come on, get your coat on and let's go,' Toni said, her words clipped.

Sarah raised her half-empty glass and peered at the contents. The interior of the gastropub was gloomy, night-lights providing the only low-level lighting. Her ice had melted, diluting her Jack Daniel's. She wanted another one. 'I'm . . . we're having a good time, aren't we? One more drink?' She clasped her hands together in mock prayer. 'Antonia . . . let me enjoy a night of freedom and . . .' Sarah turned and gestured to three shadowed men who were leaning casually on the granite bar. 'If we're lucky we might not even have to pay for our beverages.' She pretended not to notice Toni's disapproving look as she downed the watery contents of her glass.

According to Toni's earlier lecture, when they had arrived at the pub three hours ago, getting drunk wasn't constructive 'under the circumstances'. But it wasn't as if things could get any worse. For the past month she had felt like a prisoner in her own home. She deserved some respite from the stress and if Jack Daniel's was able to assist, why shouldn't she indulge? She looked over at the men again, straining her eyes to make out their faces under the dim lighting. 'Come on, let's go and talk to them,' she said, trying to stand.

Toni pulled her back down. 'Sarah, just sit down. I will get us a drink . . . one drink, then home.' Sarah opened her mouth to argue but couldn't speak. She didn't have the energy. 'You need to rest,' Toni said as she bent forward and kissed Sarah on the forehead. She watched Toni walk to the bar, ignore the blatant stares of the three men and get the barman's attention in one smooth motion.

As she looked again at the three gawking men they seemed to jump into focus. They didn't look old enough to be here. If she squinted she could just see the fluff on the tall one's pubescent chin. He winked at her.

'No,' she whispered to herself, distressed to hear the slur in her voice.

A group of young girls walked past her, shimmering in their sparkly dresses with matching handbags and accessories. The three men, no, boys, didn't waste a second. They looked at the group of girls, nodded to each other and followed.

'Here you go,' Toni said, pulling her chair closer to Sarah as she sat down.

She reached for the glass with a shaking hand and took a long drink, grateful for the sweetness of the Coke. 'I'm just so tired,' she said, aware of the flood of emotions crashing inside her, breaking her apart.

Toni took her hand and squeezed it. 'I know you are, sweetheart. This is my fault . . . I shouldn't have let you drink so much.'

'I wanted to,' Sarah said, taking a defiant gulp of her drink.

'I know, but has it helped?' Toni asked, raising her hands.

Sarah swallowed hard, her throat aching. 'No, it hasn't,' she said, pushing her glass away. 'Let's go.'

As they struggled into their coats, hats and gloves, the boy and his friends reappeared. They must have failed with the group of sparkly girls so now it was her and Toni's turn to suffer their advances.

'You're not going, are you?' the tall spokesman said.

She looked at his lanky frame, jeans barely covering his arse, the obligatory three inches of designer boxer shorts on show, and shivered.

'Yes, we're going. Have a nice evening, gentlemen,' Toni said, using her arms to encircle and guide Sarah away from the group.

'Awww, come on, one drink . . . we're paying?' He held his hands up to his heart, as if the pain of them leaving would shatter the poor boy.

Sarah could feel her stomach starting to twist back and forth. Her skin felt hot and her hands were shaking again. 'Who the hell do you think you are?' she said, taking a step towards the group. 'Does it look like we want to drink with you?' The vehemence in her tone startled her.

'Chill out, grandma, we ain't that bothered, trust me,' the spokesman said, turning to leave, his silent friends following.

Words bubbled up in her throat. She couldn't stop. 'You think, just because we're in a bar, drinking, that we deserve this? Have you ever stopped and asked yourself how it makes us feel, to be slobbered over?' She could feel Toni trying to pull her away. The three boys were staring back at her, their mouths open like goldfish. It was then that Sarah started to panic. She gulped for breath, stars dancing in front of her eyes, her legs unable to hold her as she swayed back and forth. She could feel everyone in the bar staring at her.

'You don't understand,' she said, hot tears blurring her vision, her legs giving way. As she slumped, Toni caught her and put a supportive arm around her waist.

'Let's go home. Come on . . . it's OK.' Toni's soothing voice floated around her mind as she allowed herself to be led out of the bar, snow crunching under her feet as she was bundled into a taxi and strapped in like a child. She closed her eyes, relishing the confinement. She wanted to be home. The trouble was it didn't feel like her home any more. It was just another thing he had taken from her.

As the car pulled away she remembered the day she had picked up the keys from the estate agent. She had been so excited. Those first few months, getting to know her neighbours, making the guy in the corner shop smile, everything had been perfect. She had spent hours in B&Q selecting just the right paint and fabric for every room in the house. Atlantic cream and Arabic Stone for the kitchen, New England white for her bedroom, Country Garden green for her lounge and a striking stripe of Bubblegum pink down the stairs in the hallway. It was hers.

'We're here, honey.'

Sarah forced herself to open her eyes and look at her street. There was nothing left of the happiness she had felt. All she saw were dark trees, shadowed cars covered in snow and eye-like windows staring out at her from all the houses.

As she climbed out of the taxi, listening to Toni make

small talk with the driver, she noticed a car on the opposite side of the street, parked next to the corner shop. Two people sat motionless inside. She leaned against her gate post for support as her legs threatened to give way again. She jumped as Toni took her hand and pulled her into the flat.

'Come on. Let's get you into bed,' Toni said, turning to shut the door.

As the front door was closing, Sarah's eyes settled on another car, six or seven cars in front of the other one. She could see a single shadowed figure, just visible through the darkness.

22

2 February – Sunday

He sat alone in the darkness and waited. It was the first time he had pulled an all-nighter but he had no choice. She hardly ever went out and when she did she was rarely alone, but he couldn't wait a moment longer. Today had to be the day.

She had been increasingly withdrawn in the last few weeks, spending hours sitting on her lounge windowsill, staring out into space. It felt, at times, as if she was looking directly at him. Perhaps she knew and desired to be taught the lesson as much as he longed to teach it. But it wouldn't be enough. He knew that now. It wouldn't be enough to sustain him. He knew she wanted him to do more, to widen their cause. Every good teacher had men to follow him.

He turned in time to see her walking towards him. Had she seen him? She was concentrating on walking in the deep snow and it was still dark. Dawn wasn't far away, though. He would need to hurry. He climbed out of the car, closing the door silently and brushing the snow off his jacket. The road was slippery. He steadied himself and followed, a safe distance behind. The road was quiet; only a few cars and buses struggled up the hill in the snow. As he passed one of the university buildings he shrank into the shadows. The windows, square and black, looked down at him.

She, on the other hand seemed oblivious. He was sure he could walk right behind her and she wouldn't notice. In a way he hated this lack of awareness. However, if they expected it, he would lose the joy of seeing the fear in their eyes. They would look genuinely shocked, at a loss to understand why he would do this to them, of all people. They had done nothing wrong; they would plead again and again. Watching that innocence turn to understanding was a vital part of the lesson. She had taught him that.

He increased his pace. The girl was finally alone.

23

2 February – Sunday

Hayley pulled on her boots and tucked her jeans in with a neat fold. It had snowed most of yesterday and, looking out of her bedroom window, it looked as if it had continued long into the night. The snow had covered the litter, the crappy cars and dirty concrete that normally decorated Aubyn Square. This morning it was an untouched winter wonderland.

She tiptoed past Louisa's bedroom door and down the stairs, into the hallway. As she pulled on her coat, it dragged the sleeves of her jumper up her arms: the waxy material of the jacket was cold against her skin. She wrapped her pale green scarf around her neck and pushed the ends inside her zipper. She felt a bubble of excitement in her stomach. Richmond Park was going to look amazing. She took her keys from the hook by the front door and let herself out as quietly as she could. Waking Louisa at 7.15 on a Sunday morning would not be a good idea.

The walkway at the back of the flat was slippery. She lifted her feet and planted them square to the ground. If she hurried and didn't fall too many times on the way, hers might be the first footprints to break the blanket of snow in the park. The thought spurred her on as she negotiated the concrete steps leading down into the estate.

The snow was so deep that she was having trouble figuring out where the pavement ended and where the road began. She tripped and stumbled her way past The Maltese Cat pub and out onto Roehampton Lane. As she watched the early morning traffic struggle up the hill, turning the snow into slush, she thought about how out of place she felt in London. How many students got up when it was still dark, because they couldn't wait to go for a walk in the snow? Certainly none that Hayley had met in her six months at Roehampton Institute. She crossed and stopped at the bollards in the centre of the road. The number 72 bus seemed to be having trouble stopping. The driver looked like he was using the kerb for traction. As the bus finally came to a sliding halt, the woman standing in the shelter seemed to reconsider her travel plans and walked away. Hayley could hear the bus driver shouting his vehement disapproval.

At home in Devon she had thought of herself as a confident and self-assured nineteen-year-old. There she had been safe, protected. Everyone here was so different. She crossed over to the pavement on the other side. There were four people walking up the hill in her direction but none had come out of the park. She sped up, thinking that if she did fall, what did it really matter? No one she knew was here to see.

When she reached the gates she walked in, as though entering the vaulted splendour of a cathedral. She didn't know where to look first. The park lay out in front of her like an enormous cloud. To her right the avenue of oak trees provided the only colour. Their canopy was so thick that the woodchip path beneath had been left untouched by the snow. It looked like the entrance to another world. The undulating parkland stretched out into nothing. The air was still so dark and thick with snow that it was impossible to decipher where the ground ended and the sky began. It would take four hours to walk around the entire park. Not that she wanted to do that today, but even if she did, it would be impossible. She would be lost within minutes. Movement to her left made her turn. A man with three terriers walked towards her.

'Morning,' he said.

'Good morning,' she said, not feeling any of the cheer that she had managed to put into her voice.

'Beautiful morning, isn't it?' With a sweeping arm gesture he indicated the scene before them.

'Yes, it is.' That was all she could say. She turned away from him, without smiling, and walked towards the trees. He had clearly walked the left-hand route, ruining it with his clumsy feet and pesky dogs, so she was going to opt for the fairyland entrance. Once she was further in she could go off the path and find snow that no one, not even dog walkers, would have spoiled.

As she looked down and watched the snow disappear beneath her feet she let the muffled sounds of the morning wash over her. Everything looked clean as she entered the cover of the trees. She thought about home, about her mother, and then she thought about him and that night. She had been partying in the Wandsworth Palais, a total dive of a club. She'd never been back. In her quest to discover the perfect drink she had mixed wine, spirits and cocktails, all night. *He* had looked at her from the other end of the bar and smiled. She hadn't known what to do. She had felt sick, so a half smile, half sneer was all she could manage. But, as if by magic, he had picked up his drink and begun making his way through the crowd towards her.

Hayley kicked the woodchip at her feet. Small brown flecks clung to her boots. The sky through the trees was getting lighter. She wouldn't be alone for long. She veered off to the left and clambered over a fallen tree, sending icy flakes down the top of her boots. She found an almost level route and with her head down, she kept on walking.

The remainder of that evening had been a total blur. When she had finally made it back to halls in the early hours of the morning she had been ambushed by Louisa for the 'goss' but could only dredge up small flashes; him walking over, him talking, a cab, a house, more drinking, loud music, a bedroom, an incense candle and finally a lot of pushing and shoving. She hadn't even known his name. She wished that was the worst part. Tears filled her eyes. She swallowed hard. What was the point in crying? It was done. She could never take it back.

She dug her headphones out of her coat pocket, pulled off one glove and scrolled through her iPod to Chicane's new album. With her already freezing finger, she set the volume as loud as it would go and shoved the earphones as far into her ears as she could. Music was her version of white noise. She replaced her glove, tucking it into her sleeve.

As she entered a small alcove of trees she saw movement out of the corner of her eye and turned. A heavy clump of snow fell from a branch; a shower of fine powder hung in the air. Sometimes there were deer in this part of the park but she couldn't see any this morning. They were probably all huddled together somewhere, keeping warm. The snow was deep here, up to her ankles. She lifted her feet higher. Her muscles ached with the effort of each step but she smiled. This was exactly what she had needed; fresh air, the cocoon of her music and the clean white landscape all around her. She might even go the whole hog and lie down and make a snow angel. Another movement to her right made her turn. All she could see was white and the bark of the tree trunks.

She reached into her pocket for her fags as the next song came on. The pulsing beat was so loud it made her wince. She held a cigarette with her teeth, digging around in her pocket for her lighter. As her fingers closed around it she felt something heavy hit the back of her head. She fell to her knees and turned in time to see a man towering over her.

He pushed her face down and was on top of her before she could react; her right hand was stuck in her pocket, pinned underneath her. Her left arm was stretched out in front of her. He was heavy. She tried to move but he was astride her, holding her legs down with his own. His powerful hands pushed down on her shoulders, so all she could do was lift her head away from the snow, freezing against her face. She could see his mouth moving but couldn't hear what he was saying. Her music blared in her ears, now accompanied by the pounding of the blood that was rushing to her head. When she tried to speak, she choked on the snow. She looked up at the side of his face. He was smiling.

She let out a strangled sob as she watched his lips move, transfixed. It was like watching someone talk under water.

She could feel the vibrations of his speech: a low hum against her spine. His hand reached around to her face. Oh God, she thought, please don't touch me. He pulled at her scarf, yanking her earphones out. He exposed her neck to the cold, to his hands. Hayley closed her eyes. He's going to strangle me in the park, in broad daylight on a Sunday morning, she thought. And there's nothing I can do about it. She tried to scream but he bent forward at the same time and pushed the air out of her lungs with his body.

'Shhhh . . . Hayley.' He stroked her lips with the tip of his gloved index finger. Her whole body shivered with revulsion.

A scratch, followed by a burning pressure against her neck made every muscle in her body tense. She then felt her whole body relax and her eyelids became heavy. She could see her earphones lying in the snow next to her face.

'Shhhh,' he said again.

She didn't want to hear any more.

24

Lockyer paced back and forth in front of the corner shop, his boots turning the snow into slush. They were here to arrest Malvern Turner.

Russ, the head of surveillance, had phoned Lockyer late Wednesday night to say they had identified a potential suspect in the Grainger case. DVLA records on the vehicle being used confirmed the registered owner as Rosemary Turner. However, as she lived in a residential home in Wandsworth and the car hadn't been reported stolen, it was a safe bet that it was her son, thirty-seven-year-old Malvern Turner, who had been seen on numerous occasions at Grainger's address.

Lockyer's decision not to alert Sarah to the surveillance had weighed heavily, but there was no other way. He hadn't wanted to risk her inadvertently alerting the stalker to the police presence. She wouldn't have been able to stop herself looking for Russ and his team. If she spotted them, it followed that her stalker might too. Whether it was the right decision was moot now.

Questions circled in his head like vultures. Was Sarah's

stalker just another dead end, like Hodgson? He could have wasted precious time and resources for nothing. On the other hand, what if this guy was Debbie and the other girls' killer? The surveillance team was only authorized to observe Sarah's home address. Every time she was out on her own she was at risk.

He smacked his hands together to force blood into his freezing fingers. This wasn't where he wanted to be right now. He wanted to be where the action was. Instead he was listening to the surveillance team as they fed back information via a piece-of-shit handheld radio. As he looked over at Jane, who had chosen to stay in the car, he saw that she was looking at him with her head cocked on one side. She was probably wondering what would possess anyone to stand in several inches of snow, in the dark, for an hour, when they could be sitting in the warm, with her. But Lockyer couldn't stay still. Adrenalin had his body humming with energy.

He looked at the almost frozen fruit and veg on display outside the corner shop before walking in, stamping the snow off his boots and nodding a greeting to the woman behind the till. She smiled but immediately turned away to resume a muttered telephone conversation while staring up at a television set that showed a black-and-white Bollywood-looking film, the volume turned down to nothing. It was clear that the police presence outside the shop for the past hour hadn't fazed her in the slightest.

The aisles were so narrow, piled high with toilet rolls, Brillo pads and Kleenex Aloe Vera tissues, that Lockyer decided going any further in would be a mistake. Instead he stared into the refrigerated unit. Behind the thick strips of plastic that kept in the cold, he could see milk, yoghurt, cheese and row upon row of unrecognizable pieces of meat. He tuned out the chattering woman as he picked up an energy drink. He was thinking about the footage he had seen yesterday. One section showed Turner getting out of his Nissan, approaching Sarah's front door and touching her doorbell, although it looked more like he was caressing it. Even the thought made Lockyer's skin itch. Some of the surveillance showed Turner talking to himself, covering his mouth with his fingers when he laughed, like a schoolgirl at a dance. He put the drink on the counter. 'Do you have any energy bars?' he asked. The woman continued her telephone conversation and pointed to a shelf in front of the till. He picked up one bar after another, reading the labels and ingredients to pass the time. The waiting was killing him.

The radio at his hip crackled. He waited but it fell silent. Nothing yet. He paid for his drink and two energy bars before walking back into the freezing February evening. As he approached the car he tried to picture Turner as a highly motivated killer. Phil's psychological profile detailed someone of above-average intelligence, an accomplished problem solver. If Turner had possessed either of those qualities, surely he would have spotted Russ and Amir in the maroon Volvo and the other officer sitting alone in a white van for the past four days? But he hadn't. It seemed that Malvern Turner was so preoccupied with watching Sarah's flat that he was oblivious to everything and everyone around him. That wasn't the behaviour of a calculating killer.

He pulled back the sleeve on his coat to look at his watch and let out a frustrated breath. An hour and a half he'd been stood here and nothing had happened. 'Sod this,' he said, opening the door to the squad car, climbing in and turning up the heater to full blast. It was only when the warm air hit his face that he realized just how cold he was.

'Feel better, sir?' Jane asked.

'I can't just sit here all evening waiting. It's driving me nuts.' He pulled off his gloves and handed Jane one of the energy bars before cupping his hands over the air vent. His fingers tingled as they came back to life. 'Do we have any idea when she's meant to be home?'

'No, sir. All Amir said was that Grainger left the flat with the Italian woman this afternoon.'

'Great . . . do you think Turner has anything to do with these murders, Jane?' he asked.

Jane paused but only for a second. 'Well, he fits some of the profile. He's a predator in the killing zone.'

'Yes, I know that, but what do you think?' He waited.

Jane finally turned to face him. 'I don't think he's our killer, sir, no.' She shrugged. 'As for him being your "watcher", I just don't know.'

'Neither do I,' he said, turning his face into the heater. What had he expected from Jane – reassurance, or a confirmation she couldn't possibly give? The radio crackled. Lockyer sat up, his mind suddenly clear, his body ready.

'Target in sight, red Mazda, registration X-ray, one, three, three, mike, bravo, delta,' Russ said, his voice quiet.

'And the suspect?' Lockyer asked.

'Yes, suspect in sight, blue Nissan Micra, registration Mike, four, five, four, papa, uniform, delta. He's parking up . . . five cars up from target . . . engine stopped. Target out of her vehicle with one female, five foot five, long black hair. They're entering the flat, 10A Surrey Road. Target is carrying a handbag, green. Target and other now inside, door closed.'

Lockyer's muscles jumped beneath his skin as he listened. Something inside him was firing up.

'Target closing front blinds. Porch, hall and lounge lights all on. Suspect has a camera, seems to be using the zoom to look at the target. No flash, no pictures taken that I can see. What do you want us to do, sir? How long do we wait?' Russ asked.

'You and Amir stay put. We'll be there in three.' Lockyer pulled his gloves back on and opened the car door. 'Jane, we're on.'

He jogged down the street, favouring the centre of the road where the majority of the snow had melted. He could hear Jane close behind him. As he approached the end of Surrey Road he slowed and stopped. He peered around the corner at the quiet street. He could see the surveillance van parked on the opposite side. He held the radio up to his mouth.

'I'm at the corner, Russ. Am I going to be able to get across to the van without Turner seeing me?' he asked in a hushed voice.

'Yes, sir. You could dance up and down the street naked and this guy wouldn't notice.'

'Good,' he said, pulling up his collar and reaching back to take Jane's hand.

As they crossed the street, beginning their charade of a husband and wife out for an evening stroll, he resisted the urge to look down Sarah's street. He found himself wondering whether Grainger had ever been married, but the thought

162

vanished as they took position behind the white van. 'Right,' he said into the radio. 'I want to take him quietly. Amir will run interference on the passenger side, allowing Russ to approach and make the arrest before the suspect has time to react or run. Jane and I will provide back-up.' With a bit of luck this would be quick and simple. In and out and back to the station before the first curtain twitched. 'On my word, move in on the suspect.' He put his arm around Jane's shoulder and held her close as they began walking up the street, talking and laughing about what a great night they'd had and how good the food was at The Green now it was under new management. Lockyer kissed her forehead, using the opportunity to take a sly look at the blue Nissan.

Once they were a good distance past Turner's car, Lockyer stopped, checked the road behind them and then crossed, both of them immediately crouching behind a long line of cars. 'We're in position, Russ,' he whispered into his radio.

Russ and Amir climbed out of the Volvo and began walking up the street. Turner was motionless, his face turned up to Sarah's lounge windows. The guy was totally oblivious. Still, Lockyer held his breath as Amir knocked on the passenger-side window of the Nissan.

'Just need some directions, mate,' Amir said, in a loud voice.

Turner barely reacted. He just turned to look at Amir, leaned over and rolled down the passenger window. 'What do you want?'

Lockyer was struck by how normal he sounded.

'I need to get to Lordship Lane, top end, near the curry house,' Amir said, leaning into the Nissan.

Turner nodded his head. He seemed unfazed, unthreatened by the intrusion to his vigil. 'All you need to do is walk to the end of this street,' Turner said, pointing to the far end of Surrey Road, 'make a right and walk all the way down to the end till you come to the traffic lights and the edge of the Rye.'

'Yeah, down 'ere, right, to the end, lights, the Rye, got it,' Amir said, looking in the direction he would be going.

'That's right. Then you need to take a left . . .'

Russ was approaching Turner on the driver's side but as he reached for the door the radio attached to his belt came to life, crackling and giving off high-pitched feedback. Turner's head whipped round and everything seemed to happen in slow motion as he kicked open the car door, flooring Russ with the impact. Amir still had his head stuck inside the car, so was helpless when Turner cracked him on the head with what looked like a steering-wheel lock. Lockyer looked on in stunned silence as Amir's legs crumpled beneath him.

The slow motion suddenly jumped to real-time as Turner got out of the car and set off running. After a moment's hesitation Lockyer was chasing after him, shouting, 'Stop, police!' as Turner disappeared around the corner of Sarah's street, sliding in the snow and slush.

When Lockyer reached the corner he saw Turner take a right past Nunhead Cemetery. He pushed his muscles to go faster. Despite the shock of an impromptu run, he could feel his breath steadying as he got into a rhythm. His radio banged against his right leg, his boots alternately collecting and dumping slushy piles of snow with each step. As he made the right past the cemetery he could see that he was gaining. Turner was no more than a hundred yards ahead now. Lockyer used his arms to give him extra momentum and sprinted down the centre of the street.

'Stop, police!' he yelled again. As he pounded the wet tarmac he could see curtains twitching. So much for a quiet take-down.

As Turner reached the end of the road he slipped and fell but was up and running again in seconds, heading straight down the alleyway that led from one side of the cemetery to the other.

'Gotcha,' Lockyer said on an exhale of breath. The path ran for a good half mile. There was no way off it. A high wall on the left and an even higher fence on the right. He swerved onto the path and raced up the steady incline. Unless Turner was super-fit, sprinting uphill was going to slow him down considerably.

As Lockyer rounded a corner he saw him, now only fifty yards out in front. Turner stopped and began trying to scrabble up the fence on his right. When that didn't work he tried the wall to his left.

'It's over – stop!' he shouted but his words only seemed to spur Turner on as he managed to get a hold on the wall and heave himself a couple of feet off the path.

Lockyer jumped, slammed into Turner's side and both of them came crashing down onto the footpath. There was a loud crack when they landed but that didn't stop him positioning his knee firmly in Turner's back, broken arm or not.

'My arm, my arm,' Turner screamed, struggling beneath Lockyer's weight.

'The more you move, the more it'll hurt,' Lockyer said, turning to look behind him at the sound of footsteps. It was Jane and a limping Russ.

'Sorry, sir,' Russ said, holding his stomach, clearly out of breath. 'Bloody radio tuned into another frequency.'

Turner's protests had become dull whines as the shock of the break and the exhaustion of the chase caught up with him.

'Where's Amir?' Lockyer asked, easing the pressure on the prostrate man's right arm. He wasn't going anywhere, so there was no need to crush him, although the idea appealed.

'Left him in the car, sir. He took a blow to the head,' Russ said, glaring down at Turner lying on the ground.

'Harassment, resisting arrest and assaulting two police officers. Who knows what else you've been up to, Mr Turner?' Lockyer said, talking quietly into Turner's ear.

25

Lockyer waited behind a line of rush-hour traffic for the temporary lights to change. It was an act of will, resisting the urge to turn on the sirens in order to power through the gridlock.

He would be interviewing Malvern Turner at 11 a.m., provided he actually managed to make it into the office at all. He cursed as a courier bike hurtled past him, clipping his wing mirror in the process. Pedestrians were slipping around on several inches of snow. King's College A&E was going to have a busy day tending to broken ankles.

It had been easy to keep Turner overnight. Lockyer had a veritable smorgasbord of charges to choose from. So many, in fact, that the original reason for Turner's arrest – the alleged harassment of Sarah Grainger – had barely been discussed when the thirty-seven-year-old was booked in, after his own trip to A&E to set a fractured radius. Lockyer inched the car forward. It was going to take another ten minutes to get to the office at this rate. He leaned on the horn. He could see the station car park ahead of him. His hand hovered over the switch for the siren again.

When the lights finally changed, Lockyer revved his engine and shot through, swinging his car onto the wrong side of the road and into the station car park. His phone began to ring on the passenger seat. He grabbed it and pushed answer.

'Lockyer,' he said.

'Morning, sir. Where are you?' Jane asked.

'I'm pulling in now. I'll be there in five. I want to run through the questions for the interview with Turner. Bring his arrest sheet, will you?' There was a long silence and Lockyer held the phone in front of him to see if the signal had dropped out. It hadn't. 'Jane, you still there?'

'Yes, sir. You're going to have to postpone the interview.'

Lockyer doubted that very much. He had already lost twelve hours because of Turner's hospital visit and overnight stay at the MPS's local holding facility. He didn't want to waste any more time. 'Why?' he asked.

'I just got off the phone with DI Baker. His team were called out when a body was found over in Richmond Park earlier this morning . . . from what he's just told me, it sounds like our guy.'

Lockyer felt as if his whole body was being squeezed like a wet rag. 'But it's only . . . that's not even two weeks since Debbie,' he said, ramming his car into reverse.

'I know, sir. Dave's on his way there, so we can wait for confirmation if you want, but . . .' Jane stopped short. He could hear the adrenalin in her voice. She was ready to move and he needed to get into the same mindset.

'Right. You come with me and tell the rest of the team to meet us there.'

'I'm on my way,' she said, hanging up before he could say anything else.

Twelve days, only twelve days. Phil had said that the time gap between murders for cases like this would get shorter, but this felt crazy. He looked up to see Jane running across the car park. Turner would have to wait.

26

3 February – Monday

Lockyer pulled up behind Dave's battered white BMW and turned off the sirens. It wasn't even 8.30 a.m. but Roehampton Lane was swarming with squad cars, three SOCO vans and a plethora of other on-site officers' cars. There were also two press vans.

No one in the melee in front of him seemed at all bothered by the three inches of snow. Before he had a chance to engage the parking break, Jane was out of the car and talking to three of the on-call team. He followed her, turning up his collar against the chill. The snow had finally stopped but from the look of the sky, it seemed the break might be short lived. He walked towards the main gates of Richmond Park, stopping at the outer cordon to put on shoe covers. Jane was close behind him, scribbling in her notebook. He wanted to hear her initial, un-biased reactions but he was also conscious that she hadn't been with him when Debbie was found. If today's victim was in a similar state, it was a lot to take at this time on a Monday morning. He watched her as she grabbed her own pair of plastic shoe covers from the waiting constable. She leaned on Lockyer's arm to slide them over her sensible shoes. It hadn't escaped his notice that Jane never wore heels any more. She looked calm and focused. He didn't need to babysit her. He never had.

'Jane. I want you to talk me through the scene, start to finish. Anything that comes to mind I want to hear it, OK?' he said, gesturing for her to go ahead of him.

'Yes, sir.'

They both ducked under the perimeter tape, and as they crossed the threshold into Richmond Park Jane said, 'Wow.' She was looking up, down and all around her. 'I feel like I've wandered into Lapland. Hardly any of the snow has melted.'

He looked out at the snow-covered parkland. Dozens of footprints broke the surface of the icy crust where they were standing, exposing brown, sodden grass. It looked like the SOCOs had put down as many walkways as they could, but as he and Jane moved further into the park it was clear that the evidence trail was going to be a nightmare. There were numerous footprints, all going in different directions. No doubt some of the prints belonged to the person who discovered the body, some to the first responders to the scene, and some would be the killer's, but deciphering which would be impossible now.

'Tell me,' he said, walking towards the cover of trees to the right of the entrance.

'Well,' Jane began, opening her notepad, 'I spoke to Baker's DS and she said that the victim is Hayley Marie Sawyer; nineteen, five foot five, petite build, reddish hair. She lived in a flat across the road, Aubyn Square, with two other girls. She was a student at Roehampton University.'

'OK, what else?' he asked, trying to ignore the reaction his stomach was having to the news that it was another redhead.

'Most of the Aubyn Square block is second-year accommodation, if they aren't in halls of residence. One of the flatmates...' Jane flicked through her notepad, 'Louisa Samad, said she heard Hayley leave the flat at about seven on Sunday morning. The other flatmate was staying with her boyfriend in Islington, North London.' Lockyer watched as Jane put the pad to her lips, resting it there. 'It would still have been dark. Sunrise isn't till about 07.45 and the park opens at 07.30. It had snowed heavily overnight, so it would have been even deeper than it is now.' Jane looked at him with one eyebrow arched, her lips pulled down to accompany a shrug of her shoulders.

'An odd time for a walk, then,' he said.

'I would think so,' Jane said, chewing the end of her pen.

'She could have been meeting someone . . . a guy, maybe,' he said.

'I don't think so,' Jane said. 'The flatmate's statement says Hayley was shy, not good with guys at all. Family's from a small village in Devon. Hayley had struggled to cope in London. The flatmate was surprised she even came back this term.'

'And what does that tell us?' he asked.

'Maybe she wanted to be alone, enjoy the quiet. She might have seen the park as a little piece of home.'

'Maybe, but the thing that feels odd to me,' he said, walking towards the tree line, regaining his composure, 'is why she would come here, alone, in the dark, when we've had warnings on the news every night for over a week?' He looked at

Jane for some kind of answer but she just shook her head. He continued, 'Either she doesn't watch the news or read the papers, or she doesn't give much credence to her personal safety, don't you think?' His voice was muted as they entered the cover of the trees.

'The warnings have focused on south-east London, sir. Maybe she didn't think they applied to her. And the attacks have been late at night. Perhaps she thought being out that early in the morning was safe,' Jane said.

He looked up at the arch the trees had created, thirty feet above their heads. The boughs swayed and creaked. He walked down the woodchip path, Jane close at his side, muttering to herself as she scribbled notes into her pad. The path itself was clear of snow due to the canopy of trees. As they both followed the route marked out by the SOCOs, Lockyer took great lungfuls of air, clearing his mind, focusing on Hayley's last walk and, in turn, the killer's movements, not too far behind her.

'What else do we know about her?' he asked, looking ahead to the throng of officers around the body. They were all here to help Hayley but he couldn't help thinking that they resembled a pack of vultures, their backs arched as they picked their prey clean.

Jane flicked back several pages in her notepad. 'She was studying psychology and social studies.' He looked at her but neither of them voiced what they were thinking. All that learning about how people think and how the world works, and she still managed to end up in a ditch. Jane continued reading, 'Father, mother, two older brothers. No known boyfriends either, back at home or here at uni.'

He chewed his thumbnail. 'I'll ask Dave to check for evidence of a termination in the post-mortem, but we'll need her medical records ASAP so we can add her name to the list we've got out with the local clinics and women's centres.' He watched as Jane made neat notes of his instructions. 'We need to find out if south-east and south-west London have a centralized database that could be accessed and, if so, who could access it.' He covered his mouth with his hand. 'I don't feel good about him moving boroughs at all, Jane. It means he's getting more confident . . . spreading his wings.'

As they approached the crime scene, Dave stepped out of a crowd of white-suited SOCOs and walked towards them, peeling off his gloves to shake Lockyer's hand.

'Hello, you two. Impressive, isn't it?' he said, gesturing towards the snow-covered park.

'There's no denying it looks like a Christmas postcard in here, but something tells me you haven't been examining an unfortunate Santa,' Lockyer said.

'I'm sorry to say there's nothing festive about this one,' Dave said, gesturing for him and Jane to follow. 'So, DI Baker didn't mind you taking over his case, then?'

'No. Not at all. In fact he called the chief to have me brought in because he knew my team was running the other three cases,' Lockyer said, raising his eyebrows. 'I don't think anyone wants in on this one, Dave. I'm on my own.' He managed a weak smile as the weight of another victim settled on his shoulders. 'So tell me, is it our guy?' he asked, knowing already what the answer would be.

'Yes . . . puncture wound on her neck, sexual assault, wrists and throat cut,' Dave said with a grimace.

They were close enough now to smell it: the acrid odour of blood. He stepped onto one of the platforms and turned to help Jane up behind him. Her hand felt cold and small. 'You should have gloves on,' he said, squeezing her fingers. She smiled and tucked her hands into her jacket pockets. As she did, several of the suited figures stepped away to reveal the body of Hayley Marie Sawyer lying on a combination of ice, soggy grass, mud and a lot of blood.

Her body was laid out as if crucified, her arms stretched out, her legs neatly placed together. She was naked except, on her feet, she still wore a pair of long boots, woollen socks poking out of the top, and her hair was red: not reddish, red. It could have been the damp or blood making it darker but Lockyer could already see that she must have been a striking girl. Her skin was white, which contrasted with her dark eyebrows and hair. She was tiny, a delicate frame. Her ribs stood out from her chest, covered in bruises, like the keys of a piano. He ran his eyes over the ground surrounding Hayley's body. An iPod with the headphones still attached lay off to one side. He was sure he could still hear the faint tinny music playing. He was surprised the battery had lasted this long, but that in itself might help with the time of death. A scarf, dark jeans and what looked like a Barbour were in a heap by the girl's feet. Lockyer pictured a man kneeling over her, removing her clothes before throwing them absently over his shoulder.

'She didn't die like that,' he said.

Dave shook his head. 'Well spotted. No, she didn't. The livor mortis suggests she was moved after she died.'

Livor mortis was one of the few parts of forensic medicine

that could be wholly relied upon. It never lied and it couldn't be cheated. When a person dies, their blood immediately begins to sink to the lowest point in the body. Within two to five hours the shift is permanent, leaving a purplish, red staining or lividity on the surface of the skin. If Hayley had died on her back, as she was laid now, the colouring would be on her calves, thighs, buttocks, shoulders and neck. But that wasn't what Lockyer was looking at. The staining on Hayley's young skin was concentrated on her left side; her arm was almost entirely purple.

'So, where do you put the time of death and the body repositioning, Dave?' Lockyer asked, his own thoughts racing ahead of him.

Dave spread his lips into a thin line and took a deep breath in through his nose. 'It's almost impossible to say, I'm afraid. The temperature doesn't help and there's been hardly any interference with the body by local wildlife.' Dave reached up and ran his hand under his nose several times. 'I can tell you from the livor mortis that the body was moved, maybe four to six hours after she was killed, but without the TOD it doesn't help you much, does it?'

'No, not really,' Lockyer said, hoping he didn't look as distracted as he felt. 'Are you almost ready to move her?'

'Yes, we'll just finish up photographing the scene and the body, and then I'll take her back to the mortuary suite with me.' The way Dave spoke, it was as if he were taking her home to her parents. The respect and reverence he managed to conjure in a simple sentence never failed to impress Lockyer. As Jane came to stand next to him he remembered her words: 'What kind of person would watch a murder and not intervene?' He hoped the man waiting in the interview room in Lewisham would be able to answer that question for him.

'She looks like she's about to make a snow angel,' Jane said.

27

3 February – Monday

He tried not to smile, aware of the invisible eyes and ears in the room.

The police officer interviewing him looked young enough to have attended poor little Hayley's university. He could only assume this man-boy in uniform had signed up straight out of school, hoping to work his way up the ranks, which would never happen if the intelligence displayed so far was anything to go by. He could hear her voice mingling with his own thoughts.

Inside he was feeling elated but he masked it with a calm, solemn exterior. One slip and his elation could very quickly turn to despair – it was not likely, but too cavalier an attitude was dangerous. He guessed it would only be another thirty minutes before they let him go. He had almost finished his list of answers to the questions he knew they would ask and been more than helpful, subtly pointing the finger at a number of individuals. It was clear from the boy's fidgety demeanour and the sweat stains visible beneath his jacket that he would be happy with something, no, anything that he could report back to his superiors.

As he ran his fingers through his newly trimmed hair, he paused and massaged his temples, feigning a headache brought on by the obvious stress of innocence. He was enjoying his role. The plastic chair squealed as he leaned back. It sounded just like Hayley. She hadn't screamed like the others but squealed, like a piglet being taken from its mother. There was something feral about the noise, nothing resembling a human being in peril. It had been an unexpected pleasure and he would tell his disciples.

The two-way mirror on the wall next to him was covered in smudged fingerprints. He imagined previous occupants with their noses pressed to the glass, trying to see through to the other side like they did in the movies. His reflected image looked pale. Of course, Constable Chris would assume this was from fatigue and anxiety, rather than exhaustion. When it was over he had looked at her, lying on her side in the snow. He had almost felt tempted to lie down next to her so they could rest awhile together.

The door opened, the overpowering smell of musk invading the room before the boy appeared, a friendly smile on his face and two cups of coffee in his hands.

'Here you go. It's not as good as Starbucks across the road but it's got more caffeine than a can of Red Bull.' The officer took a slurp of his own drink. 'Just a few more questions and then you can get back to your day.'

'Thanks. I'm working this afternoon, extra shift, need the money,' he said, giving the constable his best 'we're-all-in-it-together' look.

'Don't we all,' the boy replied.

As he picked up his coffee he winced as the heat of the

bowing plastic burned his fingertips. They looked red, chaffed from the hours spent stitching Hayley's precious addition into place. It looked beautiful, the colour complementing its neighbours. A contented sigh escaped his lips before he could stop himself. He covered his mouth with his hand and coughed.

'Hot,' he said, still coughing.

The boy nodded, his eyes empty of understanding.

This interview was becoming an inconvenience but he had to be patient. All he need do was tolerate Constable Chris's questions for a few more minutes. He disguised his growing smile with the moulded rim of the little plastic coffee cup.

28

3 February – Monday

Sarah lifted herself onto her kitchen counter and stared out at the trees swaying in her back garden. They were smothered in snow, the branches bowing under the weight. It had been almost a week since she had spoken to the Detective Inspector, Lockyer. Bennett had called several times to reassure her that 'investigations into her case were continuing'. Her head ached. She couldn't eat and had barely slept. When Toni had left her early this morning Sarah had sat on the bottom stair, hugging her knees for an hour, waiting for the nausea in her stomach to stop.

As she pushed herself off the counter, her bare feet connecting hard with the cold linoleum, she heard a car engine start. She ran through to the lounge and resumed her vigil by the window. A red Peugeot 306 was pulling away. It belonged to No. 11. She was a nurse. Her shift would be starting soon, no doubt. The white panelled van that had been parked down by the shop for days had gone. Sometimes it looked empty but sometimes she was sure there was a man sitting in the driver's seat. She took her new notepad from the sofa and wrote down the time and the registration. Her eyes drifted up the page to a dozen similar entries.

She knew Surrey Road and its inhabitants better now than she ever had before, in her previous life here. She knew that the bald man from No. 8 drove a red Ford Ka and that he was having an affair with the girl across the street in No. 15. The family living in No. 17 had been visited by the bailiffs. Sarah could have told them they wouldn't find anything, because the mother's friend had visited the previous day and loaded up her car, a silver Vauxhall estate, with two flat-screen televisions, an Xbox and a load of other stuff. Sarah had a list of each item. A twisting pain under her ribs was followed by a loud rumble. She should eat but she had nothing in the house and she couldn't go out. One of the people she was watching was there, watching her right back. One of the people out there was her stalker. And he was angry. The note told her as much. He was angry with her, following her, terrorizing her for reasons she couldn't understand. If only she knew who he was. Perhaps then she could face him. Walk out onto her street and confront him, ask him what he wanted from her.

A maroon Saab pulled up, reverse parking into a space five houses down from hers, on the other side of the road. She recognized it immediately. Without thinking she jotted down the reg, the make and model, and a description of the two figures sitting inside. They had been here before but they wouldn't stay for long. The young guy from No. 23 would join them in a moment. But the Saab people didn't bother her as much as the others. She wasn't being stalked by two or even three people, that was a ridiculous notion. Mass stalking. As soon as the thought entered her head she made a note to do a Google search. It could be a new trend, a new way of torturing victims. Her mobile started to ring, skittering across the floorboards away from her. She leaned forward and grabbed it. It was Bennett's mobile number.

'Hello,' she said, realizing she was whispering. 'Hello,' she said again in a normal voice but crawling out of the lounge so no one from the street could see her.

'Sarah, it's DS Bennett . . . how are you?'

She waited until she was safely in the hallway before she answered. 'I'm fine . . . I'm OK.' Neither statement was true but what did it matter? Bennett wasn't really asking after her health. It was just something you said. A British way of starting a conversation.

'I have some news,' Bennett said. 'Good news.' Sarah couldn't speak. Her throat had closed, her breath stuck in her lungs, waiting to be released. 'A suspect has been arrested in relation to your complaint.'

The only emotion she recognized these days was fear, so any other feeling was hard to process, to deal with. 'What . . . who?'

'The individual is in custody. I'm afraid I can't release his identity to you until he is formally charged, but I wanted to let you know as soon as possible so you could . . . I thought you would want to know.'

She couldn't register what Bennett was saying and her mind was jumbling every word that travelled over the airways between them, but she definitely knew she wanted to know. Her eyes filled with tears. She let them come as she listened to Bennett talk, not really caring what she was saying. It didn't matter now. 'It's over,' she whispered to herself.

29

'Just tell me if it's possible?' Lockyer asked for what felt like the millionth time. He had been on the phone to Phil for ten minutes and so far had bugger all to show for his efforts.

'It's difficult for me to say, Mike. You haven't given me a lot to work with,' Phil said in an indulgent tone as if he was speaking to a five-year-old. Lockyer was tempted to march over to Phil's office and put his foot right up the guy's arse. 'Why don't you try telling me what you're thinking and then I will tell you, in my professional opinion, if it's a possibility?'

He forced himself to sit down. Despite his reservations, other than Jane, Phil was probably the best person to talk to regarding his theory, so he may as well get on with it. 'Fine. We've discussed my theory regarding the fingerprint on Debbie Stevens, the third victim?' he said.

'Yes . . . that the stray fingerprint is from someone who witnessed the murder and touched the body post-mortem, rather than the killer himself.'

Phil's ability to talk without compassion or empathy made Lockyer ball his hands into fists. He took a calming breath and decided to push through. 'Right . . . and you agreed that it was a possibility. I certainly remember you saying the fingerprint could be . . . significant,' Lockyer said, figuring if he used Phil's own words he might get a positive response.

'I certainly agree on the basis that I do not think your boy would have been so careless. He went to the trouble of cleaning his victims. I very much doubt he would have removed his gloves to indulge himself in skin-to-skin contact. That would be too amateurish for a man of his . . . talents,' Phil said.

The way he said 'talents' sent a chill over Lockyer's shoulders. 'OK, so we can agree . . . in theory that the fingerprint came from a third party. I want to take it a step further,' he said, absently rearranging the folders on his desk according to colour. 'Perhaps the . . . excitement of observing the murder and approaching the body intrigued the "watcher". Maybe he follows the culprit, begins a ritual of his own, wanting to be there to see what our killer does next.' He stopped and let his words travel to Phil and settle. 'So?' he asked after a few seconds.

'Mmm,' Phil said. Lockyer would swear he could hear him tapping his chin, deep in thought. 'The personality traits necessary to observe a violent assault and not act could mesh with an individual pursuing the perpetrator, with a view to being present for the next . . . instalment, shall we say.'

'Good. So, today's victim, Hayley Marie Sawyer . . .'

'I haven't had the notes on this scene, as yet, Mike,' Phil said, as if excusing himself from any further involvement or responsibility.

'Yes, I know, but just listen. Dave confirmed that someone

returned to the body several hours after the attack and repositioned her.'

'What kind of position?' Phil asked. The pitch of his voice rose half an octave, his interest obviously piqued.

'Well, she was naked, apart from a pair of boots, and she was laid out as though crucified.' It sounded absolutely insane even to say it out loud. 'So, either the killer came back to check on his handiwork and moved the victim into the pose for his own reasons, or . . . the observer from Debbie Stevens' attack had, given his interest, followed our guy to Richmond, witnessed the murder and, just like before, approached the body, but this time he repositioned her.' He pushed his thumbs into his eye sockets with more force than he had intended. As white stars danced in front of his eyes he had a hideous vision of sitting in the pub and the entire team including Jane laughing their arses off as Phil regaled them with this conversation and Lockyer's complete removal from reality.

'Right,' Phil said. 'From a psychological standpoint it has possibilities but . . . am I to understand from your reticence that you haven't told anyone else about this, as yet?'

'Not in detail, no,' he said, relieved his office door was closed.

'Would I also be right in thinking that at the beginning of our conversation, your numerous questions about stalkers and harassment mentalities were inextricably linked to this new theory of yours?'

'In a word, yes.' He took a deep breath. 'I arrested a thirty-seven-year-old man, Malvern Turner, last night on suspicion of harassment. I'm interviewing him first thing in the morning. I think there's a chance he watched Debbie

Stevens' murder *and* was present at Hayley Sawyer's. I guess what I need from you, Phil, is a yes or no before I go out on a limb here. Is it possible?' He was disturbed by the pleading tone in his voice.

'It's possible but I wouldn't like to say more at this stage,' Phil said. 'Presumably Turner was fingerprinted when he was arrested?'

'Yes,' he said.

'Well, then . . . as soon as they check Turner's print to the partial found on the Stevens girl, you will know, without doubt, if he was present at her murder,' Phil said. 'Perhaps then we can talk more about the most recent victim and this theory of yours.'

'Right,' Lockyer said, letting out the breath he hadn't realized he was holding. 'Thanks, Phil. I'll talk to you later.'

He hung up and tossed his phone onto the table. It bounced, knocking over his coffee cup, the contents soaking his colour-coordinated files. He dabbed at the spillage, throwing the soggy paper towels into his bin. They made a sucking sound as they hit the metal. He could feel sweat collecting on the back of his neck and in his armpits. His stomach was alternating between cramping and relaxing as the apprehension and excitement of the next few hours took its toll. He wondered how Sarah Grainger was doing now Turner was behind bars. He could call her. Later, maybe.

Lockyer strode out of his office, took the lift down to the lobby and went out into the freezing car park. He hadn't put Dave's new number in his phone yet. It was on a piece of paper in the glove box of his car. He clicked the keys and the indicator lights flashed as he opened the door. As he bent into the passenger side a gust of cold air found its way inside his jacket.

He punched in the number off the torn piece of paper and waited for Dave to answer.

'You missing me or something?' Dave asked.

'Just a quick call. I know you have far more interesting things to be getting on with,' he said, leaning on the hood of his car and immediately regretting it. The layer of frost on the metal stuck to his wrist. 'Are you back in the suite with the body yet?'

'Yes, just arrived. Patrick's preparing now,' Dave said.

'Can you ask Patrick to check for trace evidence, finger-prints in particular, first? I'll need them processed ASAP.'

'Sure. It's pretty high on the order sheet anyway so he won't mind doing it first. What's up?' Dave asked.

'Nothing much,' he smiled to himself. 'But if there are any, I think I might know who they belong to.'

'I'll speak to Patrick now,' Dave said, not waiting for Lockyer to respond. The line went dead.

'Hey, boss.'

Lockyer turned to see Chris, one of his DCs, walking towards him. He pushed his door closed, alarmed the car and started over to meet him.

'How are the interviews going?' he asked. More than half the team had been in back-to-back meetings all day with anyone and everyone remotely related to local doctors' surgeries, hospitals, well-woman clinics, you name it, his team had questioned them on location or back at the station.

'Pretty good, sir. Me and Penny have been through twenty-five apiece today,' Chris said, tilting up his chin.

'That's great. Anything I need to know?'

'No, sir. Not from my end, anyway. You'd have to check with Penny – she's upstairs.'

'So where are you off to now?' he asked, noting Chris's coat and gloves slung over one arm. It was a bit early to be clocking off for the day.

'Just got to head over to Nunhead for Sergeant Bennett.'

'Oh yes, why's that?' Lockyer asked. He had a sneaking suspicion that Jane was keeping Grainger more informed than they had agreed.

Chris seemed to sense his mistake, blithely walking Jane straight into trouble. 'I just . . . she asked if I could update one of her . . . there's a case she hasn't had a chance to follow up on, what with this morning's victim. She asked me to pop through on my way home.' Before Chris had even finished his sentence his ears had betrayed him by turning bright red.

'Right, I see. Wouldn't be Sarah Grainger, would it?' It was cruel to ask. It wasn't that he was pissed off with Jane. He knew when he told her not to tell Sarah about the surveillance that Jane had an issue with it and would most likely use her discretion by speaking to her once the operation had finished. He could hear Jane now. 'You said not to inform her about the surveillance. You never said anything about not informing her once the surveillance had terminated.' Chris shifted from one foot to another, his face almost puce.

'On you go,' Lockyer said, finally releasing Chris from his crippling dilemma of dobbing in a colleague or disobeying the boss.

'Thank you, sir,' Chris said, scurrying away like a small boy after a telling-off.

Lockyer walked across the car park, up the slope and into the foyer. He wasn't really cross with Jane for keeping Sarah in the loop. He had wanted to tell Grainger himself. But then that's why Jane was his right hand. She made sure the stuff he wanted to do but couldn't because of 'procedure' was sorted without him having to do a thing. In fact he would thank her when she was back. She was out of the office now. Some problem at her son's school and an ill grandmother meant Peter was left with no one to take care of him. Jane thought it would only be a day, two at the most, but judging by her face, when she'd told him, she wasn't sure. He really couldn't spare her right now but what could he say? Her son came first. He realized that if he was half the parent to Megan that Jane was to Peter, his relationship with his daughter might be significantly better. Megan's face when he'd practically kicked her out of his flat made his head hurt. He would call her later, or tomorrow, straighten things out. But for now he needed to concentrate on his interview with Turner tomorrow morning and maybe, just maybe Dave would call with some good news in the meantime.

30

4 February – Tuesday

Malvern sat in the interview room surrounded by bodies. DC Groves, from the previous interviews, was sitting on the other side of the desk and Mrs Brunswick, the appropriate adult, was sitting next to him on his right. She was so close he could smell her perfume, a lemony scent that was so strong it tickled the back of his throat. She was wearing a long flowery dress and a thick navy-blue cardigan. The dress looked like a tent, covering her chubby body, her round face poking out of the top. Her legs didn't even fit on the chair. They bulged over the edges like a muffin rising out of its paper casing and dripping down the sides. She had explained that she was 'on his team'. He didn't feel like anyone was on his team. He also didn't see why he needed her here in the first place. He wasn't a child.

The room felt cold and unfriendly. His wrist still hurt. As he tried to wiggle his fingers at the end of the cast the door opened and the tall detective walked in. There was no mistaking this man's face. He had eyes like an owl's.

'Good morning, Mr Turner,' the detective said, sitting

down on the other side of the table. 'Remember me?' he asked.

Malvern tried to still the tremor that had taken hold in his left leg. He rested his hand against his thigh, keeping the vibrating limb in place. His cast was heavy and it itched. 'Yes, sir,' he answered.

Officer Groves leaned forward and pressed a button on the recording box screwed to the wall.

'For the record, I am Detective Inspector Mike Lockyer,' he said. 'This is interview three with Mr Malvern Turner. Also present are Detective Constable Groves and Mrs Pamela Brunswick, the AA assigned to Mr Turner by the custody officer.'

Malvern couldn't bring himself to look up so he just stared at the table top. It had been a mistake to run.

'I have some questions for you,' the detective said, leaning over the table, invading Malvern's space.

'I haven't done anything wrong,' he said, trying to put some confidence and authority into his voice. He felt Mrs Brunswick shuffle her chair closer to him.

'It's all right, Mr Turner,' she said.

But it wasn't. He had been sitting in this room for hours, days. They knew all there was to know about him; everything except Sarah, of course.

'I am duty bound to stress, again, that you are entitled to have legal representation. Are you certain you wish to refuse this right, Mr Turner?'

Malvern was already shaking his head. They had asked him this so many times. 'I told you. I've done nothing wrong,' he said, sitting up straighter in his chair.

'Right,' the detective said, shrugging his shoulders. 'As before, this interview will be recorded. Are you happy to continue, Mr Turner?'

'Yes,' he said, leaning back as far as he could. He wanted to move away. Everything and everyone felt too close; the table, the digital recorder, its red flashing light pulsing, and the detective, in his space, breathing on him.

'Then let's begin, shall we?' the detective said, crossing his legs so his ankle rested on his knee. 'You confirmed earlier that you were born and raised in London. The Wandsworth area, is that correct?'

'Yes, sir,' Malvern said, nodding for emphasis.

'Do you have family here in London?' the detective asked.

It took Malvern a moment to find an answer. 'My father died a long time ago. My mother's in a home now. She's not well.'

'I see. That must be hard. Are you able to visit her often?'

'Not that much. She doesn't like to . . . see people.' He had tried to see her lots of times but the people at the nursing home said his mother didn't want visitors right now.

'I see. Any other family, friends?'

'No.' He wasn't going to tell these strangers about Sarah. Their relationship was delicate, private, his. The detective was nodding, as if he understood.

'Do you drive, Mr Turner?'

'Yes, sir,' he said. Malvern felt tired already. These questions were all the same.

'How often would you say you use the vehicle?' the detective asked, leaning his elbows on the desk. He was too close again.

'I suppose . . . I . .' His face felt hot. He wanted to ask Mrs Brunswick what he should do, what the detective wanted him to say, but she was just sitting staring straight ahead, looking bored.

'Let me rephrase that for you,' the detective said with a little smile. 'Do you drive it every day, once a week, less than that?'

'Every day,' he said.

'Mr Turner, can you tell me your whereabouts on the night of the 22nd of January of this year?'

He tried to think, confused by the question. What date was it now?

As if the detective could read his mind he said, 'Let me help you. It is Tuesday the 4th of February today. The 22nd of January was a Wednesday. So that would be . .' he seemed to think for a second, looking up at the ceiling as if there were a calendar pinned to it. 'Yes, that would be two weeks ago, tomorrow. Where were you between the hours of 21.00 and midnight?'

Malvern looked up at the ceiling to see if it would help him, as it had obviously helped the detective. Two weeks ago, a Wednesday night. He tried to picture what Sarah had done that day. It was always easier to plot his movements if he thought of what Sarah had been doing. Her life was more ordered than his. If it had been a Wednesday she would have been working in the day. She never wasted a weekday. Well, she never used to. The detective cleared his throat. Malvern dragged his eyes away from the ceiling and the image of Sarah he had conjured there. 'I'm sorry. I can't remember,' he said.

'Right. Let me ask you . . .' The detective pulled a notepad from his jacket pocket. He seemed to study it for a long time before he placed it open, face down on the table, and looked back at Malvern. 'Do you know a . . . Sarah Grainger?'

His breath seemed to rush out of his body. How did the detective know about Sarah? What did this tall, all-eyes idiot want with his Sarah? Anger bubbled up in his throat. To hear her name on another man's lips made his blood hum with fury. Even the way he said it, as though caressing each syllable on his filthy tongue.

Mrs Brunswick leaned towards him. 'Do you understand the question, Mr Turner?' she said, her voice gentle. He pushed his hand harder into his thigh, absorbing the pain that shot through his shoulder from his injured wrist.

'Yes, I understand the question,' he said, his jaw clenched as he spat out the words.

'Then please answer it, Mr Turner. Do you know Sarah Grainger?' the detective repeated.

'Yes . . . she's a close friend of mine,' he said, trying to ignore the flash he saw in the detective's eyes.

'A close friend? I see. Can you tell me how you and Miss Grainger met?'

Mrs Brunswick was shifting in her seat. Malvern hoped she would interrupt but she stayed silent. He picked at a piece of skin on the end of his thumb and said, 'Last year, we were working together, for the same company. I mean, I was doing a painting job . . . she was taking photographs of people . . . but . . . I don't think . . . it's not.' He balled his hands into fists. 'Sarah has nothing to do with you . . . with this,' he said, gesturing at the interview room with his uninjured hand.

'I'm afraid, Mr Turner, that Miss Grainger is more than involved. She instigated this investigation.'

Malvern's brain pulsed as he tried to piece together the past few weeks. Sarah had come to the police station. When was that? It was a Friday. He could see her now, sitting on the long red-brick wall outside the police station, crying. She had been upset that day. This detective must have upset her.

'I know Sarah visited this station less than two weeks ago, Detective, but I'm afraid she didn't tell me why she was here or what the result of her visit was. So I cannot help you with that.' He felt his pulse slow in his temple. It was all right. He was back in control now. He would not let this beast get his claws into Sarah.

'So, Miss Grainger didn't tell you why she was coming to the police?' the detective asked, his mouth set in a thin line.

'No, she didn't. Sarah doesn't have to tell me everything, Detective,' he said, tilting up his chin.

'Would it surprise you to know, Mr Turner, that Sarah was here to report a nuisance in her life? A stalker, as she saw it?'

Malvern could feel his mouth falling open. A nuisance, a stalker.

'Would it surprise you further to know that the nuisance Sarah reported was calling her, following her, shadowing her every move and, for all intents and purposes, frightening her?' the detective asked.

'Detective, I think that's enough of the "surprises", don't you?' Mrs Brunswick said. 'Perhaps you can move on to another line of questioning or make your point clear?' She patted Malvern's arm like he was a small boy. Her hand was heavy.

'Yes, Detective, it did . . . it does surprise me that Sarah would come to the police about someone harassing her and that I wouldn't know about it. But I don't, so there's no point asking me about it.'

He would speak to Sarah tonight. She had nothing to fear. He imagined the smile on her face. The relief, the sheer joy. She would ask him in. Maybe they would share a drink together, on her sofa, her telling him all her worries and him stroking them away. He felt a tightening in his trousers. The detective seemed to have noticed too but had turned his head away to allow Malvern to pull his chair forward, the table now shielding his predicament. At least the man had some manners.

He heard a buzzing sound. It was loud and insistent, like a hornet trapped under a glass. As he looked around the room for the origin of the sound the detective took a fancy-looking iPhone out of his jacket pocket.

'DI Lockyer,' he said. 'Yes, I'll be right there.' The detective was on his feet and pushing in his chair before the phone was even back in his pocket. He leaned over Officer Groves, his finger hovering over the button on the digital recorder. 'Interview suspended at . . .' He looked up at a clock on the wall high above them. '09.15. Mr Turner, I will be back in a moment,' he said, stopping the tape and disappearing out of the door before Malvern even had a chance to reply.

Lockyer jogged past the reception desk, jabbed the 'down' button on the lift and paced back and forth waiting for the doors to open. He looked at his watch. He was meant to be seeing Bobby today. There was fat chance of that happening.

He pressed 'lower ground', aware of his heart beating hard in his chest.

As the lift shuddered into movement he let the various charges scroll back and forth in his mind. He needed to talk to the custody officer again. The CPS would make him drop the resisting arrest charge but they would probably agree to a twelve-month suspended sentence and a fine, say two hundred and fifty quid for the ABH assault charges. A judge would hear those charges and the harassment plea when Turner was released. It was obvious the guy wasn't going to plead guilty to the harassment charge so that hearing would be set for a later date. Turner would no doubt get another suspended term and then whatever kind of restraining order Grainger wanted. The doors opened and Lockyer walked down the hallway, rubbing his hands together, shaking his head. None of the charges kept Turner in custody.

He dodged down another hallway. It was like a rabbit warren down here. All he could hope was that Dave had good news. If he didn't, Turner was liable to be back on the streets first thing in the morning and Lockyer would be right back where he started. Dave was sitting at his desk tapping away at his keyboard.

'Dave, tell me you've got something for me,' he said, closing the door behind him.

'Take a seat and I'll tell you,' Dave said, indicating the moth-eaten chair. 'Patrick has done the initial sweep for fingerprints on Hayley Sawyer and there aren't any.'

Lockyer looked at Dave. 'Nothing?' he asked.

'No, not even a smudge. The suspect was wearing gloves

and, as with the other victims, he cleaned the body post-mortem.'

'Was the body cleaned before or after the repositioning?' he asked, knowing the answer already.

'After,' Dave said. 'I'm guessing this isn't the news you were expecting?'

'Not exactly, no,' he said, shaking his head. His theory about the 'watcher' being present at Hayley's murder had been a distraction. He realized he had been using the idea to avoid the reality now staring him in the face. The killer's confidence was growing. There was no other way to explain it. To return to the scene of the crime some four or six hours later, to reposition the body in broad daylight. Those weren't the actions of a killer who felt threatened. Those were the actions of a man who was just getting started.

'It's not all bad news,' Dave said, smiling, accentuating the myriad lines around his eyes and mouth. 'The partial fingerprint on the Stevens girl. You have a match. It's Turner.'

Lockyer banged his fist on the desk as relief flooded through him. 'I knew it.' He let the revelation settle in his mind. Turner might not have been present at Hayley's murder but that didn't matter now. Lockyer had a witness.

Dave leaned back in his chair. 'Are you sure Turner isn't the killer? This fingerprint puts him at the scene.'

'Sure? No, I'm not one hundred per cent sure, but . . . look, Turner doesn't fit the profile and from what Phil's told me there's no way Debbie's killer would have removed his gloves. He's too careful for that.' He could feel Dave's doubt, could see it in his eyes, but Lockyer knew his 'watcher' theory was right. For him, Turner's fingerprint was all the confirmation he needed.

Dave shrugged his shoulders. 'OK. So do you think Turner is going to be able to identify the killer?'

'That, Dave, is what I'm about to find out.'

The detective had been gone for ages. No one had told him anything. No wonder Sarah had looked so upset when she had been to the police station. She had probably been subjected to the same appalling treatment.

Officer Groves had left the room not long after the detective but she was back now, staring straight ahead, not speaking. Nobody was speaking. Mrs Brunswick had said some soothing, annoying words when the detective first left the room but now she was trying to file a raggedy nail without anyone noticing. Malvern's ear twitched with each stroke of her file. If he was forced to stay here much longer he was going to bang on the door and demand to be set free. All the time he was here, Sarah was out there, alone. Someone was following her, upsetting her. He should be with her, protecting her. The door opened, jarring his thoughts.

'Sorry about that, Mr Turner,' the detective said, pushing the door closed and sliding into his chair. He nodded to officer Groves, who pushed the button on the digital recorder.

'Interview resumed at 10.03 a.m.,' she said before reeling off everyone's names, again.

The detective looked almost happy as he said, 'Mr Turner, are you OK to continue?'

'Yes,' Malvern said, leaning back in his chair, trying to copy the detective's body language, but the detective suddenly shot forward in his seat and put both of his very large hands on the desk with a thump.

'Have you ever seen a dead body, Mr Turner?'

'Detective?' Mrs Brunswick said, holding up a chubby finger.

Malvern had no idea what to do or what to think.

'I'm not sure I know what you mean,' he said, disappointed to hear a waver in his own voice.

'Detective, is this really necessary?' Mrs Brunswick said but now the detective held up one finger to her, as if it was some secret code that only they were in on.

'I will repeat the question. Mr Turner. Have you, in the course of your life, ever seen a dead body?' The detective sat back, his eyes boring into Malvern like little lasers.

'In my life . . . I . . .' His mind emptied of everything.

'Surely, Mr Turner, on television, in films?'

'Oh yes. I have. Films, television, yes, I have, then,' he said, relieved.

'Good. So, you have seen a dead body at the cinema, DVDs at home, that kind of thing?' the detective asked, pulling a pen from his jacket and turning over his notepad that was still face down on the table.

'Yes,' Malvern said.

'Have you ever seen a dead body that wasn't on the television, or in a film?'

Malvern felt exhausted and confused. He longed to see Sarah, to calm his nerves and restore his peace.

'Mr Turner, please answer the question.' The detective's words were hard.

As Mrs Brunswick was about interrupt again an image

flashed into Malvern's mind. A girl, lying naked, surrounded by mud and rubbish. Her face had been beautiful; her mouth open as if she would speak. He had reached out to her, touched her skin but it had been cold. She hadn't been as lovely as Sarah but there had been something about her that had made Malvern's heart ache. Her blood had felt sticky on his fingers. Everything had been so quiet.

'Mr Turner,' the detective said.

'Mr Turner?' Mrs Brunswick said. 'Are you all right?'

Malvern could hear voices and he could see the detective's mouth moving but he felt as if he was floating above himself, watching. 'I . . . I don't know, I can't remember,' he said.

'You can't remember if you have ever seen a dead body, Mr Turner. Is that what you are saying?'

'Yes, sir,' he said, watching as his arms seemed to lift from his lap and float like seaweed on the ocean current.

'Turner,' the detective shouted, banging the desk with his hand.

Malvern fell back into himself and looked up, startled. 'Yes,' he managed to say.

The detective rubbed his forehead with his large hand and stared at the notepad on the desk. 'Let's see if we can make this a little easier for you, Mr Turner,' he said, smiling at him and then at Mrs Brunswick. Her hand was on Malvern's arm again. He wanted to ask her to move it but he was too busy staring at the detective's smile. It stretched across his face as if it pained him.

'How often would you say you used your mobile phone, Mr Turner?' The detective rolled his hands over as he said, 'Every day, several times a week, never.'

'Sometimes every day, sometimes not,' he said, trying to remember where his phone was. Oh yes, they had it. They had taken it from him on Sunday night.

'Do you have Miss Grainger's phone number, Mr Turner?'

'Yes . . . I do,' he said.

'How often do you call Miss Grainger?' the detective asked, tapping the table top.

Malvern looked at Officer Groves; she was smiling too. 'Not today,' he said.

'You haven't called Miss Grainger today, no. Do you call her most days, Mr Turner?' the detective asked.

'I try,' he said. His voice sounded like it was in his head or he was talking under water. He felt strange, detached. It was nice.

'Do you recall making a lot of phone calls to Miss Grainger on Thursday the 23rd of January?'

Malvern thought for a moment, he made a thinking sound, 'mmm', and put his finger to his lips. 'Yes, sir. I did. That's right. I did.' He felt eager to speak, now that he knew the answers. 'I was calling Sarah, Miss Grainger, that night. She didn't answer. I think she was sleeping.' He felt warm and comforted to think of Sarah in her bed.

'Right, so you were calling Sarah that night. Can you remember why? Can you remember why you wanted to talk to her?' the detective asked, leaning forward again.

'I . . . she . . .' He pushed his mind back to that night. It had been cold, freezing in his mother's Nissan. His breath on the windows. He had called Sarah over and over, all night long, but she never answered. 'I needed to tell her,' he said, looking into the detective's owl-like eyes.

'Needed to tell her what, Mr Turner?'

'I needed to tell her about the girl . . . the girl in the alleyway.' He remembered her red hair, the bits of dirt and muck stuck in it. Her face, her eyelids blue from the cold. He tried not to think about the gaping hole at her throat.

'Mr Turner. Malvern. On the night of Wednesday the 22nd of January a girl was attacked and killed in the alleyway next to the Tesco Metro on East Dulwich Road. Do you know the place I mean?' he asked.

'Yes,' Malvern said, wiping away a tear with the sleeve of his jumper. Sarah must be desperate without him. If she was here she would hold his hand. She would help him. He didn't like to think of the girl in the alleyway, to remember how cold she was.

'Were you in the vicinity of the Tesco Metro on Wednesday the 22nd?'

'Yes, sir.'

'Why?' the detective asked.

'I was on my way . . . somewhere,' he said.

'On your way where, Mr Turner?'

'To her house . . . to Sarah's house,' he said, comforted by the feel of her name on his tongue.

'Right. And what did you see when you passed the Tesco's, Mr Turner?' The detective's voice was quiet now. He looked angry.

Malvern didn't want to remember but maybe if he answered the questions they would let him go. Let him go home to Sarah. He closed his eyes. He could see the man; he could see the girl beneath him. 'I saw a girl.'

'What was she doing, Mr Turner?'

'She was, she was hurt. The man was hurting her,' Malvern said. He knew the man had hurt her, not because she screamed; she didn't. Not because of the blood; there was lots of blood. It was her face, her mouth open, in a silent scream.

'Was the girl still alive when you saw her, Mr Turner?'

'No, I don't know. She was cold. I helped. I covered her up. I helped,' he said, realizing he was whining like a child.

'Mr Turner. Who else did you see in the alleyway?' the detective asked, his hands hovering over the table.

'A man, I saw the man.'

'Did you walk closer to the alley, Mr Turner?'

'Yes, sir, I did.'

'That's good. You're doing very well. Can you tell me what happened then?'

Malvern could feel a buzz around him, it felt like it was coming from the detective. 'I don't know. It was dark and he . . . moved away . . . I covered her up. I helped the girl. I helped, didn't I?' he said, reaching out and trying to touch the detective's hand.

'Did you see the man leave the alleyway?' the detective snapped, snatching his hand away.

'Yes, sir,' Malvern said.

'Now . . . this is very important, Mr Turner. Can you remember what the man looked like? Could you describe him?'

Malvern's head was pulsing, lights dancing in front of his eyes. 'I don't know . . . he was tall, like you. He was white.'

'What was he wearing?'

'I . . . I don't remember. Trousers. A top, a jacket or a

jumper. I don't know, it was dark. Can I go now?' he asked. He was so tired.

'I'm afraid not, Mr Turner, but we will take a break. I am going to send in one of my colleagues. You can tell him what you saw, what this man looked like, and he will draw a picture. You tell him when the picture is right. Understand?'

'Yes, sir, I do,' Malvern said, looking up at the detective who had stood up. 'Can I call Sarah, to let her know I'm OK?' he said.

The detective didn't answer him. He just stopped the tape recorder, said a few words to the officer Groves, thanked Mrs Brunswick and walked out of the room. Mrs Brunswick didn't have her hand on Malvern's arm any more.

31

4 February – Tuesday

Sarah folded up her newspaper. She had hoped for a distraction but the headlines were dominated by the discovery of the body of a young girl in Richmond. Some poor man, walking his dog, had found her just inside the park. She shivered as she looked out at Lewisham High Street, still peppered with snow. She should consider herself lucky but she didn't. It was 10.30 and she had already spent half an hour in Bella's Coffee House, waiting for Bennett. They had agreed to meet here, rather than the station. Sarah couldn't bear the idea of being in the same building as him, even if he was behind bars.

The impact of Bennett's call yesterday had been short lived. Once the shock had worn off and the relief hadn't fully come, she had been left with questions, dozens of questions. What happened now? What happened to him? There was so much doubt circling in her mind it was making her dizzy. She sipped her coffee, glad for the extra shot of espresso after yet another sleepless night.

Outside the café the temporary traffic lights changed to

green, cars edged forward, horns blaring. She leaned forward and looked up the street at Lewisham Police Station as her eyes filled with tears. She dropped her hands on the table with a thump, sending her teaspoon spinning to the floor. As she bent to pick it up, sniffing, she heard the café's door open, the bell jingling a friendly welcome.

'Sarah?'

She looked up to see Bennett's boss. His name vanished from her lips as soon as she opened her mouth. It was Mike something. 'Good morning . . . Detective,' she said before dropping her eyes back to her coffee cup.

As if by magic a young girl appeared behind the counter and cleared her throat. 'What can I get you?' she called out. When Sarah looked over she could see that the girl was blushing. She hadn't got table service.

'Espresso, please, double shot,' he said, not really looking at the girl and clearly clueless to her crestfallen expression as she skulked off to get his coffee. 'May I join you?' he said, indicating the seat opposite Sarah.

She heard herself say, 'Please, go ahead.'

He shrugged out of his jacket, slung it over the back of one of the chairs and slid into his seat. 'These chairs remind me of the dinner hall at school, but if I remember rightly, ours were nailed to the floor.' He spoke in a laughing whisper, leaning towards her as if they were old friends sharing a joke.

'We didn't have chairs. We had benches,' she said, feeling a blush flare at the base of her neck. What the hell was she talking about? Before she could say anything else banal the young girl walked over, plonked the espresso on the table and walked away again.

'I think the service is better in Starbucks,' he said, again in a stage whisper, 'but I just can't stomach their coffee.' He took an appreciative sip and smiled. Sarah wasn't sure if the smile was for her or the coffee.

'I expect you've been busy?' she asked, immediately wondering where that had come from. He wasn't going to want to talk about his job, not to her. And she didn't want to hear about it anyway. Not after what she'd just read.

He seemed to think for a minute, his lips hidden behind his cup. She thought for a second that he wasn't going to answer at all, but then he said, 'It's been a tough couple of weeks but we're getting there.' He shrugged his shoulders.

'How long have you been a detective . . . Detective?' she asked, unable to think of another topic of conversation but unable to stay silent either. Despite feeling uncomfortable talking to the detective, it was a significant improvement on crying into her coffee. She needed a distraction.

'Call me Mike.' He smiled but it didn't reach his eyes. The tiredness she had seen last week was still there. In fact now that she looked at him she could see the grey bags shadowing his deep-set eyes.

'Of course,' she said, taking a sip of her coffee. It was already starting to cool beyond the point of enjoyment but she didn't care. She was surprised by how relaxed he seemed, his arm resting casually on the back of the chair next to him. She could smell lavender and something else. Every time he moved another waft of the scent drifted under her nose. She breathed it in, pushed her shoulders down and tried to relax, if only by an inch.

'. . . I guess I'm coming up to twenty years . . .' He was

still talking about his job but Sarah found she couldn't focus. Instead, she was thinking of the other times they had met. Their first meeting had been at Bennett's desk. He, Mike, had walked over with an expression bordering on angry. He was all eyes and rudeness.

'. . . when I left university I went to the . . .' he continued.

Sarah was only half listening. The second time they met, when it was just her and Mike, she had been crying. When he had walked into that interview room, she remembered wanting to scream at him but then he had been so different; kind, softly spoken, sympathetic. She could still see his hand reaching across the table to her.

'. . . and that's when I was promoted to inspector, and I've been running the HSCC, Homicide and Serious Crime Command, quite a mouthful, I know, but no one calls it that.'

She looked at him and finally focused on what he was saying. 'Did you say homicide?' she asked.

'Yes. There are offices in Lewisham, Hendon, Barnes, Belgravia . . .'

He had probably talked for five minutes but the only word she really heard was homicide. 'Is Sergeant Bennett . . .?' she asked, feeling the coffee in her stomach begin to churn, threatening to come back up.

'Jane is my lead detective sergeant, has been for the last five years. She's my right hand.' He seemed to accentuate the end of his sentence as if Sarah had somehow cast doubt on Bennett's abilities.

'So . . . why was she assigned to my case?'

Now it was his turn to pause. She watched as tiny red blotches came out on his temples and around the nape of his neck where he had loosened his collar. 'Simple,' he said, his eyes scanning the coffee shop. 'Sergeant Bennett oversees your borough and the matter was handed to her initially. It is then up to her whether to handle the case herself or delegate to a more junior member under her supervision.' He finished speaking, raised his cup as if to indicate he needed a refill. 'Can I get you another? What would you like?' he asked, pushing his seat back with a screech.

'Americano,' she said, unable to say anything else.

Sarah watched as he walked over to the counter, staring at the board as if unsure what to order. She had a sudden desire to leave, to get out of the café before he said anything else, but before she could bolt he was back. There was only one cup. It was obvious. She was staying, he was leaving.

He seemed to be struggling to find the right words, the right sentiment to leave her with as he escaped. 'Sergeant Bennett asked me to speak to you,' he said. Sarah felt her eyebrows bunching together. He had just spent five minutes chatting away like they were old chums but he never mentioned being here to see her. She assumed it was a coincidence. Why wouldn't she? Why the hell hadn't he said anything?

'I'm sorry, Sergeant Bennett asked you to come here and see me?' she asked, aware that she sounded as incredulous as she felt.

'Yes, she isn't in the office today, I'm afraid. She was called out on some private business. She called and told me about your meeting this morning and asked if I would come and explain that she was unable to attend and could she possibly reschedule when she's back in the office, tomorrow, most likely.'

Sarah was surprised by how young he sounded when he made excuses. 'But,' she began, unsure what to say, 'Bennett told me she would explain what happened next . . . what I do now?'

He seemed to study his hands for a moment. 'I can help you with some of that,' he said, trying to smile in what was obviously meant to be a reassuring way.

'So tell me,' she said, not letting him look away. She didn't know where the forceful voice was coming from.

'Wouldn't you prefer to come into the station? I'm not sure this is the best place to talk, Sarah,' he said, gesturing to the café around them.

The place was empty. Even the girl behind the counter had vanished. Sarah felt something inside give way. She couldn't take any more games. 'It's not as if we've got half of Lewisham listening, is it?' She saw the disquiet on his face but she couldn't stop now. 'Just tell me. I really don't think I can take this any more. If I'm in some kind of danger, tell me. If I've imagined it, tell me. If he's watching someone else and I've got it wrong, tell me. If he's an old boyfriend hoping for reconciliation, just tell me. Don't I deserve that much?' She said the last sentence barely above a whisper. Her strength had vanished as quickly as it had come.

He put both hands on the table, flat, fingers spread out. It was becoming a familiar gesture. 'Sarah. I can understand how difficult this must be for you.' He seemed to be waiting for her to agree so she forced herself to nod. He was fiddling with whatever he wore around his neck. She remembered him doing the same thing when he had interviewed her last week. She realized she was watching his fingers rather than listening to him. '. . . as Sergeant Bennett told you, a suspect was brought into the station for questioning on Sunday evening,' he said, raising his thumb as if the first point on his agenda had been dealt with.

'Sunday?' Sarah said. 'But Bennett only called me yesterday. Have you still got him? Has he been there since Sunday? Who is he?' She was trying to control the rising panic in her voice.

'The suspect is still in custody. He is being questioned in relation to another matter,' he said, raising his index finger. Sarah realized she was going to get the information, what little of it there seemed to be, piecemeal.

'Another matter?' she said.

'Not relevant at this time. It is separate to your case and I am not at liberty to discuss it with you, but I can tell you that the individual was arrested, questioned and Sergeant Bennett is preparing to charge him in relation to your complaint. His identity can't be released until the charges are formalized, I'm afraid.' He shifted in his seat as a beeping sound invaded the space between them. It didn't take a body language expert to see his relief. 'At this stage it is up to you how you want to proceed. Sergeant Bennett will have to go through the details with you,' he said, glancing at his phone and then sliding it back into his pocket. 'As I say, Jane will be able to go through the procedure in detail.'

'Proceed with what?' she asked.

'A restraining order is possible. The individual has been advised that not only are his attentions unwanted but that he will be committing a serious offence if he continues. I have spoken to the suspect myself and I feel confident that he will take heed and keep his distance.' He reiterated his statement with a decisive nod.

'Why have you spoken to him?' She felt like she was either being utterly dense or going over the final edge of crazy. Why was the head of homicide speaking to her stalker?

He waited a second before replying, his voice calm but authoritative. 'I am Sergeant Bennett's superior officer. In the course of her investigation I came into contact with the suspect. As I said, I really think the charge and the warning will be heeded but, of course, when you speak to Jane you can discuss the options available to you to ensure that you feel totally at ease.'

She slumped forward in her chair, no longer able to hold herself upright.

'Sarah, go home. Get some rest. I will ask Sergeant Bennett to call you as soon as she's in the office.' Before she could respond he had risen from his seat. When he held out his hand she took it almost without thinking. They didn't so much shake hands as hold hands for what felt like several minutes. He looked at her and she looked right back at him. And then he was gone, the jingling bell the only proof that he was ever there.

32

4 February – Tuesday

He slipped on some surgical gloves and stopped outside the house, squatting as if tying a stray shoelace. In fact his eyes were focused on the front window of the Victorian terrace. He could just see a young woman standing in the hallway, a phone pressed to her ear. The front door stood open; peculiar, given the temperature. The snow had gone but the temperature wasn't much above freezing. The plants in front of the house looked frozen solid.

As he looked back the woman was finishing her call. She stepped towards the door and, without looking at him, slammed it shut. How unobservant, he thought. He watched her walk through to the living room, plumping cushions and, from what he could tell, singing to herself as she did so. Her black hair was long but unkempt. She repeatedly tossed her head to keep her tresses out of her pinched features. The dress she was wearing looked as if it was stretched to bursting over her rotund figure. A shiver took hold of his shoulders. As he watched her rearranging ornaments on the mantelpiece he realized she was the antithesis of Hayley. Where this woman was round, Hayley had been slim, her skin supple, white and perfect. This creature's skin was stretched, puckering at her neck. Her wrists looked swollen.

When she finally disappeared back into the hall he moved to the left of the house and walked calmly down the alleyway. There was a gate, of course, tall and sturdy. Without so much as a missed step he put one hand on top and used the wall to his left to launch himself up and over. He landed with barely a whisper of noise and not a nick on his gloves.

The French doors that led into the lounge were unlocked, as he knew they would be. He checked the bottom of his shoes for any traces of dirt. There was a small amount of a red clay-like soil, so he wiped his feet carefully on the mat that said 'Benvenuto'.

'Thank you,' he whispered, stepping into the house and listening. The woman's humming was still audible but other than that the house was quiet. The carpet beneath his feet had once been plush. Thankfully now it was almost threadbare. No impressions of his shoes would be found. He approached the doorway and peered into the hallway. The girl was on the phone again, gesticulating and babbling away, completely unaware of his presence. Her back was turned to him. Without hesitation he made his way up the stairs, slowly, wrinkling up his nose at the flock wallpaper. The chattering woman never turned or noticed the slight creak of a floorboard near the top of the stairs so he continued down the hallway.

When he found the room he was looking for he opened the door and looked around him, fingering the tiny object in his hand. He looked at the shelves, cupboards and surfaces where he might leave his present. There was an abundance of pottery and canvasses covered in bright slashes of colour. The owner was obviously proud of their handiwork. As he looked back to the precious item in his hand he sighed. He was reluctant to part with it. He turned it over, the metal cool against his skin, resisting the urge to put it in his mouth, to let his tongue search for the taste of blood.

Footsteps on the landing made him turn and shrink back against a bookshelf. The humming woman walked past the door. He heard a door close and a lock slide into place. Before she could return he placed his prized possession on top of a pile of books He smiled, turned on the bedside lamp with a flick of a switch and looked pleasurably upon the metal catching the light. It couldn't be missed.

The sound of rushing water broke his reverie and he left the room and walked down the stairs, in no hurry but with quiet steps. Within seconds he was vaulting the garden gate, walking down the driveway and vanishing into the grey suburban streets.

33

5 February – Wednesday

Lockyer looked at the e-fit in front of him and groaned. The breakthrough of a witness was a coup. The idea that Turner could identify the killer was another. But the e-fit was a joke. The man in front of him could be anyone. Did he recognize the face? Yes. Was it utterly generic? Yes. A physical description was detailed beneath the large black-and-white image. It stated that the individual wanted for questioning was Caucasian, average height, average build, brown or black hair, cut short. The clothing listed was laughable: jeans, blue or black, a jumper black or grey, a coat, black or navy. Shoes, blue or black trainers, or black boots. He turned the paper over so he didn't have to look at it any more.

Malvern Turner, once he had stopped crying, had sworn he would be able to identify the man, but Lockyer suspected he would say anything to get out of the station and back to his beloved Sarah. He shifted in his seat and looked up at the ceiling, pushing aside the anger that swelled inside him whenever he thought about Turner watching Sarah.

The helpline attached to the e-fit had been inundated with

calls. More staff had been drafted in to help. There was a little old lady who was positive it was her postman, an electrician who was sure it was his boss and even the headmistress who was almost certain the man in the picture was her year three History teacher. Every lead had to be checked, no matter how unlikely. Everything was taking too much time, time he didn't have. According to Phil they had less than two weeks to find the girls' killer before another body would be added to their number. Four girls in less than two months. It was crazy, senseless. The abortion link couldn't be the only motivation for murder. He needed to get into the guy's head to catch him. He had the distinct feeling the e-fit was doing nothing but slowing the investigation down, stretching his manpower and budget to the limit.

He turned to look out of his office window. It was snowing again. People were rushing along the pavements, using their hands, newspapers or briefcases to cover their heads. There was a line of five men standing outside the curry house, their backs flat to the glass window. The overhang of the sign was keeping them out of the snow, just. All five were smoking, their combined smoke adding to the plume of steam coming out of the kitchen vent. The smell of cooking meat, oil and spices made Lockyer's stomach grumble. As he watched a gang of kids climbing onto the number 176 bus, shouting at each other, practically throwing their money at the driver, he realized he was wasting time. He looked away and forced himself to go back to his desk.

He needed to forget about the e-fit, forget about dead ends and forget about yesterday, his disastrous meeting with Sarah. 'What a moron,' he said to himself, covering his face with the e-fit. The suspect's face was turned away from him, replacing his own. Anyone walking into his office might wonder if this was how he got into the psyche of a killer. He remembered the pathetic excuses he'd used to justify Jane's and his involvement in Sarah's harassment case. He never told civilians about his work and he certainly didn't make a habit of revealing sensitive information about a case. His intention when he walked into Bella's was to reassure Sarah. Instead he had essentially told her that her stalker was connected to his murder investigation. What a way to terrify an already vulnerable woman. There was something about her that seemed to unhinge him professionally, incite his sympathy. The phone on his desk started to ring. He glanced at his mobile but there were no missed calls. Hardly anyone used his office line.

'Lockyer,' he said as he picked up the receiver.

'Dad?' Megan's voice was quiet.

'Hi, honey, what's up?' he said, pleased to hear actual cheer in his voice, rather than the forced joy he was getting uncomfortably used to. He hadn't called her since last week when he had kicked her out of his flat. He simply hadn't had time with Turner's arrest and the discovery of Hayley's body.

'I know you're busy but have you got five minutes?' she asked, barely above a whisper.

'Megs, I can hardly hear you. Where are you?' he asked, putting the phone closer to his ear.

'I'm in that café, just down from your office, Bella's,' she said. 'Could you come down and meet me? Just for five minutes?' Her voice sounded croaky. She sounded like she was or had been crying.

'I'm coming down now. I'll be with you in two minutes.' He slammed down the phone, grabbed his suit jacket off the back of his chair and jogged out of his office, across the open-plan room towards the lift. 'Penny, back in five,' he called over his shoulder. He didn't even know if Penny was at her desk but either way someone would have heard him. As he pushed the lift's call button, he noticed a few beads of sweat on his forehead reflected in the metal doors. His heart felt like it was leaping about in his chest. 'Calm down,' he told himself. This was exactly what he was like as a father. Either he barely noticed his daughter's distress or he went completely overboard. A classic case of guilt-fuelled parenting. He crossed the foyer and went out of the automatic doors, a swirl of falling snow now catching him full in the face. He patted his pockets to check he had his wallet.

The bell jingled as he pushed open the door to the café. Megan was sitting in the same place where Sarah had been the day before. The place was empty but for an old couple at the back of the room in a leather-lined booth. The waitress seemed to recognize him.

'Espresso?' she asked, smiling.

'No, thanks,' he said, looking over at Megan. 'Do you want a cuppa, hon?' he asked, trying not to panic when his daughter looked up at him with puffy eyes and a red face.

'Latte, three sugars,' Megan said.

That made him smile. She only took three sugars because he used to. When she was a little girl she had wanted to join him in his ritual of morning coffee from the age of three. He had managed to hold her demands at bay until she was ten but then she had devoured a small morning coffee with three sugars with as much gusto as her father. She obviously still did.

The girl behind the counter passed him Megan's drink; he added the sugar and dropped a fiver on the counter. 'You can put the change in the tin,' he said, walking over to join his daughter. He took off his jacket, slung it over the back of his chair and sat. Neither of them said anything. Megan wasn't even looking at him. This was the second day in a row he had sat across from a distraught woman and not known what to say.

'OK, Megs, come on, why the tears?' he said, reaching across the table and giving her hand a squeeze. Megan shook her head and resumed sipping her coffee. 'You're going to have to give me something, Megs? I'm not a mind reader.'

'Would it be OK if I came and stayed at yours for a few days?' she said, finally looking up.

'All right,' he said, trying to remember the last time his daughter had stayed at his place, let alone asked to stay. 'What's happened, Megan?' He watched her take a deep breath, pulling her hair over one shoulder, playing with the ends with her thumb. She was so like Clara it was scary.

'Nothing. Well, nothing major. Mum and I had a row, that's all. Things got a bit heated. I thought it would be a good idea if I made myself scarce until things calm down.'

As she was speaking, he was racking his brains trying to figure out what they could possibly have argued about that would have this much impact. She'd failed her driving test, or an exam. Did she have some coming up? He was ashamed to admit he didn't have a clue. Had she been caught with marijuana or some other illegal substance? 'What did you row about?' he asked, not sure he had the mental capacity to deal with anything too big. Of course he might already know if he had actually taken the time to listen to her last week instead of making it all about him, his case, his work. Why did he always do that? He wanted to be there for her but somehow he always fell short.

Megan wiped her nose with a napkin, took a deep breath. 'It was stupid, she has . . . I'd rather not talk about it, Dad, if you don't mind?'

He reached across and tilted up her chin so she was actually looking at him. 'Come on, Megan. You and your mother hardly ever argue these days. What's this all about?' He could see how upset she was but he could also see how hard she was trying to suppress her emotions.

She rubbed her forehead with her fingers. 'It's so stupid . . . childish, really.' She shook her head. 'Mum's got a new partner . . . well, not new, it's been going on for a while,' she said, looking into her coffee cup. 'She told me last night that he's moving in with us.'

He didn't know what to say. He knew Clara dated but there had never been anyone significant. She hadn't had a serious relationship since their separation and they had never even discussed divorce. His hand went automatically to the ring around his neck. It was his constant reminder of what he had lost. This was his fault. If he had been a better husband none of this would be happening.

'Are you OK?' she asked, reaching across the table and resting her hand on his.

He could almost hear the tug of loyalties in her voice. 'Megs, it's fine. Your mum and I have been separated for what, five, six years.'

Megan nodded her head. 'It was just a shock, that's all, and we both said some pretty shitty things. It got out of hand.' The regret in her voice reminded him again just how much she had changed, how much he had missed. She wasn't his little girl any more. 'Would it be OK if I stayed . . . just while Brian moves in and they get themselves sorted?'

'Yes,' he said, not trusting himself to say anything else. Just hearing the guy's name was making his palms sweat. He needed to get out of here and get back to work. He wanted to push all thoughts of Clara and Brian to the back of his mind. Turner's disastrous e-fit would be a welcome distraction at this point.

Megan pushed her empty coffee cup away from her and stood up. 'Thanks, Dad, and I'm sorry for dragging you down here. I know how busy you are.' She bent down and kissed his cheek. 'I'm going to get the bus back and try to patch things up with Mum. Any chance you could pick me up Tuesday night? I'm going to Rachel's this weekend and Brian isn't moving in till Wednesday.'

'Of course, hon . . . absolutely,' he said, still feeling numb, '. . . and give my regards to your mother.'

'Regards?' she laughed. 'OK, Dad.' She bent down and kissed his cheek again, and then was gone. So that's what a hit and run feels like, he thought, listening as the bell over the door jingled, marking his daughter's departure.

34

Lockyer repositioned the petrol nozzle and squeezed the trigger but again the flow clicked off, stopping as if the tank was already full. The garage was packed, cars lining up, two or three deep behind each pump. The snow had caused problems with fuel deliveries so half of Lewisham seemed to be panic buying. He tried to ignore the numerous car horns and revving engines.

'Come on,' he said through clenched teeth, as he shoved the metal nozzle in as far as it would go with barely restrained violence. 'All I need is some bloody fuel. Do you think you can manage that?' He snatched at the trigger, his tension easing when the pump finally kicked in and the litres ticked away.

'Do you wanna get a move on, mate?'

He turned to see a huge guy leaning against the petrol pump, arms covered in tattoos, a beanie hat rammed low on his head. Rather than say what he was sorely tempted to say he nodded, removed the petrol nozzle, locked the fuel cap and walked towards the shop, searching for his wallet in his jacket pocket. Beanie man continued to voice his disapproval, muttering obscenities as he climbed back into his van. Lockyer decided challenging him was not worth the effort. He pushed open the glass door to the shop and joined the back of the queue.

'Number four,' he said when he finally got to the till, cash ready in his hand.

'Anything else?' the girl behind the counter said in a sing-song voice, pronouncing her 'th's as 'f's. She didn't seem bothered by the onslaught of impatient petrol-buyers.

'No, thank you.'

Beanie-guy had arrived and was now standing perilously close behind him. Lockyer took his change, nodded his thanks to the cashier, turned, looked the guy right in the eyes and then walked out of the shop. He climbed back into his car, slamming the door hard, dissipating some of his frustration.

The traffic crawled through Lewisham, not unusual for this time of day. Anything from 4 p.m. to 6 p.m. could be considered rush hour in south-east London. The snow was turning to slush as countless wheels pushed it out of the road and piled it up against the kerbs like a grey sludge. He had to be back at the station for a briefing at 19.30 so he was going to be cutting it fine. If he got half an hour with Bobby he would be lucky. There was a press conference at 18.30 releasing a reconstruction of Debbie's last movements, not to mention the interview with Hayley's parents who had arrived in London from Devon the day before. 'That's all I need,' he said to his reflection in the rear-view mirror as he changed up into fourth gear, zipping through the lights at Sainsbury's.

As he drove into the suburbs he passed hedges covered

in blankets of snow. It made him think of Richmond Park, of Hayley's body lying on the ground, white all around her, as if she was sleeping under a freshly washed sheet. He indicated and turned onto Bobby's street, pulling in behind Alice's car. Her back window was littered with stickers ranging from 'Nurses do it stat!' and 'If you can read this, you're literate!' He managed to smile, cheered by the yellow smiley faces looking back at him.

He took the keys out of the ignition, climbed out of the car, alarmed it and walked carefully up the driveway, avoiding the ice patches he knew would be lurking beneath the snow. He searched his coat pocket for his phone before scrolling to the notes page where he kept the combination number for Bobby's front door. 'Five, four, seven, eight,' he said, punching the buttons with his already freezing fingertips. As he pushed open the door he called out to announce his presence. 'Hellooo,' he said, walking across the hallway into the communal lounge. All the lights were on, including some Christmas lights that had lasted long past advent. 'Hello,' he said again, walking to the end of the room and poking his head through the doorway that led back into the hallway.

'One second, one second.'

Just hearing Alice's voice lifted Lockyer's mood. 'It's Mike, Alice,' he called.

'Michael, I'm a-comin',' she said.

He looked up to see her walking down the stairs, her thin blonde hair flying around her face, her eyes and smile wide to greet him.

'How are you doing?' he asked. 'And how's the new man?'

'Pretty good,' Alice said, stopping on the bottom step. 'It's going well, so far.' Her smile said it was going better than that. 'So, if you are here to see me, I'm afraid you've missed the boat, my friend.' She gave him a wink.

'I hope he's good enough for you,' he said, happy to settle into the familiarity of their banter.

'Not too good, I hope,' she said, giving him another playful nudge.

'How is he?' he asked, gesturing up to the landing.

Alice collapsed into laughter as he realized his gaff. 'None of your business,' she said as she disappeared into the lounge, still chuckling to herself. 'Of course, if you meant your brother . . .' she shouted, poking her head back through the doorway, 'sandboys would be jealous.'

'How did he enjoy the trip to Greenwich?' he called after her.

Alice reappeared. 'Everyone had a great time. Bobby absolutely loved the *Cutty Sark*. With his birthday coming up I'd say a book on sailing would make his day.' She put her hands on her hips and said, 'You know, you should come with us one day. Invite's always there for friends and family.'

Lockyer opened his mouth to deliver an excuse so familiar he should have it tattooed on his forehead. 'I will. I'm just really busy at the moment.'

Alice smiled. 'OK. Say bye before you go.'

'Will do,' he said, leaning on the banister to drag himself up the stairs. He suddenly felt exhausted. For those brief seconds, chatting to Alice, he had been able to forget about Clara and the case. But the respite didn't last long enough.

As he walked along the landing he ran his hand over the old-fashioned wallpaper that always reminded him of the house he grew up in. He knocked on his brother's door and waited for a few seconds. There was a muted shuffling sound and the creak of a chair. Lockyer took this as his signal to enter. 'Hey there, buddy. How are you doing today?' he said as he pushed the door closed behind him.

Bobby was already in his seat, a pack of blue patterned playing cards in his hand. 'Cards,' he said, holding the pack of cards in the air but keeping his head down.

'Not today, I'm afraid. I can't stay long.' He wasn't surprised when Bobby didn't react. A familiar crushing sensation enveloped his chest. 'Let's look at one of your books instead, shall we?' He walked over to a tall pine bookcase and waited. Bobby slowly stood, shuffled to the side of the chair and stepped back two paces to join him. 'So, what do you fancy?' There wasn't one book on the shelf that Lockyer didn't recognize. 'I know. We haven't looked at your *Book of British Birds* for ages. Why don't we look for birds you see in the garden? Although I guess there aren't so many, now it's winter.'

'Lots,' Bobby said.

Lockyer loved seeing the excitement on his brother's face. 'Nah, I don't believe you,' he said, gently nudging Bobby's arm.

'Twenty,' Bobby said.

'You're havin' me on, twenty birds in this tiny garden? The next thing you're gonna tell me is that they're all blue.'

For what felt like the hundredth time Lockyer saw a smile and a flicker of understanding on Bobby's face. He knew the autism restricted his brother's brain function to a certain extent but Lockyer was convinced Bobby could comprehend more than the doctors gave him credit for. Bobby seemed to snap out of a trance. He reached forward, picked up the book, shuffled over to his bed and sat down, already flicking through the pages, his eyes darting back and forth. Lockyer walked over and sat in the chair Bobby had vacated and watched his brother scanning the bird book.

'Here,' Bobby said, standing up and holding the book out, his head turned away to the door.

Lockyer took the book and rested it on his lap, looking down at the open pages. 'Nice. A brown-and-red bird. I've even seen them in my poor excuse for a garden,' he said, putting his finger to his lip in mock concentration. 'Now what are they called? They're on Christmas cards . . . there's a song about them . . .' He knew the hook would work. Bobby was tapping his slippered feet. 'Why don't you come over here and help me? I bet you know what this one's called,' he said, gently patting the chair opposite the card table.

Bobby stood up, took three sidesteps to the right and one step forward so he was next to the chair. He ran his hand over the top, back and then the arm of the chair. Lockyer realized he was sitting in Bobby's chair. Should he move? He wasn't sure. Alice said getting Bobby to try new things was an important part of his care. Lockyer could see the hesitation on his brother's face, as if he was wrestling with an invisible demon, blocking his way. God, it was painful to watch. It took every bit of his restraint not to move but Bobby finally lowered himself into the 'alien' chair with slow, minute movements. He was constantly touching the fabric, as if to reassure himself that the object was real, that he wouldn't fall to the floor when he trusted the chair with his full weight.

As soon as Bobby was sitting, Lockyer handed over the

book, placing it on his brother's lap and turning it the right way up so Bobby could look at the picture of the robin standing on a branch, a red berry in its beak.

'What is it?' Lockyer asked.

Bobby looked up at the window, then back down at the page of the book, running his fingers over the robin's head.

'Have you seen one of these in the garden, Bobby?' he asked.

Bobby nodded vigorously but didn't speak.

'Are there lots of them?'

'No,' Bobby said, shaking his head.

'How many have you seen?' Lockyer waited, leaning forward in his seat so he could see his brother's face.

'One,' Bobby said.

'Just one. Wow. They must be rare. Maybe they don't play well with others, eh?' Lockyer said, laughing.

His heart squeezed when Bobby smiled. The bugger was that Bobby could be smiling about what Lockyer had just said or something that had happened an hour ago or, in fact, nothing at all. It was frustrating and despite reading up on the Internet, looking through any literature he could get his hands on and talking to his own GP, Lockyer just couldn't get his head around the idea that his own brother was somehow locked away from him. It wasn't fair.

Bobby stood, the book sliding off his lap onto the floor with a thump he clearly didn't hear. Lockyer watched him take one sidestep to the right and walk over to the window. 'Robin,' he said, putting both hands flat against the glass.

Lockyer leaned back in the chair and rested his head, closing his eyes for a second. Visits to Bobby normally lifted his mood but today he had all but plummeted right back into the fug. With his cheek resting against the soft leather of his brother's chair he opened his eyes and looked at Bobby, still standing motionless at the window. The look on his face was one of total contentment.

He reached under the table to pick up the *Book of British Birds*. There was a pile of books next to Bobby's chair, a lamp resting on the top. Lockyer picked up the lamp with one hand and slid the bird book onto the top of the stack with the other. He heard something fall to the floor. He flicked on the light and bent down to see what he had knocked off. Bobby was very particular about his room and his things. One small item out of place could cause an enormous amount of stress. He ran his hand back and forth across the carpet until his fingers touched something hard. He picked it up, sat back and looked at it under the glow of the lamp.

'What's this, then?' he said, more to himself than to Bobby, who was still transfixed by whatever was outside the window. He turned the object over in his hand. It was an earring; silver with a butterfly clasp and a turquoise stone. Alice or Amber must have dropped it. If Bobby found it he would naturally have added it to his collection of things. Bobby loved knick-knacks, especially anything shiny, or his ultimate favourite: tiny animal figures made of glass. There were dozens dotted around the room: swans, elephants and even a peacock.

'Collecting women's jewellery now, are we?' Lockyer said, holding the earring up for Bobby to see, if Bobby had been looking, which he wasn't.

'I'll just give this back to Alice, buddy. She's probably been looking for it. And I'm sorry to say that I've got to go.' He stood and walked over to Bobby, patting him softly on the back. 'I'll see you next time,' he said, turning to leave.

'Cards,' Bobby said.

Lockyer smiled, turned back and said, 'Next time, buddy, next time.' He touched his brother's hand and walked away, leaving Bobby to go back to his window and his birds.

As he pulled the door closed behind him, a lump formed in his throat and his vision blurred with tears. He took a deep breath, leaned against his brother's bedroom door, tipping his face up to the ceiling, hoping the gravity would stop the tears that wanted to fall. It took several big swallows to push back the flood of emotion that threatened to engulf him.

'Get a grip,' he said out loud.

'You do know that talking to yourself is the first sign of madness?'

Lockyer opened his eyes to find Alice standing at the end of the hallway looking at him. There was something in her expression that made him think she had been standing there for longer than he would have liked. 'Madness,' he said, clearing his throat. 'I think I'm way past the first sign.'

'Aren't we all,' she said.

'I've got something for you,' Lockyer said, holding out his hand, feeling the weight lifting from his chest as his emotions returned to normal. He held up the earring, an inch from Alice's nose. She looked at it and then at him.

'Most of the men I know would buy me two earrings,' she said, smiling, taking the tiny piece of jewellery out of his hand.

'I found it in Bobby's room, assumed it was yours.'

'Nope, it's not mine. Must be Amber's,' she said, turning the earring over in her fingers. 'I'll give it to her tomorrow. Will we see you next week?'

'You sure will,' he said, tipping an invisible hat as he walked down the stairs.

Lockyer pulled the front door closed behind him. A freezing gust of wind found its way under his coat, cooling his kidneys. He pulled his collar up and eased the zipper as high as it would go. In lieu of gloves he shoved his hands in his pockets and walked down the driveway. The car's side lights flashed as he released the central locking. He climbed in and started the engine, turning up the fans to help clear the windscreen.

As he sat back, watching the half-moon patches of clear glass spread, he looked at the clock on the dashboard. He had twenty minutes to get back to the office. He put the Audi into reverse, his other arm draped over the passenger seat so he could look behind him. But something stopped him. He turned around slowly and sat, staring at the now clear windscreen.

'What the . . . ?' With slow, deliberate movements he turned off the engine, slid the key out of the ignition and climbed back out of his car. He walked up the driveway and rang the bell. He could hear Alice's footsteps inside as she walked across the hallway, towards the front door. When she opened it her face seemed to freeze mid-smile.

'What's up?' she asked, stepping backwards. 'Is something the matter?'

Lockyer walked in, closed the door behind them and held out his hand.

'Alice, I need the earring I just gave you?'

'Why?' Alice said, her eyes now wider than the bay windows.

'Alice, can you just give me the earring, please?' he said, his voice on a monotone.

She put her hand in her pocket, brought out the earring and held it out to him.

'What's wrong?' she asked again.

'Alice, I need you to . . . let's sit down,' he said, gently ushering her into the lounge. He was uncomfortably aware that he was using his 'work' voice. She sat down in a large armchair that seemed to engulf her tiny frame.

'Mike, you're scaring me.'

'There's nothing to worry about,' he said, as his mind raced through a dozen different options. How was he going to explain this? No one in the office even knew he had a brother and Alice didn't know he was a police officer, but that wasn't the problem. How the hell had the missing earring from Deborah Stevens' crime scene found its way into his brother's bedroom?

35

6 February – Thursday

'Oh, come on,' Sarah said, throwing her mobile onto the kitchen counter. She had already left four messages for Bennett. In the meantime she was slowly going insane wondering if he was still in custody or outside her flat, right now, watching her. She resisted the urge to go into her lounge and check, again, especially as she still didn't know who she was looking for. How long was Bennett going to make her wait? She hadn't left the flat all day. In fact she hadn't been out since her impromptu meeting with Mike on Tuesday. She picked up her phone again and dialled the only other number Bennett had given her. Her nerves vibrated with each ring.

'DI Lockyer.'

'It's Sarah, Sarah Grainger?' she said, hoping that would be enough of an explanation for her call.

'Sarah, hello. What can I do for you?' he asked, his tone all business.

'I've been trying to get hold of Sergeant Bennett. I've left a couple messages but she hasn't called me back.'

'I see . . . I'm sorry about that, but listen, I was just

heading into a meeting. Can I call you back in five minutes, ten tops?'

Sarah could feel her cheeks heating as she said, 'It's been days and I really need . . .' She drifted into silence as the determination drained out of her. 'Fine. It's . . .' She dredged her mind for the number. Toni had forced her to buy a pay-as-you-go phone. It's 07978 . . . 433 . . . 909.'

'I'll call as soon as I'm done.'

The dial tone sounded in her ear before she could respond and a weight dropped in her stomach. She shouldn't have called him. He was heading up a murder investigation. There were four girls now. Sarah had seen Mike on the news last night, standing at the back of a press conference about the girl killed in Richmond Park. He had looked so calm. What must his job be like? She shook her head as she realized she couldn't think about it; the agony, the grief the girls' parents would be facing. Guilt settled on her shoulders like a coat soaked with water. She walked over to the kitchen window and stared out at her garden. The family of foxes was back, playing in the snow and tearing up her lawn. They were making themselves at home before their afternoon nap in the shed.

'You're welcome to it,' she said, turning her back to them as they barked up at her. She was too tired to fight anyone or anything. It was months since she had even opened the back door. She stared at the floor, a wave of sickness making her whole body sway. Why was she still hiding?

She padded through to the lounge, phone in hand. The television was already on showing typical afternoon television. It was some house makeover show and they were at the reveal stage. The homeowner was crying, overcome by the transformation of her bathroom. As Sarah sat down on the sofa she pulled a fleece blanket over her knees. The heating was on full blast but her old-fashioned sash windows, though beautiful, did very little when it came to keeping the heat in or the cold out. She looked at the woman weeping with joy as the presenter showed her round her new garden, pond, decking. Sarah thought about her own appearance. She barely recognized the person staring back at her from the bathroom mirror each morning. Her long blonde hair had lost all of its shine; split ends stood out at all angles. She had lost weight, about a stone, making her normally slim frame look emaciated. Her ribs stuck out like sharpened twigs. She pulled the blanket up to her chin, covering a body she no longer knew.

She jumped as her phone started to ring. It was an automatic response, a muscle memory she couldn't shift. Would she ever be able to hear a ringing phone again, without panicking? She made herself push 'answer'. 'Hello.'

'Hi, Sarah. It's Mike,' he said. 'Sorry it took me so long to call you back.'

Sarah dropped the blanket and pulled up her sleeve to look at her watch. It was already 3.30, half an hour since her call. She looked up at the television and realized another programme had started and was now finishing, without her even noticing.

'That's OK,' she said.

'I'm sorry Sergeant Bennett hasn't returned your call. She's still out of the office. I know she intended to speak to you on her return but she's not due back until tomorrow.'

His voice sounded different, harder somehow. 'Can you ask her to call me then?'

'Of course, but is there anything I can do? I am happy to help,' he said, but Sarah thought his offer sounded tentative. '. . . Sergeant Bennett's cases are my responsibility when she's out of the office,' he said, his voice softening but only marginally. Why would he want to waste his time trying to reassure a hysteric? That's what she was now. There were so few rational marbles rolling about in her head that it could be hours, sometimes days before she managed to grab hold of one.

'A constable dropped off some paperwork; on restraining orders . . . I just wanted to ask . . . it doesn't matter.' She blew out a long breath.

'Sarah, it's OK. Could you come into the station in, say . . . an hour?'

Panic rushed through her veins. 'Oh . . . I would, but my car is in the garage . . . the buses aren't running properly because of the snow and . . .' As her list of pathetic excuses abandoned her, she realized she was crying.

'Sarah, are you all right?' he asked, his voice soft.

She took a deep breath. 'I'm fine.' She struggled to find the right words. 'I haven't been out of the flat since . . .'

'Since when?'

'Since Tuesday,' she said on an outward breath as the admission drained her last ounce of energy. All she could hear was Mike breathing at the other end of the line.

'Tuesday, after we met?'

There was a significance in his words that she didn't fully understand but he sounded concerned. 'Yes,' she said, too tired to care what he thought any more.

'OK,' he said, stretching out the final syllable. 'How would it be if I came to you? I could be with you by five, five-thirty.' Sarah opened her mouth but no words came out. 'Is five-thirty OK with you?' he asked again.

'Yes . . . but . . .' How could she take him away from those girls? They needed him more than she did. She didn't need him. She just wanted him, his time.

'I'll see you then. I'll bring all of the relevant paperwork with me,' he said, again hanging up before she could reply.

She pulled the blanket back over her hands and stared at the television, as if in a trance. Six months ago she had been independent, successful. Ever since Bennett had called to tell her that a suspect was in custody she had been waiting for some feeling of relief, elation maybe. It had never come. Instead, there was a void. A void where *he* had been, whoever *he* was. She stood and let the blanket fall to the floor. With a force of will she pushed her shoulders back, tipped up her chin and walked through to the kitchen. She poured herself a small glass of chilled white wine. As she took a numbing sip she looked around her. God, the place was a mess.

Lockyer put down his phone and stared at it. Why had he done that? All he needed to say was, 'Yes, I'll get Sergeant Bennett to call you first thing in the morning.' Instead he had practically insisted on seeing her, taking precious hours away from a multiple murder case. Ever since the discovery of Debbie's body he had wrestled with self-doubt, with the thought that he was losing his edge, but now he was begin-ning to wonder if that wasn't all he was losing.

'Brilliant, just brilliant,' he said, shuffling the files on his desk as he tried to justify his actions. The release of the reconstruction of Debbie's last movements had been a great success. The phone lines had been jammed all morning as half of Peckham called in to say they had been to the Tesco that day, or that week. Obviously, not all the calls were helpful but half a dozen members of the public had been interviewed already, with another tranche booked in for later today. He could spare the time. Besides, with Turner's release Sarah needed to know how to move forward with a restraining order. He didn't relish the thought of telling her that Turner was out, as of this morning, free to roam. But what could he do? The judge had let him keep the guy for a further forty-eight hours after Turner admitted to interfering with Debbie's body, but that was it. It would be weeks, maybe months before Turner's hearings were even set. Until then Sarah was on her own. It wasn't good enough but there was nothing Lockyer could do about it.

Raised voices in the outer office made him look up. Chris and Amir seemed to be having a heated discussion but they weren't looking at him. When he first heard their voices it was as if the shouts were in direct protest to his thoughts. Sarah wasn't a priority. She wasn't his priority but he had to see her. More than that, he wanted to see her. He pictured her pale face in the café last week. She had tried so hard to hide her fear. Surely, she deserved his time just as much as Debbie, Hayley and the other girls.

He logged off and waited for his computer to shut down. As the screen went black he saw his reflection. The strain of finding the earring was etched on his face. And he still hadn't told his team or his SIO, Roger. The office had been so busy last night and this morning, what with the press conference, the reconstruction and his interview with Hayley's parents, that he hadn't had time. He shook his head. That was a lie and he knew it. He stood up and walked over to his window, out of his team's line of sight. He had done everything by the book since Thursday morning; giving the earring to the exhibits team (ignoring their curious looks), requesting DNA analysis on the skin cells left inside the butterfly section and typing up extensive decision logs for each step. He just hadn't uploaded the information to the case file, as yet. As soon as he did, Roger, Jane, the whole team would know and numerous questions would follow. It was the questions he was dreading most because one would undoubtedly lead to another, and another.

He paced his office, finally settling next to his filing cabinet. The metal was cool against his palms. The sun that had been shining into the room suddenly disappeared. He turned and lifted the blinds with the back of his hand. The sky above Lewisham High Street was grey. It was going to snow, again. As the thought entered his head the first few flakes started to fall. He pushed his fingers into the corners of his eyes, his pulse pushing back at him.

The exhibits team had confirmed the DNA on the earring as a match for Debbie, as he knew they would. But there was no other trace evidence, nothing to lead Lockyer to the man who had taken it from Debbie's ear and planted it in his brother's room. There was no doubt in his mind it was planted, but why Bobby? There was really only one answer to that question and the ramifications were turning Lockyer's heart into a jack-hammer. He took his jacket off the back of the chair, snagged his coat and scarf from the hook on the far wall and walked out of his office.

As he waited for the lift he stared at his reflection. 'You idiot,' he said to himself. He had turned a potential lead, a significant development in the case, into an almighty cock-up. He shook his head, blowing out a frustrated breath. He would file the paperwork the second he was back from Sarah's and face the consequences. Would he be taken off the case? Could his actions and personal involvement derail a future prosecution? Lockyer didn't think so, but he would need Roger's help to convince the chief. Of course, how forthcoming Roger's help would be after he'd been kept in the dark remained to be seen. The doors opened, he stepped in and pressed the button for the ground floor. Bobby would have to be checked out and eliminated from the inquiry, Lockyer knew that. The idea was hideous and he could only imagine the distress Bobby would face. But it had to be done. Only then would the focus shift back to catching a killer before he took another innocent life.

Sarah sat on the sofa, crossing her legs as she carefully balanced the glass of wine on her knee. The oil burner's lavender scent made the room feel warmer somehow. Lavender always reminded her of her grandmother's garden. She leaned back, closed her eyes and took a long drink, letting one of the ice cubes slip into her mouth. She played with it on her tongue and in between her teeth as it slowly melted away. The sound of the doorbell made her jump right out of the chair, sending her wine glass flying into the air. She made a grab for it, which only served to increase its momentum, wine covering her, the sofa and the floor. The glass shattered into a million pieces as it hit the painted floorboards. He was early.

She thumped down the hallway and the stairs, pulling open the door to find Mike standing on the doormat, his hair, face and shoulders peppered with snow. She realized, as she looked at him, that it was the first time in months that she had opened her front door without checking who it was. 'Come in,' she said, stepping back. 'I didn't realize it was snowing.'

'It's been chucking it down since we spoke earlier,' he said, taking off his coat as she shut the door.

'Here,' she said, reaching out and taking his dripping jacket. She hung it up and turned. 'Come on up,' she said, walking up the stairs, conscious of him behind her. She went towards the lounge but then remembered the glass, turned on her heel and bumped straight into him.

'Sorry,' he said, backing up against the wall.

'I dropped a glass – let's go into the kitchen,' she said, without looking at him. She was sure he would be able to smell the wine. She pulled out a chair at the kitchen table and gestured for him to take a seat. 'Can I get you a coffee, tea?'

'Coffee would be great,' he said.

'How do you take it?'

'Industrial strength, no sugar,' he said, smiling.

The smile seemed to crack his face. Now he was under the harsh spotlights he looked knackered: grey, his expression strained. She filled the kettle at the sink and took two mugs and the coffee from the cupboard. She still didn't look at him as she spooned in the coffee and stirred in some milk.

He took some papers from the inside pocket of his jacket and spread them out on the table. 'I've got all the information with me,' he said. 'There are a number of options open to you.'

'OK,' she said, feeling incapable of saying anything else. She wanted him here, she wanted to talk, but now he was here she felt unsure.

'Do you mind if I take my jacket off?' he asked.

Was he hot? She was freezing. 'Go ahead.' The kettle boiled and she filled both mugs.

As she walked towards him with their coffees she debated whether to sit in the chair next to him or opposite. Still undecided, she placed his mug on the table and retreated behind the work surface. Before she could speak his phone began to ring.

'Sorry,' he said, 'I won't be a second.' He stood and walked out into the hallway, his phone already in his hand.

She sipped her coffee and pretended to look out of the window when really she was straining to hear what he was saying. He was muttering, his sentences short and sharp. 'Of course not,' he said, turning to look at her. He walked further down the hallway until she couldn't see him, obviously keen to keep his conversation private. She opened the fridge and looked at some limp-looking lettuce, a packet of wholemeal pitta breads, a tub of tzatziki and half a pint of milk. Toni had offered to take her to the shops and had even dropped round a food parcel earlier in the week but it was all gone. She couldn't bring herself to go to the supermarket. Too many people. She shut the fridge with a bang.

'Sorry about that,' he said.

'Is everything all right . . .?' she asked. His eyes widened and his mouth opened but he didn't speak. 'Never mind. You said I had options,' she said, watching as his face settled.

'Do you want to sit down?' he asked, pointing to the chair next to him.

'I have some paperwork relating to restraining orders and injunctions for you,' he said, handing her a few sheets of paper.

Her breath caught in her throat. At the top of the page, printed in capital letters, was a name. 'Malvern Turner,' she said, looking over at Mike.

'Yes . . . do you recognize the name?' he asked.

Sarah shook her head. 'No . . . I don't . . . who is he? How does he know me?' The name was bouncing around her brain like a dodgem car.

'According to the suspect, you met last year at an advertising firm in Camden. CBS Outdoor.'

She stared at her hands, trying to remember. 'CBS . . . I had a job there in July last year, maybe June.' Questions flooded her mouth. 'Does he work there? Did I photograph him? I don't remember him . . .'

'It's all right, Sarah,' he said, pulling the paperwork away from her. 'He was painting some of the offices . . . he says. There's no reason you should remember him.'

She shook her head again. It was impossible to believe that something so insignificant, a job she barely remembered, could have led to all of this. She searched her memories for something, anything, but nothing came to her. All she had was a faceless name to go with her fear. 'Please carry on,' she said, hearing the defeated tone in her voice.

'OK,' he said, folding his arms and leaning back in his chair. The pine creaked. His shirt had come untucked on one side. She caught a glimpse of his stomach. 'Let's talk through your options,' he said, resting his arm on the table, covering the papers.

'I know what my options are,' she said, rubbing her eyes, trying to erase the ache building up behind them. 'I just need someone I trust to tell me what I should do.' A flush of embarrassment heated her neck. She was saying she trusted him. And she did. She braved another glance in his direction. He seemed as struck by her words as she felt.

'Absolutely,' he said, nodding.

When he didn't elaborate, Sarah stood, pushed her shoulders back, walked over to her desk, picked up a pad and pen and returned to her seat. 'OK,' she said, sitting down, 'I'm ready.' She wasn't going to let a name unglue her. Nothing had changed.

For the next thirty minutes Sarah listened and took notes. No one could accuse Mike of skipping the details. He showed her the forms she needed, where to get others, how to fill them in and when she needed to send them. As he spoke she found herself staring at his mouth. She was nodding, trying to concentrate on his words, but she was immediately drawn back to his lips. When she had first met him she had thought his features almost cartoonish in their extreme. But now, looking at him, she could see that, in fact, his face had perfect symmetry. His eyes were set quite wide apart, his nose refined and centred. His cheek muscles seemed to flex with each syllable when he spoke. It was only when he began talking about court appearances that Sarah really tuned in to what he was saying, rather than how he looked when he was saying it.

'I have to go to court?' she asked, her voice heavy with the panic that had just struck her, off guard.

He held out his hands. 'It's OK, Sarah. You don't have to. The judge will examine the petition beforehand. Even if you decided you did want to attend, the defendant would be behind a Perspex screen. You'd be quite safe.'

She was puzzled by his phrasing: quite safe. Of course, she knew what he meant, but why didn't he say 'very safe' or 'totally safe'? That would have sounded better, felt more re-assuring. She pushed her coffee cup away. 'I'm going to have a glass of wine. Do you want one?' she said, already walking away.

'Actually, I could go for a dash of that, if you don't mind?' he said, pointing to a half-empty bottle of Jack Daniel's on her kitchen counter. The familiarity of his tone made her smile.

'I'll join you.' She took two glasses down from the cupboard and poured them both a small measure. As she handed him his glass their fingers touched for a second. Her eyes drifted to the clock over the cooker. It was half-past seven. They had been talking for over an hour and she was knackered. 'I'm so sorry, I've kept you so long.'

He shrugged. 'It's no problem. I'm heading straight home after this . . . hence the beverage,' he said lifting his glass. 'Going back to the office smelling of whiskey is frowned upon.' Despite his smile, Sarah could see just how tired he was.

A thought entered her head; she debated for a second but then asked, 'Well, if you're not going back to the office, do you want something to eat? It's the least I can do.' As soon as the words were out of her mouth she felt her cheeks heating. 'Don't worry if you have to go,' she said, giving him the out so she wouldn't be further embarrassed when he made an excuse.

'Well, now that you mention it, I am starving, and this . . .' he said, gesturing to his half-finished drink, 'goes down better with something to line the stomach.' His smile was fuller now, more real.

'I guess drunk driving is worse for you guys,' she said, returning his smile. 'I was actually thinking you look like you need a drink more than I do.'

He chinked her glass with his and said, 'Maybe, maybe not.' She watched him take an appreciative sip.

They both fell silent but it didn't feel uncomfortable. In fact it felt nice; having a detective inspector in her kitchen gave her a sense of safety. She stared out of the window sipping her drink. The snow had eased off but it would still be hellish for driving. The traffic would be a nightmare. He should probably wait an hour for it to stop before he set off home. Her mind strayed to thoughts of him staying much longer than an hour. She turned and began rummaging around in the fridge. What was she thinking? He wasn't staying. He was going. As she looked at the pathetic snack selection in her hands she realized she never usually ate on dates. But then this wasn't a date. As if her body was listening, her stomach growled in anticipation.

'Have you eaten at all today?' he asked.

She didn't need to look at him to know he was mocking her. His tone sounded relaxed, intimate. Her stomach rumbled again, increasing her embarrassment. 'Yes, maybe, no.' She turned her back and busied herself with the toaster but a smile was playing on her lips.

The silence between them now was anything but comfortable.

'Hey, it's OK. I live the life of a bachelor. I never have anything in my fridge either.'

As she turned she saw his cheeks flush for a fraction of a second. His grey complexion had vanished, he looked revived. She brought over two plates, the pittas, dip and carrot sticks piled on top.

'Dig in,' she said. And he did, hungrily plunging into the tzatziki.

A deafening thud made Sarah stand, dropping the food that was midway to her mouth onto the floor.

'What the hell was that?' he asked, putting down his pitta, brushing off his hands and heading down the hallway.

Sarah couldn't follow. She stood rigid, her heart beating so fast it made her dizzy. All she could do was listen and wait. She heard and saw Mike run down the stairs, heard the door open and felt the rush of cold air coming up the stairs. She waited, numb with fear.

What felt like hours later she heard her name.

'Sarah?'

She heard his voice but couldn't move, couldn't focus.

He walked back into the kitchen, his expression filled with concern. 'Sarah, are you all right?'

She couldn't speak.

He seemed to hesitate but then approached her, putting his hands on her upper arms, bending to look into her face.

'Sarah, it's OK. Two people had a shunt outside. Everyone's fine. Everything's fine. They're exchanging insurance details now. It was just a bump, no real damage done.' His hands felt firm on her arms. If he let her go, she thought she would slither to the floor like a discarded rag. She leaned into his body and closed her eyes. He whispered her name as his fingers tangled in her hair. He was telling her that everything was going to be all right. Sarah let his words seep into her bones. 'You're all right,' he said.

'I thought . . .' She stopped, unable to go on. A tremor seemed to take hold of her spine, her hands shaking.

'I know,' he said, 'I know.' He pulled her into his arms.

As he held her, she listened to his voice and let the tears come. She cried from the shock, from the fear, from the exhaustion, from everything. He fell silent but continued to hold her, stroking her back gently. Sarah finally pulled herself away, pushing her hair off her face. She dragged it up into a ponytail, walked unsteadily to the table and sat down. 'I'm sorry,' she said.

He sat and took her hands in his. 'It's all right. You've had a shock. Given what you've been through it's no wonder. Just take some deep breaths. I'll get you a drink.'

Sarah rocked back and forth on the chair and stared down at her hands as she calmed her breathing. When he returned with her drink she sat back, took a large breath in through her nose and blew it out through her lips. She did it again, took the drink and looked up. 'Thank you,' she sighed. 'I'm OK. Sorry, it was just a shock, that's all.'

'Really, stop apologizing. It's fine.'

Sarah looked at his face. He didn't look fine; he looked

uncomfortable, but then what guy wouldn't be when faced with a crying woman?

'I should go, let you rest,' he said, standing to leave.

'Please,' she said, before she could stop herself. 'Can you just stay for a minute? Just until I get myself sorted?'

He seemed to think for a second, but then said, 'Yes, of course. Take your time.'

Sarah clutched her glass to her chest, taking small sips, her hands still shaking. The whiskey warmed her throat, relaxing her aching muscles. Mike sat quietly in front of her. When she looked up she saw something different in his expression. They stared at each other, neither looking away, neither speaking. She could hear the seconds ticking by on the kitchen clock. In the small gap between them Sarah could almost see a shimmering haze, as if heat was radiating off her body or his or both. His eyes were dark, his pupils large black circles.

Without speaking, he reached up and touched her face. The warmth of his skin sent an unfamiliar shiver over her whole body. He held her gaze. She leaned towards him. He responded by brushing her lips with his. The kiss was gentle, caressing. He kissed her again, firmer this time. As Sarah closed her eyes she felt the tip of his tongue on her lips, a moan escaping her mouth as he pulled her to him. Without thinking she wrapped her arms around his neck, her fingers burrowing into his hair. It felt coarse, his scalp hot to the touch.

He stood, lifting her easily into his arms, his lips never leaving hers. She pulled him closer. She could hear his breaths coming in quick gasps as he grappled with her shirt. A button broke away from the fabric and skittered across the kitchen floor. He pulled back and looked at her. There was a moment, Sarah could see it. He seemed to be wrestling with his own indecision but it only lasted for a few seconds and then he was back in her arms.

36

7 February – Friday

Lockyer pushed his front door closed and walked down the hallway, turning on lights as he went. It was still early: 7.15 on his kitchen clock. He flicked the switch on the kettle and looked out of the window at his snow-covered garden. An image flashed into his mind of Sarah, lying naked on her bed, reaching out to him. His body reacted to the memory. He pulled out a kitchen chair, sat down and put his head in his hands. 'What are you playing at? Are you trying to get fired?'

As the kettle boiled he stood up and made himself a cup of tea and walked through to his bedroom, taking small gulps as he went. If Roger hadn't called and cancelled their meeting last night, Lockyer would have left Sarah's house hours earlier. 'Christ,' he said, slapping his forehead. Was he really trying to blame his boss? No one had made him do anything. He had chosen to exclude Jane, his team and Roger. The sound of his doorbell saved him from any more mental remonstrations.

He pushed himself up off the bed and walked out of the room and down the hallway, trying to decipher his visitor by the shadowed form beyond the opaque glass. He couldn't. He turned the latch and pulled open the door, immediately wishing he had been in the shower, or asleep, or anywhere but right here, standing at his front door facing his SIO. Roger didn't even bother to greet him. Instead he pushed past and walked down the hallway and into the lounge.

Lockyer followed and closed the door behind him. He didn't need any nosy neighbours hearing the dressing-down he was about to get. This wasn't the first time he had been on the receiving end of Roger's fury. His SIO could never be described as quiet.

'Can I get you something to drink, boss?' he asked, deciding it was probably best to keep it formal.

'No, thank you. This won't take long,' Roger said, not even bothering to look at him.

'OK,' he said, debating whether he should sit or remain standing like Roger. He decided at this point it made little difference, so lowered himself into an armchair. Sunshine streamed through his floor-to-ceiling Georgian windows, forcing him to shield his eyes as he mentally braced himself for what was to come.

'I assume we can skip the preamble about why I'm here?' Roger said.

'Yes, sir. I . . .' Before he had the chance to finish or even start his apology, Roger was shaking his head and pacing back and forth, periodically blocking the sun's path into Lockyer's face.

'Let's not bullshit each other, Mike, OK? You are no doubt going to tell me that I've nothing to be concerned about . . . that you filed all the necessary paperwork and dealt with the evidence in an expedient manner. And of course, that you didn't tell me because it's your case and you're running it, so you decided to take it upon yourself to get the item of jewellery checked out and verified before you bothered someone in my position with it. Am I close?'

He ran a hand through his hair and sighed. 'Yes, boss. Sounds about right.'

'Good. So now we've skipped the shit, you can tell me what the hell you think you're playing at?' Roger's face was puce, his hands balled so tightly into fists that his knuckles were white.

Both men faced each other in the silence until Lockyer finally gave in, sat back in his chair and said, 'You'd better take a seat, Roger.' His boss obliged by sitting on the very edge of Lockyer's new sofa, rearranging his suit trousers as he did so. 'I found the item of jewellery in an assisted living facility, just outside Lewisham. It's called Cliffview and . . .' He stopped when Roger held up his hand.

'Spare me. We're way past you giving me a normal rundown . . . I've read your report,' Roger said, putting both hands flat against his thighs. It looked like he was struggling to hold his temper. 'What I want to know, Mike . . . what I need to know is why I had to find out about this from some exhibits clerk?'

Lockyer didn't know what to say. The excuses he had been flooding his mind with for the past twenty-four hours were pathetic. He shook his head and stared down at his feet.

'Is all of this . . .' Roger waved a hand in the air, his eyebrows high on his forehead, 'this nonsense because of your brother?' he asked, incredulity in his voice.

'I guess so,' he said, ashamed of the weakness in his voice.

Roger stood up and started pacing the living room again but before he could speak Lockyer decided to get it over with. 'Look, Roger, I've only known him . . . my brother, for the past five years. My parents sent him to live with an aunt when I was four. I only found out he existed when my father died. Bobby's autistic. I moved him down here, to Cliffview. It's a nice place. He gets to live a relatively independent life.' He paused, unsure how to continue. 'I guess I panicked,' he said. 'I found the earring, realized it had belonged to Debbie . . . one of the victims . . . and I panicked. The last thing I wanted was SOCO swarming all over Cliffview, not to mention my brother being treated as a suspect, which he'd have to be. I just couldn't handle the idea of that, sir.' He finished speaking and braved a look in Roger's direction. His boss's face was no longer puce so he decided to keep going. 'The killer planted that earring, boss, for me to find. My face has been all over the papers for weeks and Phil said the suspect would be following the media coverage. This guy has obviously decided to fixate on me. He's playing games with me, trying to implicate my brother. It was him. I know it.'

Roger took a deep breath, stopped pacing and put both of his hands in the air. 'You seem to have forgotten, Mike, that I have been on the force for thirty-seven years. I am not braindead and I know a plant when I see one,' he said, closing his eyes, the frustration evident on his face. 'The point is . . . you should have informed me. Instead, I hear about it from some exhibits clerk. It didn't take Jane long to find out the rest.' Roger was clenching his jaw. He looked like he was going to burst. 'If you're right, which I don't doubt . . . and Lewisham's very first serial killer was in your brother's room, then wouldn't it seem important that SOCO dusted the house for prints immediately?'

He realized shutting the door to the lounge had been a moot effort. There was no way his neighbours or in fact anyone on his street could have failed to hear Roger's last sentence. 'Boss, I have never and would never do anything to jeopardize a case.' An image of Sarah flashed into his mind. 'I know I screwed up, Roger, and I'm sorry. SOCO are at the house now. I was literally just changing before heading there myself.' He could see Roger's colour returning to some semblance of normal but he wasn't out of the woods yet. 'I guess what I'm saying is, I needed some time.'

'Not a good enough excuse, Mike,' Roger said, shaking his head and opening the door to the lounge. 'Now, I have to go. I have a meeting with the chief in an hour. I have to find a way of spinning this so you don't end up unemployed and I'm not left high and dry without one of my best detectives.'

They walked to the front door in silence. Lockyer pulled it open and shook Roger's hand. 'Thank you, Roger. And for what it's worth, I really am sorry.'

'This isn't the first time I've saved your arse, Mike, but do me a personal favour and make it the last, OK?' Roger said, stepping out into the cold, the snow still covering the pavement. 'You will have to brief your team. I don't care how you handle it but I don't want to hear about this again. And . . .' He looked at Lockyer. 'Your brother is going to have to provide fingerprints and a DNA sample.'

He could feel his anger bubbling up but swallowed it down. 'I know. I'll sort it the second I get over there.'

'Fine.' Roger turned and walked away.

Half an hour later Lockyer was standing on Cliffview's driveway looking at the front garden. It was buried under several deep flurries of snow.

The SOCO guys were already on site, combing through the house and gardens looking for any evidence left by Debbie's killer. Was the planted earring meant to freak him out, implicate his brother or just mess with the investigation? He walked up to the front door, stepping onto the plastic sheeting the SOCO team had put down. He stared into the hallway, at the white-suited bodies buzzing around, filling his brother's home with alien sounds and smells. It wasn't right. He had spent years keeping his job away from Cliffview, away from the people living and working here. They didn't deserve to be embroiled in the crap he dealt with every day. This was his fault. He had brought the killer here. He let out a frustrated sigh and rubbed his temples before reaching into his pocket for some more painkillers.

As he crossed the hallway to the back stairs leading up to his brother's room, he thought about Sarah, the way she looked at him. He couldn't stop seeing it, thinking about it. She had needed him and, more importantly, she had wanted him. Sarah had reawakened a sensitivity he didn't know he still possessed. But she was a victim. As much as she hated to hear the word and he hated using it, she was. Had he taken advantage? Under the circumstances it would be understandable if she had just wanted someone to comfort her, someone to share her burden. He hoped that wasn't how she felt.

'Sir?'

He turned at the top of the stairs to see Jane walking up towards him. When she was standing beside him she finally looked up, meeting his eyes.

'Why didn't you tell me, sir?' she asked.

He realized there was more than anger in her expression. She was upset. Disappointed. He would have done anything at that moment for a time machine or a hole in the ground, anything to get him out of this. This was worse than facing Roger. She stared at him without blinking.

'How did you find out?'

'You weren't in the office yesterday afternoon, so exhibits called, spoke to Roger and he told them to send the full DNA report to me, sir. It didn't take much to get a list of residents,' she said, a trace of her own guilt visible in her eyes. 'I had to tell him.'

He debated his answer before holding up his hands and saying, 'I'm sorry.' He found himself staring at his hands like a naughty schoolboy. He had never apologized so much in one day.

Jane dropped her head and sighed. 'You don't have to apologize to me, sir. I . . . I just don't understand why you couldn't tell *me*, considering what you know about me and Peter.'

It was then that it struck him. Jane wasn't upset with him for withholding the evidence. She was upset about Bobby, questioning why Lockyer hadn't trusted her when she had trusted him. He had almost told her so many times, when they were alone in the car, or cooling their heels at a crime scene. 'I honestly don't know, Jane,' was all he said.

She seemed to compose herself at that, standing up straighter, snapping on a pair of gloves. 'It doesn't matter, I guess I just thought that we'd . . . never mind. Where have we got to, sir?'

'Jane, there's no way my brother is involved, it's ludicrous and a total waste of time. SOCO have been here since 07.00 . . . there are a million prints, of course, so we'll need to print the residents to eliminate them, but hopefully we'll find our suspect in the process.' He made it sound so straightforward, as if none of this was a bother, just a minor inconvenience. 'I've got to help one of the nurses print my brother now and take a sample for DNA.' He closed his eyes. He felt ashamed. How could he do this to his own brother? Bobby would never and could never understand all this. A circus had invaded his sanctuary and there was nothing Lockyer could do to stop it. 'Have you told the team?' he asked as he started to walk down the corridor.

'No, sir. I figured you'd tell everyone in today's briefing,' she said from behind him. 'Where do you want me?'

He turned and looked at her. He should thank God that he had her, that she was so loyal. 'Can you help the SOCOs get fingerprints from the rest of the residents and staff and then start the questioning?' He still couldn't believe he was here, doing this. 'I'll be along in a minute . . . after I've sorted this,' he said, pointing to his brother's door. Alice was already inside, waiting for him. His heart felt like it might explode out of his chest as he pulled back the emotion that wanted to come.

'You'll do fine, sir,' she said, touching his arm. 'I'll speak to SOCO. We'll get everyone out of here as soon as possible.'

'Thank you, Jane.' He watched her walk away before turning back to his brother's door and knocking three times.

'Come in,' Alice called.

As he pushed open the door he thought he was going to be sick. Fingerprint dust seemed to cover every surface; the air was thick with it. Why hadn't they cleaned up after themselves? He could feel his blood heating, but then he saw his brother. Bobby was standing by the window, looking out at the garden. There was no sign that the invading guests were distressing him. He was fine, untroubled. Although for how long Lockyer wasn't sure. The fingerprints, they would be tricky, but it was the cotton swab in Bobby's mouth that was going to be the real test. In a way it made him feel worse. The SOCOs weren't bothering Bobby. The dozens of police officers combing through his precious garden wasn't disturbing him, but what Lockyer was about to do would. The lengths to which he had gone to protect his brother; had they all been in vain?

'Come on,' Alice said, giving his arm a gentle nudge. 'We'll get it done quickly and quietly . . . he'll be fine, Mike,' she said. 'Trust me.' He took comfort from her smiling face and stood back as she approached Bobby at the window. 'Bobby, Mike's here . . . we're going to play a game together.' She took his brother's hand and led him over to his favourite chair. 'There you are, you sit here . . . Michael, you sit over there.'

He sat down opposite his brother, leaned forward and picked up the cards. Alice had already spoken to him and run through how they would do it. Fingerprints first, then the cheek swab. The on-site test kit lay open on the table, the paper for the prints next to it. 'Let's play,' he said, dealing out the cards. He watched Bobby's eyes dart back and forth, following his every move.

'Now, my man,' Alice said, bending down next to Bobby's chair and taking his hand. 'First things first. You put your thumb here,' she said, placing his thumb on the ink pad, rolling it back and forth. 'Good, now we put it here.' She lifted Bobby's hand but let him hold its weight, hovering over the paper. 'Now, we put our thumb here,' she said, putting her hand over his. She rolled his thumb again, leaving the ridges and swirls of his brother's thumb on the page. 'Good . . . now take a card.' Bobby seemed to pause but then he reached forward and picked up several cards at once, turning them to show Lockyer.

'Oh, that's good,' he said, nodding his head, trying to catch Bobby's eye. 'Really good. A two, a four and a nine. That's a good score.' He watched as his brother sat back in his chair and held out his hand to Alice. It looked almost like Bobby understood, as if the game was for their benefit more than his.

Alice took Bobby's hand and started the process again, repeating it with each finger before starting on the other hand. He watched, overwhelmed by her patience, the gentle tone of her voice. His part was simple. All he really did was hand out the cards, add up Bobby's scores. He felt like a cheerleader, standing on the sidelines. Even when Alice began to wipe away the ink Bobby didn't flinch. She had to rub hard to get the stain off but his brother just sat in his chair and let her. Lockyer realized there was more than simple cheeriness to Alice. She really cared for the people who lived here.

'Now for the interesting bit,' she said, pulling Lockyer from his thoughts. 'I'm going to need you over here for this.' She pointed to the back of Bobby's chair. He pushed himself out of his seat and walked around so he was standing behind his brother. He could feel his heart starting to beat harder in his chest. He tried to take deep breaths. Bobby needed him to be calm. 'OK, Bobster . . . we're going to try a new game,' Alice said, reaching for the swab kit.

'Cards,' Bobby said, reaching for the cards still on the table. Alice beat him to it and pushed them just out of his reach.

'We'll play cards again in a minute but I want to see if you can help me with something first,' she said, touching Bobby's arm. 'Michael, can you get us a book, please?' Lockyer felt lost. He didn't want to do this. The fingerprints had been OK because of Alice. This wasn't going to be the same. He didn't want to be a part of it. 'Mike, how about that one there? It's a new book on boats. Bobby got it in Greenwich, didn't you?'

'Boats,' Bobby said, tapping his feet. Lockyer knew what that meant. It meant he was excited. He thought something good was about to happen.

Lockyer looked on the shelf next to him until he spotted a book on the *Cutty Sark*. He pulled it out, leaned forward and opened it on Bobby's lap. His brother's foot-tapping increased as he looked down at the pictures, his fingers tracing the masts, the sails.

'What we're going to do, Bobby,' Alice said, taking out the first swab, 'is you are going to turn the pages until you find your favourite picture and then you can show me and Mike and then . . .' Her sentence was cut short when Bobby started to flick the pages. He rushed to the end of the book and then back to the beginning. Alice gave Lockyer a nod and then leaned towards Bobby. 'Now you show us your favourite and while you do, I'm just going to put this little brush in your mouth . . . it's just like brushing our teeth,' she said, the swab only an inch from Bobby's lips. 'That's good, we love boats, don't we, Mike?' She looked up at him and whispered. 'Talk, keep talking.'

Her words seemed to drift over Bobby's head in slow motion. He couldn't make himself speak. He cleared his throat and reached across so he could help turn the pages. 'What about this one?' he said, pointing to a picture that showed the inside of the *Cutty Sark*. As Alice pushed the swab into Bobby's mouth, Lockyer realized he was holding his breath. And then it happened. His brother's head snapped backwards, until it was pressed into the chair. He was looking up at Lockyer but his eyes had rolled back in his head.

'OK, Bobby, OK,' Alice said, putting both her hands on Bobby's arms. 'Calm down . . . come on, it's all right, nothing to be frightened of . . .'

And then there was the noise. The grinding, keening sound coming from his brother's lips. Lockyer wanted to close his eyes, put his fingers in his ears. He wanted to be anywhere but here. He watched and listened, impotent as Alice tried to calm Bobby down. Her words were constant. She pushed Lockyer over to the window. 'Just stand over here for a second,' she said, her voice hushed but urgent. 'He just needs a bit of space . . . he'll be fine in a minute, he'll be fine.'

She left him there and went back to Bobby. Lockyer couldn't bear to look. His brother was thrashing about in his favourite chair like a stranded fish. The grinding noise was unbearable. He couldn't stand it. Without knowing he was going to do it, he bolted for the door and didn't stop until he was downstairs and out in the back garden. But he could still hear Bobby's cries.

Lockyer was still standing in the back garden when Alice found him.

'Are you OK?' she asked, resting her hand on his arm.

'I'm fine. Sorry . . . I had to leave . . . I couldn't.' He felt like he was in shock.

'Don't worry about it,' she said, patting his arm. 'Trust me; it's always harder on the relatives than them. Bobby's fine, we got it done in the end. He's back at his window.' She pointed behind them. He turned and followed her finger. She was right. Bobby was standing by his window, where he always stood, looking out. None of the past hour's trauma was evident on his face. He looked the same way he always did. How could something so terrible be erased from his mind so quickly? 'I know,' Alice said, as if reading his thoughts. 'His power of recovery is astonishing.' She handed him the fingerprint and swab kit. 'There you are.'

'I can't believe he's the same guy,' he said, still staring up at his brother's window.

'That's just the way things go sometimes. It could have been anything or nothing . . . something spooks him and he can't handle it. He won't remember this, I swear . . . I mean, I won't be trying to clean his ears with cotton buds for a

266

while,' she said, laughing, 'but honestly, he's absolutely fine and dandy. You can go up and see him if you like?'

'No, no I won't. I'll let him rest, get his breath back,' he said, feeling like a coward.

'OK, no worries. I'll keep an eye on him today and you can call later, maybe, to check in?'

'I will,' he said, tearing his eyes away from the window.

As Alice turned to leave he remembered himself. 'Sorry, Alice, have you got time to talk for a minute? I need to ask you some questions relating to the break-in.'

'Sure thing,' she said, her face untroubled.

Was he the only one hanging on by an emotional thread? 'Let's talk in the lounge,' he said.

37

7 February – Friday

He arched his back, stretching out his spine. He had been watching her in the window for the past hour, an idea forming. If he closed his eyes he could see her laid out, as if crucified, like Hayley. Perhaps it had been the grandeur of the park or the untouched beauty of the snow but something had made him go back. When he had found Hayley again, lying naked and alone, it hadn't felt right. But when she was properly laid out, everything seemed to slot into place.

Despite his excitement the distraction of the past few days kept invading his thoughts. The detective had found the earring. Forensic teams had been all over the brother's house, collecting evidence. His initial intention had been to have a little fun with DI Lockyer, but then the fat woman had walked the tall detective around to the side of the house and pointed up to the bushes growing there. He knew the brother's house had security cameras. Of course he did, but he hadn't known about the one hidden above the side gate. He slammed his fist down hard on the dashboard. The lens was almost covered by an ever-expanding rhododendron. Surely it wouldn't have caught anything. He tore his eyes away from the face in the window and tried to think back to that day, walking it through in his head, to see if he could recall looking up, exposing his face. His path down the alley had been swift: ten, fifteen seconds at the most. The camera may have caught a glimpse of him as he vaulted the back fence but again it was unlikely. The lens seemed tipped in the wrong direction. He never made mistakes.

As he started the engine and pulled away he averted his gaze at the last second. It wouldn't do to unnerve her, not just yet.

When he arrived in the car park twenty minutes later he spotted two of his colleagues, hiding behind the bins, having a fag. The rules and regulations stated that employees had to leave the premises to smoke. They weren't allowed in the car park or any part of the grounds. Why was it people desired to break even the simplest of rules?

'I caught you,' he said.

Both women jumped but then tittered like five-year-olds.

'You bugger,' Evelyn chirruped. 'We thought you were the cops,' she said with a conspiratorial tone.

'Nothing to fear,' he said, his muscles aching as he dragged his facial features into some semblance of a smile. 'Mind you, it's sort of . . . exciting, isn't it?' he said, his eyes darting back and forth.

After a moment of hesitation both women laughed and began pawing him with their fag-smelling fingers, grateful to him for alleviating their fears with humour.

'Oh, you're so bad, you are,' Evelyn said, giving him a wink.

'And you love it,' he said, digging her in the ribs with his finger, repulsed by the layer of fat that engulfed his flesh.

He followed them into the clinic; both still laughing and throwing coy glances over their shoulders at him. Not long now, he thought. His next game would be much more fun. DI Lockyer would love it.

38

10 February – Monday

Lockyer's team was assembling, chairs were moved, laptops plugged in. It was a hive of activity but he felt like he was standing still. He shuffled his notes and looked over at Jane. She nodded as if to confirm her support. For the first time in his career he felt uncertain. Not necessarily about the case, although it did feel like he was travelling in ever-decreasing circles. It was more his attitude, his confidence. He hadn't been the same guy since he had seen Megan's face in that alleyway almost a month ago.

The snow had eased but the sky outside the briefing room's floor-to-ceiling windows was white, the streets unusually empty. The door opened and Phil walked in, a blue plastic folder slung under his arm. 'Morning, all,' he said, taking a seat at the opposite end of the table. There were murmurs of greetings. Lockyer stayed silent. He wasn't thinking about the case. He was thinking about the weekend. He had worked, yes. He had seen Megan for coffee on Saturday morning, yes. But that wasn't all. The majority of his waking and sleeping hours had been spent in Nunhead, in Sarah Grainger's bed.

Things had gone from bad to worse. After one night with her he had been shaken, obsessing over every little thing she said like a teenager. Now, he was four nights in and couldn't see a way out.

The sound of someone clearing their throat dragged his thoughts away from Sarah. He shook his head and walked over to the whiteboard that now resembled a collage of immense proportions. Green lines connected areas on the map. Photographs of the crime scenes and the victims were all linked with red sticky tape.

'Let's get started,' he said, nodding to Jane who was taking notes for this session. He took a deep breath as he put his hands in his pockets. 'As you are all aware the death of Hayley Sawyer puts us at four victims to date. Phil has revised his profile to account for these . . .'

Before he could finish speaking Phil was on his feet, striding up to the head of the table to join him. 'Thank you, Mike. I have indeed refined my earlier model and will be more than happy to convey that to you all now,' he said, taking the folder from under his arm and opening it with a flourish.

Lockyer coughed and held up one finger, 'Phil, can I have a minute?' he said, turning his back to the group. He waited for the team's conversations to reach a volume that would drown out his words. 'Phil,' he whispered. 'We don't have time for the revised profile now, I'm afraid. I need to brief the team on two important matters. You and I can and will discuss it later.'

Phil responded by turning back to face the room and saying in a stage-whisper, 'Well, you will have to hope that

I am free.' He then walked back to his seat, put his folder on the table and crossed his arms.

'OK, everyone, quiet down. We've got a lot to get through,' he said, approaching the table again. 'As I was just saying to Phil, his revised psych profile is now available on the bulletin board. We are all . . . grateful to him for taking the time to amend the profile on such short notice.' Heads nodded around the table and a silence fell over the briefing room. 'The first point on today's agenda concerns the exhibits team. Chris, can you update everyone, please?' he said, taking his seat next to Jane, thankful when all eyes turned away from him. He felt like his thoughts of Sarah were tattooed on his forehead.

Chris stood, walked to the head of the table and pulled down the projector screen where an image of the earring appeared, blown up to the size of a tractor tyre. 'The item you see here is the earring found at the scene of Deborah Stevens' murder. It was removed or fell from the victim's ear; however, when the team searched the area, no other earring was found.' He nodded to the officer who had handed out the exhibits bundle and the image on the screen was replaced by an almost identical picture. 'This item was photographed last week,' Chris said. 'DI Lockyer recovered it from an assisted living facility, outside Lewisham . . .' he paused, consulting his notes; the young officer looked nervous. 'Cliffview, page four of your notes.' He pointed to the screen. 'Skin cells were found in the butterfly section of the earring, here. DNA testing has confirmed that the item had been worn by Deborah Stevens.'

He tried to ignore the stares as several members of his

team looked in his direction. He indicated for Chris to continue. He wanted to get this over with, as quickly as humanly possible.

Chris seemed unsure how to continue as he said, 'Cliffview is a private facility. It houses people with varying conditions, such as dementia and autism.' He looked at Lockyer, seemingly out of words.

Lockyer took a deep breath. 'Right, let's get this over with, shall we,' he said, standing, placing both his hands flat on the table, the heat from his skin leaving traces where his fingers rested against the glass. All eyes were on him. 'I found the earring in the bedroom of one of the residents. It was lying on a pile of books, in plain view. The resident is my brother, Robert Lockyer.' Muttered conversation spread throughout the room. Their words, their doubts seemed to bounce off the glass, attacking his composure. 'Of course, you already know all of this. Nothing works faster than the bloody jungle drums in this place.' Several heads dropped so he knew who had been talking, but he could hardly blame them. He cleared his throat to make sure he had the team's full attention. 'The resident has been fingerprinted and DNA has been taken. An alibi has been given, checked and verified. Neither the DNA or the fingerprints are a match for the trace evidence found at the murder scene of Deborah Stevens.' He waited and watched this new information drip-feed around the room. 'There is no reason to believe that the resident in question has anything whatsoever to do with this murder or any of the others. Do I make myself clear?' he asked, looking from one officer to the next. A few of the on-loan officers didn't meet his eyes but the majority of the team looked back at him, their faces open, their feelings clear. At least some people still trusted him.

Trust. As soon as the word entered his mind an image of Sarah crammed in beside it. She trusted him. She had said as much. Bobby was no one's business but delaying the investigation was. What he was doing with Sarah was their business too. It was Jane's business. Conflict of interest didn't even come close to what he was doing.

'So, what we need to find out is . . .' he said, feeling his composure return, 'the identity of the man who put the earring in the resident's room. When and why?' There were more nods of agreement from his team. Jane in particular was nodding enthusiastically, already on board, back at his side. 'We're assuming the "when" was last week, Tuesday. The residents were out on a day trip so the facility would have been empty. The "why" isn't our main concern at this stage. As we know, it isn't uncommon for suspects in this kind of investigation to take an interest in police, media, anyone closely connected to the case. I have spoken to Phil on this . . .' He gestured to Phil and was relieved to see he wasn't going to fight him or attempt to heckle his way into the briefing. 'It is possible that the suspect sees me as some kind of opponent and therefore wishes to engage me on a more personal level.' Officers turned and looked at each other, concern being the dominant expression. 'I would ask you all to take suitable precautions. The case is not to be discussed outside of this office, even with other departments, without direct sign-off by me or Sergeant Bennett.' He didn't know what they looked so worried about. Lewisham's first serial killer hadn't taken a personal interest in them. Hands started to go up around the room; concern had clearly been replaced by mild panic.

'OK, OK, I can see that you all have questions. I would ask you to direct them to Sergeant Bennett . . . after the briefing, please,' he said as the entire room prepared to bombard Jane. He clapped his hands together once, twice, three times until he finally had their attention. 'We've got CCTV footage to go through . . . nothing has been found, as yet. Jane and I have already talked to the staff at the facility. As I said, we're assuming the earring was planted on Tuesday between the hours of 10.00 and 17.00. We already have a list of individuals who knew the house would be empty.' He thought back to his conversation with Alice. Her new boyfriend had known about the trip. She had even invited him to come along, but he had declined and she hadn't heard from him since. Lockyer had run a check on the mobile phone number Alice had for the guy but it was disconnected, a pay-as-you-go, no way to trace the owner. Another dead end or maybe just a false start?

'Are there any questions?' he asked. Chairs moved and papers were shuffled but nobody spoke. 'Good. Then let's move on. The second item on today's schedule involves the entire team. We're still waiting on Sawyer's medical records, to confirm if she had a termination, so we will have to hang fire on that for now. The hospitals where Phoebe, Katy and Debbie had their procedures have confirmed that records are confidential and aren't on a centralized database. Given this new information, it's unlikely that the suspect selected his victims by way of their medical records.' As soon as he said 'selected' he felt a twinge in his stomach. According to Phil's profile they had four days, max, before this guy struck again, before another girl was wrenched from her family. Why did everything take so bloody long? Debbie's killer was taking risks, branching out not only geographically, with Hayley, but going out of his remit completely, with the earring and Bobby. How was he able to stay hidden?

'Sorry,' he said, realizing he was staring out of the window, worry and frustration creasing his brow. 'If he isn't finding them through records, then we have to assume he's seen these girls face to face. The hospital administrator advised that women often attend their local surgery or clinic beforehand for initial testing, follow-up appointments and counselling before and after the procedure. We know Debbie attended the Lewisham Young Women's Centre but they have no record of any of the other victims. Penny and Chris have been over there to show the staff pictures of Katy and Phoebe . . . no joy, as yet. We haven't had the go ahead to release Hayley's name to the press, so we will have to wait on that. In the meantime we need to spread our net.' He took a deep breath. 'The anonymity offered by these types of clinics doesn't help us, I'm afraid. We're left with no option but . . . door to door.' He heard rumbles of discontent. It was going to be a laborious couple of days and the team knew it. Wait until they saw the size of the list. 'We have a list here,' he said, holding up a folder-sized bundle of A4 paper, 'of all the local clinics, surgeries and support groups operating in south-east London and south-west London.' There were more murmurs and groans of protest from the room. 'We will be visiting every single facility on this list with details and photographs of each victim, excluding Hayley.' A hand shot up at the back of the room. It was Chris.

'Yes, Chris,' he said, hoping his voice didn't sound too indulgent.

'Sorry, sir. If we're thinking the suspect had face-to-face contact with the victims then we're assuming he, what . . . works at one of these places?'

'Yes, Chris, that's exactly what we're hoping, but bear in mind a lot of people go through these places . . . doctors, nurses, office staff, cleaning staff, delivery men . . . the list goes on. There are a lot of options but if we turn up a hit we'll be narrowing the field considerably.' Until then they were still looking for a gnat in a swimming pool. We just need one break, he thought. Chris still had his hand in the air. 'Yes, Chris.'

'But . . . the third victim, Deborah Stevens, we know what clinic she went to,' Chris said, looking acutely uncomfortable to have the floor.

'As I've said, we've checked the LYWC already. What we're hoping is that Debbie visited more than one clinic. It would make sense, given that Lewisham isn't her closest facility by a long way, so there may be a reason she changed and went further afield. We'll focus on the clinics in SW15 and SW18 first, as all the girls were resident in or close to these boroughs.' Lockyer took a deep breath. He hoped this wasn't a colossal waste of time but what other choice did he have? The only link between the girls was their abortions. The only way their killer would know all four of them had abortions was their records, and if not records, then it had to be face to face. It just had to be. 'Right, is everyone with me?' he said, relieved to see a room of nodding heads. 'Good. That's all for this morning's briefing. Thank you and good luck,' he said, giving the list to Jane. 'Jane will have details of your locations in ten minutes. Be ready to leave in twenty.'

The room emptied quickly as his team shuffled out and over to their desks or make-shift spaces to grab their phones, their coats and their car keys. Today was going to be a long day for everyone but, Lockyer hoped, by the end of it he would be one step closer to finding a killer.

Lockyer looked down at the mobile on his desk. He had three missed calls. They were all from Sarah.

He walked out of his office and over to the lift, his head down as if studying a message he had received. Jane looked up as he passed but he didn't meet her eyes. He couldn't. The guilt was hideous. Jane was Sarah's official case handler but she hadn't been there. There had been no one else. He had spoken to her, explained her options. What he did after that was nobody else's concern.

'Yeah, right,' he muttered.

The doors opened and he walked in, keeping his eyes lowered. It was almost eleven so half the station would be heading over the road for a bacon sandwich, cup of tea and a fix of Sky Sports. He listened to their banter until the lift finally reached the ground floor. He was so relieved to get out that he practically jogged across the foyer and into the car park. He clicked the remote central locking on his key, the Audi's indicator lights flashing twice as he climbed in and turned on the engine. All the windows were fogged. He sat back and rested his head, closing his eyes and savouring the moment of peace.

As he dialled Sarah's number he cranked the heaters up

but kept the blowers on his legs so he could enjoy the privacy of his fogged windows for a moment longer.

'Hello,' she said, her voice quiet, tentative.

'Hi, it's Mike,' he said.

'I know,' she said. He could hear the smile in her voice. 'How are you?' she asked, her tone more serious.

He tried to think of a clever or witty answer so he could make light of the situation, but his mind was empty. Humour was a tool in the office but now, when he really needed it, it had abandoned him. 'I'm fine. Sorry I missed your calls. I've only just come out of the morning briefing.' It felt strange to hear himself saying a sentence he had said thousands of times to Clara over the years. He reached for the ring at his neck. It wasn't there. He hadn't been wearing it for days.

'You left so early this morning; I wondered if everything was . . . OK?' she said.

He could hear the doubt in her voice. He should be trying to slow things down. But he couldn't say it. He didn't feel it. 'Everything's fine,' he said. 'I just didn't want to wake you.' He pictured her face as it had been this morning before he left. He had sat on the side of the bed and stroked her hair away from her cheek.

'Are you free tonight?' she asked.

He mentally listed his options. You've got work to do. You have to see your daughter. Say anything. 'Yes,' he said, slapping his forehead.

'What was that?'

'Nothing, I was just getting in my car, the door slammed,' he said, feeling weak. 'What time?' he asked.

'I'm free any time, just come over when you're done. I

had some shopping delivered today so I'll cook. We can have a bottle of wine . . .' She sounded happy. He was making her happy. He realized he was smiling.

'It might not be until about eight,' he said, turning off the ignition. The fans cut out and the cold air seeped back into the car, fogging the windows again.

'Any time is fine,' she said. 'Are you sure everything is OK?'

Could she hear his doubts, his fears? 'Yes. I'll see you later. Can't wait.'

He hung up the phone and climbed out of the car, alarmed it and made his way back into the office, trying to ignore the light feeling that had taken over his entire body.

As Lockyer walked back into his office he noticed Chris shadowing him. He turned and raised an eyebrow. 'Can I help you, Chris?' he said, sitting down at his desk.

'Sir, have you got a second?' Chris said, his voice filled with anxiety.

Lockyer cracked his neck and prayed for patience. He could understand Chris's concern. His wife had just given birth to their first child, so knowing a deranged killer was targeting members of the team was bound to unnerve the poor kid. 'Yes, Chris . . . what's up?'

'I've been going through the patient list for the clinic the third victim . . . Deborah Stevens . . . used, sir, and . . .'

'Chris, I've told you, LYWC checks out. You can leave that, for now.' His words didn't have the desired effect. Chris was shifting from foot to foot and then, much to Lockyer's surprise, he stepped further into his office and closed the door.

'It's not that, sir,' Chris said, his voice hushed. 'When nothing came back on the first check, I decided to look further back, up to a year,' he said, his eyes lowered. Probably because he knew damn well he shouldn't have requested older records without Lockyer's express permission.

'Go on,' he said.

'I noticed a name . . . a patient,' Chris said.

'Spit it out, Constable.'

'Here, sir,' Chris said, putting a piece of paper on Lockyer's desk before retreating back to the door. 'I just thought you should know and I didn't want to . . . I didn't think you'd want anyone else to know.'

He leaned forward and read the name, the date and the reason for the visit. He read it again, once, twice, three times. 'Thank you, Chris,' he said, not looking up. 'No one else sees those records . . . is that clear?'

'Yes, sir,' Chris said.

Lockyer didn't notice the door opening or closing. He just stared at the piece of paper, unable to think.

39

Malvern still felt shaky as he leaned against the wall at the end of Sarah's street, hidden by darkness. He had spent most of the weekend looking over his shoulder, jumping at the slightest sound. The notion that he would, or even could, harass Sarah was outrageous. He rubbed his eyes and looked up at her. She was standing in her lounge, her blinds fully open. She looked so beautiful, so happy. Could she sense his presence? Did she know he was back, protecting her?

After they had finally let him go, Malvern had gone straight home, climbed into his car and driven to Sarah's. He couldn't wait to see her. Their days apart had felt like years, each minute passing like a knife across his throat. He hadn't been home since; he couldn't leave her. He had found a side street, about a half a mile away, that no one seemed to use, so he had slept in his car but even then he was anxious, missing her face. He had to pluck up the courage to go and see her. He was desperate to tell her what had happened, to see if she could understand the mess the police had made. To charge him with harassment was insane.

As he watched Sarah pull her hair into a ponytail, he couldn't help smiling. She looked relaxed, carefree, like the woman he had met all those months ago in the City. The cups of coffee they had shared, chatting like two old friends. The connection had been obvious from the second their eyes met. Malvern knew it and it was clear Sarah did too. She had said she looked forward to seeing him, that he made her day, photographing strangers, more bearable. He knew when she took her breaks. It just so happened he took his at the same time. Fate. He watched as she pulled her hair through her fingers, draping it around her shoulders. Her neck was long and smooth. How he longed to touch it, to kiss her there. He sat down on the wall as his trousers tightened. He needed to be careful. If the police saw him here they might take him away again.

He stood and walked into the corner shop, his hands in his pockets. It was so cold tonight. The man behind the counter was watching him. Malvern picked up some milk and cheese from the fridge unit and pretended to be deciding on another purchase. It was much warmer in here. His hands tingled in his pockets as they came back to life. He needed to go home, to shower, to change, but he couldn't bring himself to leave. As he looked up, his breath caught in his throat. She was here. He watched as she walked into the shop. She didn't look quite so happy now. She looked like he felt: nervous.

'Evening,' she said to the shopkeeper who just nodded in response.

Malvern's hands began to shake. He stood, fixed to the spot, the milk slopping around in the plastic container. He suddenly felt very hot as he looked down at his wrinkled jacket and tea-stained trousers. He looked like a tramp. He probably smelled like one too. Before he could move, hide, she was walking towards him. The aisle was too small for the two of them. She picked up a carton of apple juice, some milk and a tub of something. He froze as she raised her eyes to meet his. She seemed to hesitate, looking him up and down.

'Excuse me,' she said, looking at the gap between them.

He tried to back himself into the fridge unit, his arms folded over his coat, the milk and cheese still clutched in his hands. She turned away from him and slid past. Her back brushed against his arm for just a second. His whole body seemed to come alive with that one touch. He knew he was blushing, he knew his body was reacting to her presence. As she disappeared behind a tower of toilet rolls she caught his eye; her nose wrinkled. She understood.

By the time he had collected himself, picked up a loaf of bread and followed her around the corner she was already at the till, talking to the man behind the counter.

'Could I have a bottle of Jack Daniel's as well, please?' she asked.

She spoke so softly, Malvern had to strain to hear. Her voice felt like velvet against his skin. He watched her pack her items into a small plastic bag. Her hands were so fine and delicate. He forced his feet to move towards her until she was only inches away. As he opened his mouth to speak she turned away, raised a hand to the man behind the till and was gone. Malvern was too shaken to move, to think. She was so close. He should have talked to her. She wanted him to talk to her. He dropped the milk and bread and ran out of the shop without looking back.

As he rounded the corner he caught sight of her. She was standing at her front door but she wasn't alone. A man was with her. It was the tall detective. He was taking the shopping bag out of her hand. Malvern's heart began to thud harder in his chest. He felt as if his fury would overwhelm him. They were kissing. Her arms threaded around his neck, her fingers in his hair. The detective seemed reluctant, pulling away from her, looking around them, as if ashamed. Malvern took a step forward, wanting to shout, to scream, but they were gone, disappearing into Sarah's house, the door slamming behind them.

He walked up the street and stood on the opposite side of the road, impotent with rage. This was his fault. He had led this man to her. But how could she betray him, humiliate him like this? He swiped at a tear as it trickled down his face. When Sarah was alone again he would come back and this time he would have the courage to act. To do what needed to be done. She had left him no choice.

40

Lockyer beeped his car horn again and waited. He didn't know what he was going to say. As soon as he had read Megan's name on the piece of paper Chris had given him his mind had been in freefall. He had almost told Sarah when he saw her earlier, but how could he? They were still getting to know each other. Besides, he could tell she was disappointed that he couldn't stay for dinner. They had barely had time for a drink before he was rushing out of the door, promising to call her later.

He shook his head. He still couldn't believe it. His eighteen-year-old daughter had had an abortion in March of last year. Over twelve months ago. She had gone to a clinic, got tested, made a decision and had the procedure, all without him knowing a thing. Lockyer had spent the drive over from Sarah's trying to remember whether Megan had been different last year, when she was only seventeen. She would have been over the age of consent. He knew she had boyfriends. Clara no doubt knew all about it, which made him even more furious. How could she not tell him?

He looked up and saw Megan in the doorway, wrapped up in a winter coat, a colourful scarf wound round her neck. He suddenly saw an image of her when she was seven years old, going away to Brownie camp. 'One second, Dad,' she shouted before disappearing back into the house. He had to get a grip. Megan was fine. He could always talk to her about it; make sure she was all right. Even the thought terrified him.

It felt odd, sitting outside his old house. The house where he had shared a life with Clara, a life he had ultimately sabotaged. It felt like he was being unfaithful to Sarah, even being here. His hand automatically went to his chest, to touch the ring that was no longer there. As snowflakes landed on his windscreen, pushed aside by the automatic wipers, he realized things could never change back.

'Hi, Dad,' Megan said as she climbed into the car, dragging a rather large overnight bag with her. How long did she say she was staying for?

'Hi, honey, you look good.' Why did he say that? He felt nervous. He started the car and pulled away, the tyres slipping as he pushed past a small drift of snow.

'How's everything going?' she asked, pulling at the loose strands sticking out of the end of her scarf. 'How's work?' She looked pained. He didn't know if she asked about his work because she thought she should or because she really wanted to know. Either way, he didn't want to talk to anyone about the case, especially his eighteen-year-old daughter.

'Everything's fine,' he said. 'Thanks for asking,' he added, as he pulled out onto the main road. He saw her nodding out of the corner of his eye. These stilted conversations were becoming a bit too habitual.

'I called you on Saturday, after our coffee, but you weren't answering your mobile or the flat phone . . .'

'I was at . . .'

'No, I called your office too, Dad . . . you weren't there,' she said. He could hear mocking in her tone but before he could react she said, 'Don't tell me you're seeing someone?'

Lockyer tried to indicate but only succeeded in turning off the windscreen wipers, the snow immediately blinding him. He slowed down, turned his lights on and then off again, found the indicator and finally managed to get the wipers going again. It was all he could do to keep the car on the road. 'I don't know what you're talking about.' He decided it was best to keep quiet. She was only fishing. 'What do you fancy for supper?' he said, putting on his most casual voice.

Megan dropped the ends of her scarf. 'Hey, it's none of my business,' she said, shrugging her shoulders. 'I was just telling Mum how different you were on Saturday.'

'What did your mother say?' he asked.

'Nothing . . . Mum didn't say anything. I was just saying you seemed different . . . more relaxed, maybe? Let's drop it before you crash the car.' She leaned forward and turned on the radio. 'There's a programme on in a sec that I need to listen to for college . . . do you mind?'

'No, no, I don't mind at all,' he said. He doubted he would ever have the courage to discuss the other matter. Their father–daughter relationship had turned on its head as it was.

41

12 February – Wednesday

He watched her as she brushed her hair, long strokes, her eyes closed. He wanted to reach out and touch her. How could the handsome detective have been so careless? He thought again of his disciples as he looked at the face in the window. The calm he saw there wouldn't last until tomorrow.

His dreams had been filled with visions of her, distracting him. It was strange. The images coming to him were ones he had buried long ago but they refused to quieten. Instead the memories crippled his mind. The doctor had said he could touch her but he hadn't wanted to. He had felt trapped behind a two-way mirror, viewing himself, viewing her. Her red hair, once so vibrant, now hanging limp over the edge of the gurney. Her shape beneath the sheet. Her breasts creating the faintest undulation of the material, her hip bones another, then her feet, creating a final point. He remembered the stain on the sheet. It spread like a flower opening its petals to the morning sun. He hadn't been able to stop himself thinking about the blood. How it would have congealed around the meaty slices she had made in her wrists. He had wondered if it had hurt, if she had felt pain.

His eyes filled with tears as he was transported back to that hospital corridor. He had needed those walls for support, unable to understand, unable to forget the black-and-white outlines, the flutter of a heartbeat. Tears dropped onto his cheeks. They trickled into his mouth and down the side of his neck into the collar of his shirt. Blood pounded in his ears, his right eye twitched, his skin itched, prickling as adrenalin surged through his system. He allowed the heat of his rage to surge through his body.

42

Sarah scrolled through the messages on her mobile, waiting for the traffic lights to change. She tried to block out the persistent horns outside the car. Everyone around her seemed to be in a hurry, but then that was London. She clicked into her inbox. Most of the messages were from Mike, a couple from Toni, but Mike's name dominated the screen.

She couldn't remember the last time she had been so attached to her mobile. It was her new one, and she had only given her number to four people so far: her mother and father, Toni and Mike. Right now she was content to have a phone that, for the most part, remained silent. When it chirruped to let her know she had a message or a voicemail, instead of feeling dread, she felt excitement. Her feelings of panic were replaced with a calm self-assurance, a renewed confidence. It was a welcome change.

Sarah turned into the car park at Lewisham Police Station and parked up at the end of the row. Her meeting with Bennett was at 5.30. It was only 4.30 now. She wanted to see Mike. When he was with her, her fears, her worries, everything seemed to vanish for those few hours. In the past week she had been able to laugh, to chat. It had been so long since she had felt even close to normal.

She pretended to be searching for something in the glove compartment when a group of officers walked by, close to her driver's side window. She wasn't hiding. She just wasn't ready to go in quite yet. She climbed out of the car and walked out onto Lewisham High Street. Without thinking she headed straight for Bella's coffee house. She pushed open the door, listened to the bell jingle and walked to the counter. The same girl was serving.

She smiled at Sarah. 'What can I get you?'

'Americano, please,' she said, digging in her handbag for her purse. To hear her voice sounding so normal was comforting.

As she waited for her coffee she searched for her phone in her handbag. She would call him. It would be stupid to arrive unannounced. He might not even be in the office. Although he had told her yesterday he would be spending most of the day reviewing CCTV footage. She found his number, pushed 'call' and put the phone to her ear, turning away from the counter. He answered on the second ring.

'Hi,' he said. 'How are you doing?'

Sarah could feel the smile spreading across her face. 'I'm good, really good. You?'

There was a pause before he answered. 'OK, but today has been a very long day.' He sounded tired. 'I'm with people right now.'

'No problem . . . you'll be done soon,' she said, looking up at the clock on the wall of the café, immediately realizing it was a lame thing to say. 'I'm in Bella's if you get a second,' she said, but when he still didn't respond, she hurried on. 'I'm here to see Bennett, thought I could pop in and say hi,' she said with a tentative smile. Silence greeted her question. She listened as he cleared his throat.

'That would be great but . . . I'm right in the middle of things. I really don't have time to take a break, I'm sorry.'

Sarah tried to ignore the change she could hear and feel in his voice. 'Of course, it was only on the off-chance. It doesn't matter. Will I see you tonight?' she asked, blushing, aware of the waitress behind her.

'Actually, I'm going to have to rain-check,' he said. Sarah tried to ignore his business voice. He was in the office, people were with him, he was hardly going to sing down the phone to her. 'I'll probably end up pulling an all-nighter at home,' he said.

'No worries at all,' she said, distressed to hear her voice sounding forced, falsely upbeat.

'If I'm around when you see Jane, I'll say hi, just depends on what I'm doing,' he said.

'If you change your mind you know where to find me. Or . . . I've got a bottle of wine with your name on it, so I can always come to you. I'll bring dinner.'

'I'll give you a call later on, OK?'

The dial tone sounded in her ear before she could respond. She stared out of the café windows at Lewisham shoppers, walking in and out of town. She closed her eyes, took a deep breath and then opened them again. He was just busy. His case. She knew how important it was. She knew what was at stake. When a bus stopped outside, darkening the windows, she caught sight of herself, disgusted by her own selfishness.

She barely heard the bell as she left the coffee shop. She crossed the road, walking up the street to the police station. It wasn't until she reached the car park that she realized she had never even touched her coffee. The waitress, the one who fancied Mike, must have overheard their telephone conversation. She hurried towards the station but as she walked past her car she noticed something under the windscreen wiper. She trudged over and yanked the piece of paper towards her, unfolding it at the same time. Her breath caught in her throat. She saw the four, slashed angry lines, scoring the page, underlining the words meant for her.

YOU ARE MINE

43

Lockyer sat back, not even slightly surprised when the creaks and pops came from his spine rather than the chair. He had been reviewing a week's worth of CCTV footage taken from Bobby's home for the past five hours. He blinked his eyes, trying to rehydrate them. Chris and Penny were doing exactly the same thing out at their desks. Every time he looked up he could see that they too were sagging under the strain, but it had to be done.

He was finding it impossible to concentrate and he knew he wouldn't be able to settle until Malvern Turner was back behind bars. The fact that Turner was so brazen, putting the note on Sarah's windscreen on police grounds, showed just how unhinged the guy was. Lockyer should have known that the warnings to stay away from Sarah wouldn't work. She had been calm, considering. He had watched her walking across the office, stealing glances as she talked to Jane. It had been Jane's face that told him something was wrong. Two squad cars were already out looking for him. Lockyer had arranged for a squad car to make a pass on her street, on the hour, every hour until Turner was brought in.

With a shake of his head he looked out at the open-plan office. It was more like the *Marie Celeste* today, as nearly the entire team were out doing door-to-doors from the list, or Bible, as it was now called. He looked at his watch. It was already gone eight. Megan would be waiting for him at home. He picked up his mobile to call her just as it started to ring. 'Lockyer,' he said.

'Just checking in, sir. All quiet this end.'

It took him a second to recognize the voice. 'Russ, great . . . I really appreciate you checking in with me, I know it's not procedure.'

'No problem at all, I'm just driving round, got nothing better to do,' Russ laughed.

'Cheers, mate, I'll be home in an hour, I hope. I'll text when I'm en route.' He thanked Russ again before hanging up, the relief palpable.

On some level he had been worrying about Megan ever since he'd left her in his flat this morning. Even on the drive back from Clara's he had felt acutely aware of every car, bike or pedestrian in his rear-view mirror. They hadn't been followed – he would have noticed – but he would still feel a lot better when Megan was home with her mother. Several other officers had also been drafted in to keep an eye on key members and their families after the incident at Bobby's home, but Lockyer wanted Russ. The guy was way too senior for the job but Lockyer didn't trust anyone else.

His mind drifted back to Sarah. What would happen when Jane found out? What would Roger do? But it wasn't really himself he was thinking about. It was Sarah. None of this was fair on her. He could tell by her voice when he said he couldn't go to hers tonight that she felt abandoned. The sound of her pain was so familiar it made him reach for the place where Clara's ring had been. He would never be able to really know what he put Clara through; late nights in the office, forgotten anniversaries, weekends when he barely managed an hour at home. He fired off a text saying he hoped she was OK, that there was no news on Turner yet and that he would be heading home to work but would call her. He rubbed his face, trying to push away his tiredness. He turned back to his computer. He felt like his eyes were beginning to twitch in rhythm with the constant jumping of the screen. With a sigh he tipped himself forward, clicked the 'play' button and put his elbows on the desk, mainly so he could hold his head up with his hands.

The black-and-white screen sprang to life. It was footage from the camera in the back garden of Bobby's home. The scope caught everything from the top of the French doors to the end of the garden, the view that Bobby loved so much. He had called Alice to check in on his brother. All was well, as Alice would say. What wasn't quite so good was Alice's mysterious boyfriend. Still no contact. Lockyer had made the decision not to tell her why he wanted her to come into the station on her way home from work. He wanted to show her the e-fit.

He stopped the tape, pressed rewind, screwed up his eyes, blinked a few more times until he was sure his vision was working properly and then pressed 'play'. He watched for a couple of seconds, stopped the tape, rewound it and watched it again. On the sixth playback he realized he wasn't breathing. He enlarged the image, taking out as much of the background as he could until he was left with the right-hand side of a man's face. He tipped his head on one side and then the other, leaning into the picture.

He cursed when his phone started to ring again, snatching at it, still staring at the grainy image on the computer screen. 'Lockyer.'

'Sir, there's a call for you . . . a Catherine John,' the receptionist said.

'Put her through,' he said, without thinking. He looked out into the office to see who he could pass the call to but Penny and Chris had vanished and Jane wasn't at her desk.

Before he could hang up the line crackled and a very quiet voice said, 'Hello, is that Detective Inspector Michael Lockyer?'

'It is,' he said.

'My name is Catherine John. I work at the LYWC, the Lewisham Young Women's Centre . . . I don't know if you're the right person to speak to, but . . .' The woman trailed off. He wondered for a second if they had been cut off. That would be a blessing, he thought, still staring at the man's face. 'I didn't know whether I should call . . . my husband said I would only be causing trouble but I couldn't sleep last night . . . worrying about it, you know . . . so . . . I don't know if it'll be important but . . .' Lockyer was half listening. He was preoccupied with the eye and jawline on the screen in front of him. There was something familiar, he could feel it. He realized the woman was still speaking. '. . . I've only been back in the office a few days, you see . . . I've been signed off for . . . medical reasons,' she said. Lockyer pinched the bridge of his nose. He would guess she had been under the doctor for her nerves. She sounded about ready to break down. 'I clean for Mr Walsh, at the clinic and at his house. I heard on the news last night that they released the name of the fourth girl, the girl killed over in Richmond.'

He sat up in his seat, suddenly alert. 'Yes,' he said.

'My husband said I shouldn't bother anyone unless I was one hundred and fifty per cent . . . but I'm as sure as I can be . . .'

'Please, go on,' he said, holding his breath.

'Well . . . a couple of weeks ago, just before I went off sick, I was cleaning at Mr Walsh's over in Dulwich Village, sorting through the recycling and I noticed . . . I noticed some shredded papers in with the normal rubbish.' He heard her take a deep breath. 'They were clinic records, patient records.' He waited, watching the image flicker on the screen as the woman sniffed on the other end of the line. 'I knew that's what they were because they use carbonated paper for those . . . oh dear,' she said. 'I didn't think anything of it at the time, I just thought Mr Walsh had been working from home or something, so I . . . I took them out and put them in with the paper and cardboard for recycling.'

'Did you see any names on the records?' he asked, still not taking a breath, leaning forward as if to catch her words better.

'Well, as I say, they'd been pretty much shredded, Detective but . . . one of the names was H . . . Hayley Sawyer, I'm sure of it . . . I think one of the others was Pearson but I can't be sure. When I heard the girl's name on the news last night I almost died.' He heard her take a ragged breath. 'My husband says I'm not remembering right, that I'm being dramatic, making it up, but I'm not, I swear to you, I'm not.'

He thought about his next question carefully as he tried to remember the woman's name. 'Miss John . . . Catherine . . . have you told anyone other than your husband about this?'

'No,' she said.

'You didn't tell Mr Walsh?'

'Goodness, no . . . I haven't . . . I didn't know what to do.'

The tingle had spread throughout Lockyer's body; he was practically humming. 'Miss John, I'm going to put you on with a colleague of mine to arrange an interview, as we'll need to formalize this conversation.' He craned his neck, relieved to see Penny walking back into the office.

'Of course,' she said. 'I'm just so glad I called, I've been worried sick.'

'Good, that's good. Please bear in mind that this is an active investigation and until we have formalized your statement you shouldn't talk to anyone about this call. Do you understand?' he said, standing and signalling to Penny by waving his arm in the air frantically. His expression must have been clear because she was next to him in a second, her hand held out for the phone.

'Yes, I understand, Inspector. I shan't tell a soul.'

He thanked her for her time and handed his mobile over to Penny before darting back to his desk.

Lockyer's mind was running so fast, he felt dizzy. He couldn't believe it. Walsh had been all but eliminated from the inquiry.

The past hour had been a blur, Jane dashing in and out of his office, the phone ringing constantly. It was crazy. They had both stood in front of his computer staring at the image from the CCTV and comparing it with the e-fit. Was it Walsh?

It was impossible to tell from the CCTV footage. There simply wasn't enough of the man's face in shot. As for the e-fit, both he and Jane felt a stir of recollection, a sort of déjà vu, but neither of them thought it looked like Walsh. They had both met him, talked to the guy at length. Turner's recollections and description had been worse than useless, but surely, if it was Walsh something in the e-fit would have jumped out at them?

'Sir,' Jane said from his doorway. 'Alice is here.'

He looked into the office beyond and saw Alice standing by Jane's desk. She looked so out of place. 'Send her in, Jane.' Jane turned and waved Alice over. As he watched the poor girl walking towards them he felt his gut tighten. She might look frightened, but, if he was right, she was going to feel a lot worse.

'Come in, Alice,' he said, half rising out of his chair. She didn't speak. She just sat down in the chair opposite him and stared at her hands. 'Are you all right?' he asked.

'Yes,' she said.

It was like listening to a different person. 'I need you to look at something for me, Alice,' he said, keeping his voice as gentle as possible.

'I know,' she said, wiping a tear off her cheek. 'It's about him, isn't it?'

He shouldn't tell her anything, but after all she had done for Bobby he couldn't lie to her. 'Yes, Alice . . . I assume you haven't heard from your boyfriend?'

'Don't call him that,' she said, shaking her head, more tears running down her face. 'No, I haven't. Of course I haven't. He used me . . . he used me to hurt Bobby, to hurt you . . .' Her shoulders were hitching as her sobs took over her small frame. He pushed away from his desk, walked over to her and put his hand on her shoulder.

'We don't know that, Alice . . .'

'Show me,' Alice whispered. Without speaking Lockyer turned his screen to face her and handed her the e-fit off his desk.

'Just take your time,' he said, his eyes fixed on Alice's face. She didn't react at first, almost as if she was frozen. He watched her eyes move from the e-fit to the CCTV image and back again. She leaned towards his computer, her nose inches from the screen, her fingers poised over the man's face. 'I think it's him,' she said, closing her eyes. 'I know it's him.'

'I'm sorry, Alice,' was all he could think to say.

An hour later Lockyer was sitting at his desk with his head in his hands. He felt crushed. Crushed for Alice. She couldn't confirm it was Walsh, obviously, and Lockyer didn't have a picture to show her, but she seemed certain that the face on the screen and the e-fit were the same man, and that he was the man she had dated, however briefly.

'Sir,' Jane said from the doorway of his office. She was clutching her laptop to her chest, her face flushed.

'What have you got?' he asked, adrenalin rushing into his bloodstream, making his whole body hum.

'Two things,' she said, walking in and sitting down. He could see that she was just as jacked up as he was.

'Go on,' he said, using all his restraint not to scream the words at her.

'I sent two squad cars to the clinic and four to his home address. No sign of Walsh,' she said.

'He's got to have a car. Find it, get an all-points out and get traffic to assist. The ASU can scramble one of their helicopters to chase him down, but only once we know where he bloody is,' he said, pushing back his chair and pacing back and forth in front of his window.

'Done, sir. Two vehicles are registered in his name. I've already contacted traffic. They'll call as soon as they have something,' she said.

'Is there anything else in the info you've pulled that could lead us to him? Family, friends, anything?' he said, letting out a frustrated breath when Jane shook her head. He was about to protest when she held up her hand.

'Second. The team reviewing cold cases, cross-referencing murder, abortion and mutilation or blood-letting, have found something. A case in Manchester came up.'

'Yes,' he said, with a warning tone in his voice. He wasn't interested in cold cases right now. They knew it was Walsh. They just needed to find him.

'I've just got off the phone with Manchester MPS. I spoke to a DS Saunders. He was part of the original investigation. It happened five years ago,' she said, flipping open her laptop. 'A woman called Joanne Taylor, twenty-five, was found with her wrists slashed. She'd had an abortion a week earlier.'

'Four years ago. Is there a link to Walsh?' he asked, mentally preparing himself for more bodies, more grieving families.

'Not yet. The death was listed as a suicide, sir.'

'OK,' he said, taking a deep breath to calm his jumping

muscles. 'What else? Because so far we don't have enough for a warrant on Walsh's home address. Without the actual papers the cleaner's statement is just circumstantial . . . hearsay.'

Jane looked down at her laptop again and said, 'Taylor had a boyfriend, Adrian Chambers. He found the body and suicide note. In his statement he said Joanne was depressed. She'd had the abortion in secret. When she told him, he was gutted. They were meant to be trying for a baby and he couldn't understand why she'd get rid of it.'

'Go on,' he said. He wanted to move.

'Well,' Jane said. 'After the inquest ruled suicide, Chambers vanished. From what Saunders could tell me, he worked at the local hospital as a receptionist and admin assistant. After the girlfriend's death he became depressed, aggressive and was eventually fired because of it.'

'Working in a hospital . . . that's good, that helps us . . . was Chambers ever under suspicion? Was the suicide note verified as the girl's handwriting?' he asked.

'Saunders wasn't sure, but because the death was never deemed suspicious the verification could have been missed,' Jane said.

'Hang on a minute,' he said, shaking his head. 'If he was never under suspicion and the death was ruled a suicide, why's the case on the system at all?' He could feel doubt creeping over him, settling on his skin like snow outside his window.

'That's where it gets interesting,' Jane said, giving him a small smile when he raised his eyebrows. 'Totally separate incident, sir. The hospital where Chambers worked called the police. Chambers kicked off when they fired him for his aggression. He punched the senior administrator; Chambers was arrested and printed but never charged. The hospital knew how much the suicide had screwed the guy up so didn't want to press charges.'

'Walsh had a prior for ABH, didn't he?' Lockyer asked, his pulse pounding in his head.

'That's right. And after Chambers left Manchester, there's nothing. He literally vanished, a regular Houdini,' Jane said, smiling again.

He managed a forced chuckle. It broke the spell of the tension that was threatening to cripple his brain. 'Do we have a description?' he asked.

'Better than that, sir. Saunders is going to send over Chambers' hospital records, photo ID, the lot.'

Lockyer ran his fingers through his hair, deciding how best to move forward. 'OK, get the warrant ready. If we get a match I want sign-off and access to Walsh's property ASAP,' he said, remembering Walsh's face in the interview, crumpled with distress that one of his patients had been murdered. And he had bought it, hook, line and sinker, Lockyer thought, slamming his fist on the desk.

44

12 February – Wednesday

He paced back and forth, the excitement building to a level he could barely control. He watched her through the window, her face flushed behind the glass. This would be the last time she would breathe without fear. As if on cue, he watched her putting on her coat.

His mouth was full, saliva wetting his tongue as the anticipation grew. He swallowed as the front door opened, closed and then there she was, alone at last. The 'protection' the detective had put on was a joke. A squad car rolling past on the hour, every hour. He had fifty minutes before the next drive-by. Enough time for his purposes.

She walked down the street towards him, flinching when he stepped out of the shadows. But instead of the fear he had hoped for, she simply sidestepped him and walked on. 'Excuse me,' she said as she passed. He stood fixed to the spot. He didn't feel angry as much as deflated. With a deep breath he unclenched his fists and forced himself to follow. She was some distance away already, so he broke into a semi-jog until he was alongside her.

'Sorry,' he said, falling in step beside her. 'This might sound odd but I noticed you walking alone and wondered if you would mind if I walked with you?' She looked at him, seemingly trying to judge if he was a Lewisham nutter or not. Before she could make up her mind he said, 'I don't like to see a young woman walking alone in the dark.' He plastered on a winning smile. The urge to drop the facade and do it right here almost overwhelmed him.

'Thanks, but I'm fine,' she said, already stretching out her strides. Traces of the fear he was waiting for were beginning to show. Her cheek was twitching and he was sure, even in the darkness, that her face had paled.

'I don't mind walking behind or on the other side of the street, even,' he said with a shrug of his shoulders, 'but my mother would never forgive me if I left you to walk alone.' This line had worked before and he could see from the softening of her features that it was working its magic again. He could see a hint of unease in her eyes, a minuscule taste of her doubt, but not enough.

'I know a mother a bit like that, but don't walk behind me. That definitely would freak me out,' she said, managing a strained smile. Her veneer of calm was cracking. Once realization dawned it would be too late. She would panic, realizing that he wasn't killing her, her own carelessness was. He couldn't help taking small sideways glances at her. 'So,' he said, 'have you lived around here long?'

'I don't live around here,' she said, her pace increasing. He hoped her mind was beginning to conjure the horror stories of women at night, alone, being taken, being killed.

'You?' she asked, but she wasn't looking at him and her

pace was definitely speeding up. They would be jogging soon.

'Oh, yes, I'm local. I know the area very well,' he said, removing all the warmth from his voice. Her shoulders rose as her muscles tensed in her back. He knew the signs of fear. She knew.

He looked ahead at the alleyway between the terraced flats, leading to the garages and bins beyond. It was only twenty feet away. A few more seconds. He carefully reached into his coat pocket and uncapped the needle.

45

At 10.15 Lockyer was still pacing around the briefing room. He had been trying to call Megan to say he wouldn't be home until later, if at all, but she wasn't answering. As he picked up his mobile to call Russ, Jane walked into his office.

'We're still waiting on the photo ID, I've chased my guy in Manchester but . . .' she said, shaking her head.

He could see that she was feeling the strain. Adrenalin only kept the body going for so long. Lockyer knew how she felt. He was exhausted, as if the past hour's intense activity had drained his energy tanks and his reserves were at critical. He thought again about Megan. He would get Russ to do another drive-by, check everything was OK. Her not answering her mobile was bothering him. Teenagers had their phones physically attached to them, his daughter included.

'Anything on Turner?' he asked, knowing he shouldn't be thinking about Sarah, knowing his mind should be solely on Walsh and finding the bastard before he hurt anyone else.

'Yes, sir,' Jane said, a quizzical look on her face. She was obviously surprised he was asking about Turner too. 'His car was spotted over in Honor Oak. I've sent the squad car over to check it out.' She seemed about to say more but stopped, shaking her head. 'Have we got sign-off on the warrant for Walsh's home address, yet?' she asked.

'No,' he said, hearing his own frustration. 'The judge said we don't have enough evidence.' He threw his hands up in the air and raised his eyebrows. The gesture reminded him of Megan.

'Christ,' Jane said, pushing one of the briefing room chairs across the room. 'What do they want?' He had never seen Jane this antsy. It was unsettling.

'A smoking gun,' he said, hoping humour would diffuse some of the tension. He could see that it hadn't worked. Jane wasn't even looking at him. She was staring at her laptop like it contained the riddle of the Sphinx.

'I'll see how the others are doing,' she said, standing to leave, picking up her laptop. But then she stopped. 'Sir.' She turned the screen to face him. 'Chambers' records are through.' Disappointment marked her face. 'This is Adrian Chambers.'

It wasn't Walsh's face staring back at him. 'I don't believe it,' he said.

Jane shook her head. 'It doesn't mean Walsh isn't our guy.' He could hear the desperation in her voice. 'The records at his house . . . everything points to Walsh.'

'The records were a plant, Jane, just like the earring, to throw us off. It isn't Walsh,' he said, looking at the face on his screen and then back at the headshot on Jane's laptop. 'But I know who it is. I've met him and so have you.'

*

Thirty minutes later Lockyer was standing in a home-made darkroom. The stench of sweat mixed with blood was overwhelming. He couldn't believe it. The bastard had actually given his home address when he was interviewed. That's how confident he was. That's how sure he was that he would never be suspected, never be caught.

Lockyer looked at the hundreds of photographs surrounding him, each hanging from a small peg, attached to a piece of string that encircled the entire room. There seemed to be no discernible order to them. The faces of Katy, Phoebe, Debbie and Hayley stared back at him. It felt weird to see them alive; at the supermarket, in the pub with friends, jogging around the park, driving.

He turned away and walked up the stairs into the kitchen. In the centre of a pine table a sewing basket seemed to take pride of place. Spools of thread were lined up carefully, a needle in front of each one. Lockyer closed his eyes. Such a mundane object and yet here, in this room, it was sinister. The sink was filled with soapy water. He dipped his finger into the bowl. It was warm. He walked over to the fridge and pulled it open. There were three shelves. Each held the same items. A head of lettuce, a packet of bacon, a takeaway sachet of tomato ketchup and four slices of brown bread. Three meals perfectly laid out, ready and waiting. In the door there were three individual pints of milk and next to them was something that stopped him in his tracks.

'Sir.'

He heard the shout from above him. He ran into the hallway and took the stairs two at a time. Chris and Penny were standing outside what appeared to be the bathroom.

He crossed the landing to them, trying to prepare himself for what he might be about to see.

'No, in here, sir,' Chris said, his skin the colour of newspaper.

Lockyer turned and pushed open the door to a bedroom. It was small but it wasn't the room's size choking his words. The wallpaper was a dusky pink, covered in small white flowers, similar to the paper he had chosen for Megan's room. He shook the thought away. The carpet was pink too, thick and deep. A mobile hung from the ceiling, little pink rabbits dancing in a never-ending circle. He looked over at Chris who was standing next to the only piece of furniture in the room. A large pine cot. He held his breath as he approached, almost too scared to look. There were soft toys surrounding the crib, a white teddy, a pink bunny with 'I love you' stitched onto its stomach. Lockyer felt bile leaking into his mouth but managed to swallow.

'There's this, sir,' Chris said, pointing to the quilt lying in the centre.

Lockyer noticed the stains before he realized what he was looking at. There was blood and mud mixing with the white of the sheet, streaks where the blanket had been moved, repositioned, many, many times. Each square of the quilt sent a shot of pain into his skull. They were the missing pieces of material from the crime scenes. Phil had said that killers took trophies from their victims, to remind them of the act itself, but Lockyer had never imagined this. The sick bastard had made a baby blanket from the bloodied remains of his victim's clothing. He closed his eyes and saw the bottle in the door of the fridge.

'Where's the baby?' he said, surprised by how hollow his voice sounded.

'We don't know, sir,' Chris said, visibly swaying on his feet.

Lockyer walked out onto the landing, leaning on the banister for support. He tried to focus to pull his mind away from the horror it had just witnessed. What did that room mean? Had he taken a baby or was he just preparing to? The bottle in the fridge was made up, ready to use. Lockyer thought about the girls in the photographs downstairs. There were faces he didn't recognize and more film to develop. How many more bodies were there? And the baby. He couldn't stop thinking about the baby.

'Sir,' an officer said, holding a phone out to him.

He reached for it, barely registering what he was doing, but as he listened he felt an ice-cold hand squeeze the air out of his lungs. He couldn't breathe. The officer on the other end of the phone was saying his name, over and over. 'Yes,' he croaked. 'We're on our way.' He dropped the phone. His brain couldn't catch up with the panic racing around his body, like a thousand needles being rammed into his flesh, all at once.

'Sir,' Jane said, appearing in front of him as if from nowhere. 'Sir, what's happened?'

He could feel her hand squeezing his arm but he could barely see her. She was a blur, everything was a blur. He took a huge lungful of air and rocked backwards against the banister, his senses rushing back to him. He looked down at Jane, refocused his eyes and finally found his voice.

'That was despatch. They've received a 999 call, five minutes ago. An attack in progress,' he said, his voice hoarse from the shock. He watched, dumbstruck, as Jane reached up and placed her hands on either side of his face. Her palms felt like hot coals against his skin.

'Where?' she asked.

'French Street . . . my street,' he said, his voice almost unrecognizable.

'Sir,' she said, pulling him towards the stairs, 'we need to go.'

He didn't answer. He didn't move.

'Sir, we need to go, now!' Jane shouted.

Her voice broke through his stupor as his eyes cleared. The paralysis of his body finally released him and he raced down the stairs behind Jane. He could hear her shouting into her phone. He wasn't listening to her words. He wasn't seeing anything. All he could think about was Megan.

Lockyer sat forward in the passenger seat, hands gripping the dashboard, his back dripping with sweat. Jane was weaving in and out of the late-night traffic, racing towards Lockyer's street, racing towards his house. All he could hear was the squad car's sirens screaming.

How could he have been so blind? When he had visited the LYWC he had been totally focused on Walsh. Danny or Daniel Armstrong, the submissive office assistant, hadn't even registered. Lockyer remembered feeling sorry for the guy, having to work under a bully like Walsh. He rubbed his face with his hands, his skin hot to the touch. He had met the guy, talked to him, shook his hand and then led him right to Megan.

'I shouldn't have left her,' he said, shaking his head. 'I should have told her what was going on.'

'We're there, sir,' Jane said, swerving to avoid a line of cars in front of them before screeching to a halt behind a squad car. Before Lockyer could leap out she grabbed his arm. 'There,' she said, pointing to a dark figure running down the road ahead of them. Jane swung the car out into the road and accelerated towards the fleeing figure. When she was almost alongside she swerved and shouted, 'Go!' He jumped out before the car had come to a complete stop. Armstrong was no more than thirty feet ahead of him. He seemed to be dragging his left leg slightly. It was slowing him down. Lockyer could hear the muted shouts of the officers behind him. 'Stop, police!' he screamed, pushing his legs to run faster, until he didn't know if he was running any more, as much as flying.

'ARMSTRONG,' he shouted, his arms pumping at his sides as he watched the dark figure disappear around the corner. His muscles were screaming at him to stop but he only pushed harder, his vision blurring. As he rounded the corner he could see that he was gaining. Armstrong was fifteen feet in front now, his hands and arms covered in blood. Lockyer was aware of running footsteps behind him, the other officers breathing hard, trying to keep pace. He was tuned to every sound, everything together and yet everything separate; tyres squealed, sirens blared, people shouted, dogs barked, doors opened and slammed closed.

With a howling shout, he threw himself forward, his hands connecting with Armstrong's shoulders. Both men rolled, barrelling through a line of bins and then down to the hard cement. Before he could stop himself he was punching, kicking, beating his fists down again and again on Armstrong's back. He didn't stop, couldn't stop. Only when several pairs of strong hands began to pull him back, to drag him off the motionless body, did Lockyer finally stop swinging his fists and take a breath.

'Sir, we've got him,' a voice said. But he wasn't listening. He was looking at the blood on his own hands, the smears covering his jacket. All he could do was sit and watch as a swarm of officers dragged Daniel Armstrong to his feet and started half walking, half dragging him away.

As Lockyer limped his way up his street, the scene before him sucked the breath right out of his lungs. There were at least twenty uniformed officers running back and forth. The flashing lights from their squad cars lit up the entire street. He could see Jane. She was standing on the pavement, waiting for him. As he closed the distance between them his heart began to beat faster and faster with each step.

'Jane, is she . . .?' His throat closed. He couldn't say the words.

Jane stepped towards him and took his hands in hers. It was a simple gesture but just then, for that second, he was more grateful to her than he would ever be able to express. The touch of her skin told him what he needed to know before she even spoke. 'Megan's fine,' she said.

Lockyer stared, blinking. 'She's OK?' he asked, squeezing Jane's hand tighter and tighter, willing her to say the words again.

'Yes, she's fine, sir. It wasn't Megan. She's safe. She's sitting in Chris's squad car,' Jane said, turning and pointing further up French Street.

The vice around Lockyer's heart opened, the cramping in

his legs disappeared and the fug in his mind shifted, blown away. He limped over to the squad car, relishing Megan's profile as he got closer. And then she turned, saw him and she was out of the car and in his arms.

'Dad,' she said, sobs racking her tiny frame. No words came to him so he just held her and stroked her hair.

'Sir, I'm sorry,' Jane said, her tone dragging him out of his euphoria. 'Sir . . . you need to see this.'

He pulled away from Megan. Chris, who had appeared from nowhere, took her by the arm and helped her back into the squad car. 'Has someone called Clara?' Lockyer asked.

'I have,' Chris said. 'She's on her way.'

Now that the shock was wearing off he knew he needed to focus. He followed Jane, glancing over his shoulder at Megan, to see her safe.

'The first victim is over here,' Jane said, gesturing to a body lying on the left-hand side of the alleyway.

'There's more than one?' he said, closing his eyes and rolling his head around his shoulders. 'Not the baby,' he whispered, 'please, God, not the baby.'

'There's two, sir,' Jane said. 'The first victim is Malvern Turner.' As she spoke he tried to process what she was saying. 'From the initial examination it looks as if he tried to stop Armstrong in the act and got a knife in the throat for his trouble, but not before he struck Armstrong in the leg with what looks like a kitchen knife,' Jane said, pointing to a black-handled knife lying in the dirt. 'We're assuming it was Turner who called in the attack.' Lockyer shook his head. What the hell was Turner even doing here? He watched as Jane lifted her hand and pointed to the second group of SOCOs, working right in front of them. 'The second victim is over here,' she said, her expression pained as she stepped aside, revealing Sarah's bloodied body sprawled out on the path.

Lockyer froze. Sarah's eyes were open, staring back at him. Her face was spattered with blood from a wound at her throat. He could feel vomit filling his mouth, a stream of foul-smelling bile rushed out, covering his hands and his shoes as he bent double.

'Sir,' she said, thrusting a tissue into his hand. 'Are you all right?'

He managed to wipe his hands as he straightened up, coughing. He couldn't look at Jane. He couldn't take his eyes off Sarah's legs, the pale skin of her thighs covered with blood.

'I didn't know she had been pregnant,' Jane said, shaking her head, her own face showing pain, regret and possibly guilt. 'She never said anything. Her name wasn't on the LYWC records.'

'No,' he whispered. 'She wasn't pregnant. That's not why he chose her. This was my fault. He killed her because of me.'

He could feel Jane's eyes on him, waiting for an explanation. There was only one. While exorcizing one maniac from Sarah's life he had inadvertently invited another in. He looked up at Jane, unable to stop the tears from falling. He shifted backwards, putting Jane between him and Sarah's ravaged body.

He didn't want to see any more. He couldn't look at her face.

46

13 February – Thursday

Lockyer sat at the head of the large glass table in the briefing room. His team were crammed in, some sitting but most standing. The room felt hot and sweaty. He was barely able to listen as Jane debriefed the team, and he no longer cared about the sideways glances he was getting, the whispering that ceased whenever he entered a room. He didn't care what they thought. It couldn't be worse than what he thought of himself.

'Daniel Armstrong, aka Danny, or Adrian Chambers, was apprehended at the scene. He's currently over at King's College Hospital having a leg wound stitched. He should be with us later on this morning. Armstrong's residence has been secured. A full examination will take place later today, but from their initial search, evidence has been recovered linking Armstrong to all five victims.'

He could see the pictures in his mind. If only he had looked harder, he might have seen the half-developed pictures of Sarah. Maybe then he could have stopped him.

'As I'm sure you will have heard by now, Armstrong had

created a child's nursery . . . of sorts. A handmade quilt is down with the exhibits team now. Armstrong used the material taken from his victims' clothing to make it.' Jane stopped. Silence greeted her last statement. 'Some items relating to an infant were recovered from the scene: nappies, a baby bottle and clothing. However,' she said, raising her hand to silence the murmurs spreading around the room, 'forensics have found no evidence to suggest a child was actually present. We can only make presumptions of Armstrong's intentions at this point.' The murmurs started again but this time they seemed filled with relief. But it wouldn't last. Lockyer watched the faces around the table. They were no doubt thinking the same thing he was. Had Armstrong been planning to take a baby? And what had he intended to do with it?

There were so many cruel images in his mind. He felt suffocated by them. Instead of seeing the briefing room he was choking on a montage of hideous pictures: Sarah's face, her legs, splayed open, covered in blood. Malvern Turner's body, three vicious slashes to his throat, his mouth twisted in fear and pain. Megan's shadowed profile, sitting in the squad car at the scene.

'Armstrong's laptop was also removed from the scene. From initial examination it appears he was visiting a number of chat rooms, all password protected. Who he was talking to and the subject matter of those conversations is, as yet, unknown.'

He looked up when Jane paused. Her eyes told him what was coming next. 'Victim number five, Sarah Grainger, was pronounced dead at the scene. Dr Simpson and his team are preparing for the post-mortem.'

He clenched his fists against the cool glass of the table top and focused on the carpet beneath. He shouldn't be here. It could prejudice the case. Jane hadn't even blinked when he'd asked her to do the debrief.

'Malvern Turner, a suspect in a harassment case and under active warrant, was also found dead at the scene.' He could hear the guilt in Jane's voice. It was faint but it was there. She felt culpable for Sarah's death too. She had arranged the squad car at Sarah's flat. She had despatched it to follow up on the sighting of Turner's car in Honor Oak. 'It appears Turner phoned 999 to report the assault and then attempted to intervene. He wounded Armstrong in the leg but was then stabbed by Armstrong, three times in the throat.'

Lockyer had been trying to protect Sarah from Turner, but instead it was Turner who had been with her in her last moments, trying to save her. The irony cut deeper than Armstrong's blade ever could.

'Finally, Manchester MPS is forwarding all their files on the death of Armstrong's girlfriend, Joanne Taylor, five years ago. The CPS wants verification of the girl's suicide note. We don't know as yet whether Taylor's abortion and suicide were a catalyst or if Armstrong, in fact, killed his girlfriend in an act of revenge for terminating the pregnancy. It may well be that Armstrong is going down for six murders, not five.'

He closed his eyes and blocked out Jane's voice.

47

14 March – Friday

Lockyer stood back, leaning in the doorway, watching. Megan was perched on the arm of Bobby's chair, showing him the present she had brought with her. It was a huge coffee-table book on ancient Egypt. From Bobby's foot-tapping Lockyer could tell that this was an even bigger hit than the boat book.

'She's good with him,' Alice whispered from where she was standing next to him.

He looked at her and smiled. There was some semblance of the old Alice in her eyes, but not enough. It would take more than a few weeks to get over what had happened. He reached down and squeezed her hand. She smiled, turned and walked away down the hallway.

'Come on, Megs. It's time we were going and I'm sure Bobby could do with a rest,' he said, looking at his watch. They had been here for over two hours. Lockyer had never visited for so long. Megan turned down her mouth at the corners, just as she had when she was a little girl.

'I just want to show Uncle Robert one thing,' she said, waving Lockyer away.

'I'm not sure the "Uncle" is appropriate, Megs, we don't want to confuse him,' he said. Although from where he was standing he seemed to be the only one who was confused.

'Confuse him?' Megan said, raising her eyebrows. 'He's your brother and he's my uncle, why wouldn't I call him "Uncle"?' As she looked at him he realized he didn't have an answer. His eighteen-year-old daughter had managed to change something he had made complicated for five years into something simple in under two hours.

'Right,' he said.

Megan smiled. 'Now, Uncle Robert . . . this is a mummy. When they died the priests wrapped them up in all this material, here,' she said pointing to a picture on the page. 'It's like swaddling . . . but they had to remove their organs first . . . they took the brain out through the nose with this hook,' she said, turning to another page.

'Steady on, Megs, you don't have to be quite so graphic. The pictures show enough, I'm sure,' he said, smiling.

Bobby appeared to be completely at ease. He had even assigned Megan an indicator. As soon as she had walked into the room and into his brother's field of vision Bobby had been taken by her hair. With his head cocked on one side he had stared, transfixed. She had such a natural way with him that, even after five years, Lockyer hadn't perfected. There was no tension or anxiety in either of their faces. As he stood watching he wondered, again, why he had kept them apart for so long. The family he had lost when he and Clara separated, the family he had longed for, it was right here. This was his family now.

'OK . . . time to go,' he said again, practically dragging

Megan out of the room. She was still talking when he pulled the front door closed. Her excitement was infectious, almost. As they walked down the driveway to his car, he felt the pain creeping into his bones.

'I wanted to say I was sorry, Dad,' Megan said.

He turned to look at her. Her eyes were shining with tears.

'You've got nothing to be sorry for, Megs. I'm the one who's sorry,' he said, tipping her chin up so she was looking at him.

'No, I mean I'm sorry about . . . Sarah.'

He stepped away as if the sound of her name was a physical blow. Of course his daughter knew about his personal relationship with Sarah. There had been no avoiding it after what had happened on French Street. Despite Lockyer's protests, Megan had attended three interviews to establish Sarah's last movements. Up until now he had avoided talking about Sarah on the premise that it would be too upsetting for Megan. He had been so wrapped up in his own pain that he hadn't realized that not only was his daughter suffering from her ordeal but she was also hurting for him, for his loss.

Megan was shaking her head when she said, 'She was . . . lovely. Really lovely. She wanted to surprise you, make you something nice for dinner. She wanted to look after you. I should have called you. If you'd known she was there, you might have come home, you might have stopped him,' Megan said, tears rolling down her pale cheeks.

He stepped forward and put his hands firmly on her shoulders, pushing away the image of Sarah standing in his kitchen, smiling and laughing with his daughter.

'Megan, you need to listen to me,' he said. 'This is not your fault, sweetheart.' The authority and the calm in his voice surprised him. 'Do you understand me? This had nothing to do with you.' If anyone was to blame, it was him.

'What will you do now?' she asked, wiping her eyes with her sleeve.

'I will be fine, honey. I don't want you to worry about anything. Everything will be fine.' He took her hand in his. It was time to start thinking about Megan, about Bobby. It was time to start putting them first.

Daniel sat on his bunk, his sheets and blanket folded at the end of the bed, resting against the bars. He stared at the blank walls but to him they were filled with colour, with images of his girls: Phoebe, Katy, Debbie, Hayley and finally Sarah. He saw their faces and bodies mingling together as one.

Phoebe had been his first real test, stretching his skills, his patience. He remembered her strength when he took her. With the graves of others surrounding them, she had kicked, screamed and flailed like a stranded fish. But he had taken her resilience and absorbed it, empowering him to do more. Katy, in contrast, had been weak. Too scared to cry out, too obedient to struggle. The remembered disappointment cramped his thoughts but Debbie and Hayley had renewed his faith, confirmed his efforts. It was Sarah who had changed everything.

Her lesson should have been easy; his preparations were faultless. He had known Turner was watching. Of course he had. The man had been following him for several days. Ever since he had let himself be seen outside Sarah's flat and everything had flowed effortlessly until she had decided to leave her flat. He sat back, the prison walls cold against his back. Instead of the pathetic amoeba Daniel had witnessed, Turner had been an enraged animal. If the kitchen knife hadn't already been in his leg, Daniel might have laughed at the absurdity of facing someone of his power with such a pathetic tool. But Turner had surprised even him with his gusto, his fight for the woman he loved.

He heard Joanne's voice, her whispers circling his cell. She had killed their baby, taken from him the one thing he craved. But now he understood. She had set him on the path, prepared him for what was to come, for what he was to become. He smiled. DI Lockyer would have found his room, his sanctuary for the innocent. No doubt he would be racking his brain to discover its purpose.

Daniel closed his eyes and let himself imagine what was to come. There were more houses, more rooms, ready and waiting for their tiny occupants.

COMING SOON

NO PLACE TO DIE

ISBN: 978-1-4472-3934-5

An exclusive extract from Clare Donoghue's
next novel follows here . . .

PROLOGUE

Maggie tried to run but she couldn't feel her feet. Her breath felt warm against her cheeks as each step pushed air out of her lungs. She could hear him. He was behind her, the sound of his arms brushing against his sides as he ran, insistent, a buzzing inside her head. She had to move faster but her body wouldn't respond. She could smell him. It was an earthy, feral scent chasing her through a labyrinth of hedges, trees and bare brick. Her throat closed up, refusing to ingest his stench. She looked up at the sky. It was black, not even a pinprick of light to guide her. The darkness pressed down; a velvet cloak soaked in terror. Her fear was collapsing her, suffocating her, trapping her inside. Her lungs burned, her eyes stung. She reached out but touched nothing. The walls retreated from her fingers. There was no way out; no trail of bread-crumbs to follow. A door appeared up ahead, its red paint peeling away from the doorknob as if repulsed. She reached out to open it, his smell crippling her body, the sound of his footsteps throbbing inside her head. The red door shook, and vanished into the blackness. She screamed herself awake until she lay panting on her back, her throat dry. The dream was fading, the door was slipping away. He was slipping away.

She arched her back and let out a low groan, expelling the nightmare. Her muscles seemed reluctant to yield, preferring to return to their constricted state. She blinked. Not even a streetlight penetrated the blackness in her room. The power must be out on the street. She should get up, find out what was going on, but she couldn't, still paralyzed by her dream. She covered her face with her hands. Her fingers felt damp against her lips, her tongue was swollen and heavy in her mouth. Memories of the previous evening began to flit through her mind like a magic lantern display. Had she had a lot to drink? She didn't think so. She had been to his house. They had eaten dinner. He had been angry. They had fought. Then nothing: only a void.

Maggie allowed her muscles to retract and draw her body back into a foetal position as she felt around for the duvet. Her hands were heavy, clumsy. Sleep was pulling at her, dragging her back under. She wanted to give in but she was too cold. Yet she was sweating, her skin clammy beneath her cotton pyjamas. As she ran her hands over the freezing bed sheet she became conscious of a familiar odour. It was earthy, the smell of her parents' front lawn after the rain. Her heart began to beat faster, a pain spreading and gripping her lungs.

This wasn't her bed.

She sat up, staring into the inky blackness. She felt as though she were falling, her body shaking, shivering. She touched her face. Her skin felt cool, slick, alien.

What?

She turned her head from side to side but there was no light to soften the darkness.

'I can't see. Please, someone, help me.' She stopped, her chest heaving. Her words sounded muted, almost lost by her leaden tongue. She listened.

What's happening to me?

Maggie tasted bile in her mouth. She tried to swallow but more came as adrenaline flooded her system. She flung out her arms as far as she could in front of her: nothing. To the sides: nothing. She tried to stand up but her head struck something solid above her. Her whole body was shaking, her teeth biting down on her tongue, but there was no pain.

She inched her palms up higher and higher until they rested against a flat, marble-like surface. She pushed against it: no movement. She snatched her hands down and began rocking back and forth.

It's all right. It's okay.

She drew her knees up to her chin, put her arms around her shins and held herself. Her head ached as she tried to pull her thoughts into focus. This wasn't real. She was still dreaming, hallucinating – something. She began to count, slowing her breathing with each number, ignoring the aching in her bones and the slur in her voice.

When her shuddering body had settled enough for her to move again she turned, until she was on her hands and knees in the empty space. God, she hoped it was empty. She let her head hang. It was too heavy for her to hold it up any more. The counting was helping but she needed more, she needed to fill the silence. She began to sing as she crawled, crab-like, to her left.

'One little elephant came out one day, upon a spider's web to play,' her voice trembled. She closed her eyes, took a deep breath and forced the words out, 'he . . . he had such tremendous fun that he called upon another elephant to . . . come.' Her head hummed, as if a hundred flies were trapped behind her eyeballs. 'Two . . . two little elephants came out one day, upon a spider's web to –' She stopped, her head pulsing in rhythm with her voice as her hip struck a wall. She sat back on her haunches and with her palm flat she ran her fingers as far along in front of her, and then behind her, as she could. She leaned her face closer to the wall until her nose was pressed against the icy surface. She took a deep breath. Soil. Mud. She touched it again. It was earth, compacted earth, smoothed to a slick finish. 'No, no, no,' she said, shaking her head, tears rolling off her cheeks. 'No.' She closed her eyes but forced them open when she realized sleep was trying to suck her under again. She raised her shaking hands above her head, humming the nursery rhyme to herself. She couldn't bear to hear her laboured words, to feel her tongue, bitten and raw in her mouth.

In the same crab-like movement Maggie followed the line of the wall to one corner, then another, and another until finally she reached the fourth: the final wall of earth enclosing her. She could taste blood and soil. Panic needled her spine, her neck, like a shard of glass in her throat, tearing at the delicate tissue. Her breaths were coming in ragged gasps, her head light. An image of a grave flashed into her mind. Her bladder let go, the urine was warm against her thighs. She began to scream, all rational thought lost.

She screamed and screamed until she didn't know if she was screaming at all.

1

21 April – Monday

'I know,' Jane said, waiting for the next line in what was a well-rehearsed piece. 'Yes, Mother, I'm aware of that.' She looked at the digital clock on the bottom right-hand side of her computer screen. She should be done soon. 'I agree. I'll call as soon as I leave.' The seconds ticked by. 'Yes, clean ones are in Peter's room.' She resisted the temptation to drum her fingers on the desk. 'That's right, where they're always kept.' Jane could sense other people in the office beginning to tune into her conversation. 'Nothing. There was no tone. Sorry, yes, you're right. I'll be home soon.' Almost there. She hoped. 'Before eight. Yes. Okay. Yes. Good. Thank you, Mum. Bye.' Detective Sergeant Jane Bennett put the phone back in its cradle, closed her eyes and let her head drop onto her desk with a thud. The polished melamine felt cool against her skin.

Her mother didn't object to looking after Peter. Far from it. She was 'happy to help.' Jane would have the words engraved on her mother's tombstone. 'Celia Bennett, beloved wife, mother and grandmother. "Happy to help".' The image relaxed Jane's shoulders and she smiled. The ten minute ear-bashing she had just endured was routine. Her mother was happy to care for Peter, but in return she was fully entitled to ring Jane up to nag at her whenever she felt like it. Jane didn't mind. To know Peter was being looked after by someone who loved him meant everything. Her working life didn't allow for routine, something Peter craved. She simply couldn't be there all the time. So every pick, veiled dig, subtle criticism or direct assault her mother levelled against her was worth it. Peter might not care who picked him up from school, but to Jane, it mattered. She wanted the best for him. Although, she couldn't deny that taking her mother's abuse also helped to alleviate the guilt that shrouded her. She should buy shares in the 'Bad Mother Award'. She lifted her head off the desk, using her fingertips to pull her fringe back into place. The heat of the day had all but gone. The office had cooled. She turned and pulled her jacket off the back of her chair and slipped it on.

Peter would be eight in June. When Jane looked at him she still saw the chubby, red-faced baby who was always hungry. That was before his autism had been diagnosed, before the invisible barrier separating mother and son had been explained. Eight years old. She couldn't believe it. She would have to organize a party, get his friends over. Her mother would help. Jane rolled her eyes. It was an involuntary action, as she pre-empted what her mother would say. She pushed the power button on her laptop and waited for it to shut down. The weather should be good in June. She might even get away with a barbecue; paper plates, no washing up.

One quick meeting with the department heads, a briefing with the team and then she should be able to head home.

She slipped her laptop into her bag and surveyed the files on her desk, deciding what she needed to take home with her. She wanted to be ready to go the second that the briefing was over. Peter had already picked out a book for tonight's bedtime story. A bedtime story Jane had promised to read to him. Her eyes settled on the most current Stevens file.

She still had one girl to find.

For the past month the young woman's face had been a shadow, following Jane wherever she went. When she was found, would she be added to the list of victims on the Stevens case or would she be the luckiest girl alive? The irony made Jane pause. She picked up the file and two memory sticks and pushed them into her bag. She wanted a glass of wine in her hand and something by Elgar playing on her stereo before she even attempted to get back into the mindset of Lewisham's first serial killer. It would take months, years, to erase the images her and the rest of the team had witnessed. The killer's two-bedroom semi could have been papered with the photographs found in his home-made darkroom. The majority were shots of his five victims; names and faces Jane now knew well, but there were a handful of pictures showing girls no one knew. It was Jane's job to identify and find them, to make sure they had been photographed and nothing more. Two girls had been found safe and well, but the third? Only time would tell. Jane looked up and spotted her boss, DI Mike Lockyer, walking towards her. He smiled but his pale skin and shadowed eyes didn't match his expression.

'Jane,' he said, resting his arms on the partition that separated her desk from the rest of the open-plan office. 'How are you getting on with the Schofield case?'

'We're pretty much there, sir,' she said, her hand automatically reaching for the corresponding case file on her desk. 'The husband's with the custody sergeant downstairs. I don't think it'll take much to get him to talk.' She watched Mike nod, and rub his right eyebrow, his fingers tugging at the skin around his eye. He had lost weight. Jane thought he had the look of a sheet that had been left too long in the dryer: crumpled.

'Are you leaving him for the morning then?' he asked, no longer looking at her, his eyes no longer engaged.

'Yes. In fact, I was going to suggest Chris ran the interview,' she said, putting the file back in its place, straightening it with her palms. She could see that her boss wasn't really interested. In fact he had done only the bare minimum since his return to the office three weeks ago.

He was shaking his head, staring across the office. 'I don't think that's appropriate, Jane, do you?' he said, still not looking at her. 'Once Schofield's admitted it, maybe, but to send Chris in at this stage, before we know for certain that we've got enough evidence to convict, with or without a confession is risky. It's a risk I'm surprised you're prepared to take considering the mess the guy made of the wife. Have you looked at the crime-scene images lately?'

Jane sat back in her chair. His words didn't bother her. Neither did the disapproval and judgement in his tone but the look in his eyes made her stop and think carefully about how to respond. She knew he was hurting, struggling to come to terms with what had happened on the Stevens case, but what more could she do? He wouldn't talk to her, hadn't talked to her. He hadn't trusted her and that hurt. More than she was willing to admit. She had always assumed that their relationship went beyond mere colleagues; that he respected her, considered her a friend. His actions had proved her wrong on both counts. Now he prowled the office like some phantom from a horror movie, his eyes black, empty of reason. This wasn't the first time he had been critical of her since his return. And it wasn't just her. Most of the office had taken tongue-lashings. But Lockyer was the boss. It wasn't unusual to hear his shouts reverberating around south-east London's 'murder squad' offices. But now he seemed to be going off the deep end about nothing whilst overlooking something vital. She had been covering for him for weeks but his behaviour had not gone unnoticed. Roger, the Senior Investigating Officer for Lewisham, had already pulled Jane into his office and asked her to 'keep an eye on him'. However, she could see that now was not the right time to address the issue.

'Not a problem, sir,' she said, her voice quiet, her words measured. 'I'll take Chris in with me on the initial interview and, if Schofield confesses, I'll let Chris take over, under my direct supervision.' She waited for some kind of response or at least recognition but there wasn't any. 'Are you happy for me to do that, sir?'

She felt almost compelled to reach out to him, to touch the arm of the statue before her but then his eyes seemed to clear and he said, 'It's your case, Jane. You do what you like; you don't need me to babysit you. I don't need the details, just get it done. I've got enough on my plate.' He ran his hands through his hair then dragged them down his face, pulling his sallow skin out of shape. 'I trust you, Jane. Just get it done. I'll see you in the briefing.' With that, he turned on his heel and walked back across the room, into his office, closing the glass door behind him. The sun was setting outside the window, and he sat motionless, his face silhouetted by the fading light. Jane couldn't take her eyes off him. She wondered how long her boss could subsist on anger and regret.

As she stood to leave, her mobile started to ring. She glanced down at the name on the screen. It was Sue, a fellow copper, albeit a retired one. They hadn't spoken in months. Jane glanced at the clock mounted on one of the pillars in the centre of the open-plan office. It was already gone seven. Peter would be going to bed soon. The ringer on her phone seemed to increase in volume as if it could sense her indecision. 'Oh, all right,' she said, dropping back into her chair. 'Sue, hey. How are you doing?' Silence greeted her. 'Sue?' Jane said, straining to decipher the muffled sounds coming from Sue's end of the line. Maybe the phone was in Sue's bag and she had dialled Jane's number by accident. It was then that she heard a sniff. 'Sue, are you okay?' As Jane spoke, a dozen possibilities rushed through her mind. Sue and Mark had had a fight, one of the kids was ill, they'd been burgled, the cat had died. Jane shook her head. It could be anything.

'It's Mark.' Sue sobbed down the phone. 'He's gone.'

Jane felt a flood of relief that she had answered the call but a tug of guilt that she wasn't going to be reading Peter the bedtime story after all. She doubted if she would even be home before he was asleep. 'Oh, Sue, I'm so sorry. What happened? I didn't realize you guys were having problems again.'

'What? No, Jane, it's not that. He's just gone, disappeared. There's blood, Jane, there's blood in the house. He's gone.'

extracts reading groups

competitions books new

discounts extracts

competitions

books

new

events books

extracts

new reading groups

interviews

events extracts

discounts

new books events

events new

discounts extracts discounts

www.panmacmillan.com

extracts events reading groups

competitions books extracts new